STABLE
AFFAIRS

STABLE AFFAIRS

*More Horse Scents and Nonsense
in Twelve Short Stories*

MARC D. HASBROUCK

STABLE AFFAIRS
MORE HORSE SCENTS AND NONSENSE
IN TWELVE SHORT STORIES

This is a work of fiction. All of the characters, names, incidents, organizations, and dialogue in this novel are either the products of the author's imagination or are used fictitiously.

Photo credit to: Gaylin Hasbrouck

iUniverse books may be ordered through booksellers or by contacting:

iUniverse
1663 Liberty Drive
Bloomington, IN 47403
www.iuniverse.com
1-800-Authors (1-800-288-4677)

Because of the dynamic nature of the Internet, any web addresses or links contained in this book may have changed since publication and may no longer be valid. The views expressed in this work are solely those of the author and do not necessarily reflect the views of the publisher, and the publisher hereby disclaims any responsibility for them.

Any people depicted in stock imagery provided by Getty Images are models, and such images are being used for illustrative purposes only.
Certain stock imagery © Getty Images.

ISBN: 978-1-5320-8284-9 (sc)
ISBN: 978-1-5320-8285-6 (e)

Library of Congress Control Number: 2019913761

Print information available on the last page.

iUniverse rev. date: 09/10/2019

"There is something about riding down the street on a prancing horse that makes you feel like something, even when you ain't a thing."

Will Rogers

INTRODUCTION

*"The events in our lives happen in a sequence in time,
but in their significance to ourselves they find their own
order...it is the continuous thread of revelation."*

Eudora Welty

Well, here we go again. I never thought that I'd be revisiting my old "friends": the characters that I created in *Horse Scents*. But they kept coming back to me. Waking me up at night. Wanting to move forward. They told me that they have more to do. Some of them, anyway. I chose to ignore one reprehensible character, although he will be mentioned in passing. You will see some familiar faces in the coming pages. You will learn a bit more about those characters. Also, you will meet some new and intriguing characters. Needless to say, the emotions will run the gamut, high to low, from cover to cover and I hope that you'll be entertained, enlightened, amused, saddened and frightened by what transpires.

I am sincerely grateful if you have read my first book. The encouraging words from you, dear readers, were very much appreciated. But then, on the other hand, I am thoroughly miffed if you *haven't* read my first book. Your loss! But now is a great time to do so.

Stable Affairs is a sequel to *Horse Scents,* following the same format, with a timespan of one year and a dozen intertwining stories. The action picks up, here, approximately fifteen minutes after *Horse Scents* ended. I've taken several detours regarding reality and/or logic, as I did in my last attempt at putting Hemingway to shame. So, please don't take everything I've written as gospel. For those of you unfortunate souls who *didn't* read my first masterpiece, I'm sure you'll catch up soon enough.

And, above all, pay attention. You just might recognize yourself here.

JANUARY

Major Changes and New Beginnings

"Change will not come if we wait for some other person, or if we wait for some other time. We are the ones we've been waiting for. We are the change that we seek."

Barack Obama

It was late in the afternoon, and the horses were getting restless. The sky, which had been milky white earlier in the day, was turning a darker gray, becoming heavy with the threat of rain. The horses could sense that it was nearing feeding time. They jostled for position at the battered metal gate leading from the pasture to the stable and their awaiting stalls. Their only instincts now were hunger and impatience, with neither a thought about yesterday nor a care about tomorrow.

The party atmosphere was winding down. Tears of joy had been shed, and then dried. Remy Major was the man of the hour, followed very closely by Bryan Dennison and his wife, Brandy. CedarView Stable was to be saved, for the time being, from those horrible developers who wanted to bulldoze the whole shebang to build thirty crappy houses. The dusty tack room still reeked of coffee and leather. The empty Krispy-Kreme donut cartons still lured a boarder or two to peek inside, hoping that a treat managed to hide in one of its recesses. No such luck.

Since Remy's wife, Zara, was killed in a tragic auto accident several months ago, each of the boarders had been taking care of their own horses on a daily basis. Although they had gotten into the lazy habit of having Zara and Remy bring their horses in every night, feeding them and turning them back out into the pasture, they had been far more attentive to their equine charges. Came as a surprise to the horses, some of which hadn't seen their owners in weeks if not months. The social aspect at the stable had actually picked up as well, with evening feeding times extending into the night with idle gossip, swapping of kid's or grandkid's photos and just basic conversation.

Now, after just hearing the welcomed news about the Dennison's imminent purchase of CedarView, the mood was ebullient. One by one, the boarders headed to the battered, rusty gate from the pasture to get his respective horse or horses in for their evening meal. The horses, jostling, stomping and snorting in eager anticipation of food, made it a bit tricky to get one after the other in. But with a bit of patience and maneuvering it proved successful.

Remy cleaned up the tack room, disposing of the empty donut cartons in a large trash can outside the tack room door and taking the empty coffee urn out to his truck. Although he would still be around for a few more days until the deal was finalized, he hugged, shook hands, and kissed the boarders thanking them all for their patience throughout the years and their help throughout the past few agonizingly sad months. Cue the soundtrack: Billie Holiday singing "I'll Be Seeing You." Sniff, sniff.

Two days later it was a done deal. The papers had been signed and notarized, funds had been transferred, hands had been shaken, and hugs had been given. Bryan and Brandy Dennison were now, officially, the new owners of CedarView Stables. Bryan, especially, was ecstatic. Ideas for improvements swirled through his mind and he had already drawn up a design for a large arched gateway he planned for the entryway to the stable's driveway. His days would be filled. The roof needed replacing… some stall doors needed repair…the plumbing in the tack room bathroom was a disaster…some wobbly fences needed mending. Oh, the possibilities!

Brandy, too, was enthusiastic; hoping to attract some new boarders to fill so many of the empty stalls vacated by the sale of Zara's multiple horses. That part made her tear up. She truly missed Zara and their many chats. But, the past is the past. Time for new beginnings. A world of possibilities, indeed. She also had to deal with the situation regarding her mother. Sara Ambridge was slowly slipping into a world of her own, where the past and the present got confused. The future was never considered.

Later that afternoon, Mary Pat and Mary (just plain Mary), were walking side by side, bringing their horses in from the pasture when they saw Mary Anne's car come bouncing down the long gravel driveway. She hopped out of the car and practically jogged up to her two friends; making their respective horses come to an abrupt halt, then snort.

"Well, aren't *you* a little bundle of energy tonight, missy? What gives?" asked Mary.

"Guess what? I'm so excited about this. Now that this place has been saved I was hoping this would happen. I convinced my Zumba instructor to get a horse. You'll just love her; she's so damn cute. She had a horse as a kid but not since. She loves them and she rides western and I told her all about our place and all about you guys, and…"

"Whoa, whoa, whoa…" laughed Mary Pat, "you're running a bit too fast there. Slow down. Take a breath."

"Oh. Okay. My instructor…oh, and she's great at that…her name is Sandi Prescott. She's a teeny, bitty thing. I think she stands probably four feet seven inches, if that. She's cute as a bug and looks like a Munchkin. On a perky scale of one to ten, she's probably a fifteen! And her energy level is out the roof. I stopped by The Tack Shack to pick up a Farmer's Bulletin to scout out the horses for sale. Sandi's going to come over here very shortly to check the place out. Oh, God, you'll just *love* her!"

Mary Pat and Mary just looked at each other and shook their heads. Mary Anne could get overly enthused about a shiny new button, so who knows what really to expect when Miss Perky U.S.A. shows up.

Twenty minutes later, a shiny black Miata slowly came down the driveway. The convertible top was down. It's January. It's 43° and windy. And yet, there was a blonde, curly-headed woman smiling and singing along with her CD player blasting out some show tunes.

"It's show time, folks," said Mary as she winked at Mary Pat.

The blonde, evidently Sandi Prescott, got out of her car, a large Starbucks coffee cup in her hand, and headed toward the stable as Mary Anne went to greet her.

"Mah, lawd," Mary Pat drawled in her best faux southern belle accent, "that li'l bitty thing could walk right under every day-um horse we have here. She probably has to jump around just to cast a shadow."

Introductions were made and, in truth, Sandi was instantly likeable even if she did sound a little bit like Minnie Mouse. She must be a hell of a Zumba instructor because she simply could not stand still. She had bounce in her step and even kept moving in some way when she stopped walking.

"Damn, lady," Mary Pat joked, looking way up over Sandi's head toward the sky, "Who the hell is pulling your strings up there? You're dancing around like Pinocchio. Do you *ever* stand still?" And they all laughed.

"I guess I was just born with the activity gene," answered Sandi. "My Daddy thought I must have swallowed some Mexican jumping beans. Yeah, I've always been this way. I sure do burn through a lot of calories in a day, though."

The three Marys were jealous of that fact, but she sure was likeable, no doubt about that. An old ruffled rooster pecked around on the ground nearby, looking for some fallen bits of horse feed. The ladies warned Sandi about Oedipus Pex and his habit of sneaking up behind folks and pecking their legs or backsides. As Mary Anne was showing Sandi around the place and explaining to her that some great changes were in the immediate future, Marty and Jessica Howce pulled down the driveway and got out of their car. Looking at the little Miata with the top down, they looked at each other and shrugged. They approached the tack room to get the evening's feed for their horses, Dan and Gemmy. Sandi couldn't take her eyes off of Marty.

"Is he a boarder here, too?" asked Sandi, never even acknowledging Jessie.

"Yes," answered Mary Anne, "Marty and Jessie have two fine horses here. Jessie rides a lot, but Marty doesn't have as much time. He used to be an art director at a packaging company around here, but he does only freelance stuff now, I hear. Haven't had too much time to chat with him lately but he is *so* nice. Well, they both are. You'll just love them. Come on, I'll introduce you." Mary Anne walked and Sandi bounced toward the tack room just as Marty and Jessie were coming out. Sandi stopped right in front of Marty and practically had to bend over backwards to look up at his face.

"Holy Moly, you're a tall one, aren't ya?" Sandi said, looking up at Marty's six-foot, four-inch frame. "Hi, I'm Sandi. Sandi with an i." And obviously nothing shy about her either. "I'm thinking of perhaps boarding here. If and when I get a horse!"

"Well, hi, Sandi with an i," Marty answered, bending way over to shake her hand and having to bow at the waist. "Very nice to meet you and this is my wife, Jessica…but call her Jessie." Jessie reached out to shake Sandi's hand but Sandi wasn't paying attention.

"Lord, what a gorgeous voice you have, Marty. Oh, hi, Jessie. Marty, have you ever done any acting by any chance?"

Marty stepped back and nearly choked because he laughed so hard. That question came straight out of left field. "Not at all, Sandi. Not. At. All. No…wait. That's not true, come to think of it. I was a pirate in the eighth grade. In 'Pirates of Penzance'", and he laughed, shaking his head. "But I give a shitload of presentations to clients. You'll discover, if you'll be boarding here, that I love to talk. I'm not shy…ha! And neither are you, I can tell. The larger the audience, the better I perform."

Jessie was *not* pleased with the way this conversation was going. She was taken aback by the brashness of this little lady. Sandi seemed cute and personable enough but *way* too assertive regarding Marty. She was going to have to keep an eye on this one. Not that she was concerned about Marty's behavior. Frankly, women had come on to her husband for years. Marty was either oblivious to it or pretended that he was. Marty and Jessica were staunchly devoted to each other and, despite other women's attentions, Jessie never doubted her husband's loyalty and faithfulness. *But.* Of course, there was *always* a "but". The male ego was a factor. Marty was approaching the age when perhaps, just perhaps, he might start to think that he's "losing it". The "it" in question, of course, was his sex appeal.

Jessie watched as Sandi kept prattling on and bouncing around like she was on a pogo stick. *She probably makes little tiny hearts over the "i" when she dots it signing her name,* Jessie thought. You never have a second chance for first impressions. Things could change, of course, but at this point, Jessica Howce was *not* impressed.

"What the hell was *that* all about?" asked Jessie, a few minutes later as they stood side by side grooming Dan in his stall. Sandi and Mary Anne had both driven away following the "tour" and introductions.

"Oh, come on," Marty laughed, "yeah, perhaps she did come on a bit too strong but, hey, someone that diminutive has to do something to compensate, dontcha think?"

"Yes. I think. On occasion. And I think that little twit needs to rein in her perky little ass about fifty percent."

Again, Marty laughed and rolled his eyes. "Do I see a little green-eyed monster creeping around here, dear heart?"

Marty had been told since he was nineteen that he had a beautiful speaking voice. He toyed with the idea, at one time, of possibly doing voice-overs but never pursued it. Just this past month, while he was speaking on the phone with one of his clients (female) she had said: "Don't be offended or take this the wrong way, but if they ever decide to do a male version of SIRI, with your voice and perfect enunciation, you'd be a shoo-in." Marty then said: Nothing. Absolutely nothing. He simply sighed and rolled his eyes.

"No little green-eyed monster here, Marty. Just be cautious, that's all," responded Jessie.

Dan snorted. And stomped his right hind leg. He really didn't like being groomed while he ate. Jessie swatted him playfully on the rump and indicated it was time to move to Gemmy's stall for *his* grooming.

"What the hell was *that* all about?" Mary asked as she leaned into Gemmy's stall and looked straight at Marty.

"Oh, good grief," was all Marty could say.

Not more than thirty seconds later, Mary Pat came up along side of Mary, leaning into the stall. "What the hell was *that* all about, huh?"

Marty threw up his hands as if in surrender. "Oh, for shit's sake!" he exclaimed.

Yes, she was a bit over the top with enthusiasm. Yes, she was *far* over the top regarding her energy level. But everyone at CedarView eventually had to admit that Sandi Prescott was likeable. She wasn't being flirtatious with the guys in any way, she was just so damn friendly…and perky… and cute. She was thirty-two but looked (and acted at times) like she was nineteen. "Acted" being the operative word there. Belonging to a community theatre group, RockMount Players, she had performed in several shows, mostly musicals, since she graduated college. She had a couple of on-again, off-again boyfriends but none of whom she considered steady. She was a personal trainer and Zumba instructor at GrayStone Body Works, a gym cleverly named for its location midway between Grayson and Stone Mountain. She and Mary Anne had found the perfect horse for her. Larger than a pony, but just barely, Sandi fell in love with this little seven-year-old dapple-gray mare the minute she saw her. The name cinched it: Fireball…one of Sandi's favorite songs that she used in one of her Zumba routines. Fireball belonged to a little girl whose interest had changed overnight from riding to cheerleading. That thrilled Sandi. Yes, surprise, surprise, Sandi had been a cheerleader in both high school and college. And had awards to prove it. After looking her over from front to back and reviewing her latest vet check report, Sandi hoisted herself up into the saddle for a "test drive". Fireball was an easy ride and responded to every command with ease. The price was right. The deal was made. Amber Givings, the youngest boarder at CedarView, volunteered to use her truck and horse trailer to bring Fireball to her new home. She and her boyfriend, Raymond, helped Sandi load up the little mare and off they went to their new adventures together.

Bryan Dennison leaned the ladder against the side of the stable, stepped up on it quickly, farting as he did so. He looked around making sure no one was in hearing distance and continued his climb. "Damn bullfrog," he muttered to himself, chuckling. "Wants to climb up here with me." It was a cloudy, cool day. Just perfect for starting to replace the tattered, battered old tin roof. It would take several days to do so, but Bryan was on a roll. A mere three weeks from taking possession of the place and he had already repaired several raggedy places along the vast fence line, put in a new toilet in the tack room bathroom, replaced the warped and torn screen door to the tack room and hauled in all the necessary materials for the beautiful archway gate that would be at the head of the driveway. He was waiting for the final building permit to be approved for that archway, although he knew that he'd probably get some negative feedback from Mrs. Critchley, the old widow who lived across the street. But he was ready to go. *Not bad for an old guy,* Bryan thought to himself. The one major change that Brandy had noticed was the lack of Bryan's heretofore-daily morning complaints about this pain or that pain affecting this body part or that body part upon awakening. However, Brandy was *not* going to poke the sleeping bear and bring it to his attention.

Bryan was excited about the fact that they had attracted one new boarder already, Sandi Prescott, and another potential boarder, Megan something or other, had left a message on his cell phone. Five minutes later he stopped what he was doing as he saw a strange pickup truck pulling a horse trailer stop at the top of the hill, then turn into the driveway leading down to the stable. A car was following the trailer and Bryan recognized it as Julia Constance's car. He left what he was doing, grumbling about having to put a halt, even if temporarily, to his work. Another little fart as he stood up and reached for the ladder to climb back down.

The truck and trailer swung around and parked as Julia got out of her car. She saw Bryan climbing down the ladder and went to greet him.

"Bryan," she called out. "Didn't mean to interrupt your work up there. I'm sorry I didn't call you last night to let you know what's going on here." And she turned, indicating the horse trailer. "But things started happening very quickly. Almost too quickly. My head is still swimming. I spoke to Brandy on the phone an hour ago and she told me you were over here working."

By this time, Bryan had reached the ground again and walked toward her, wiping his hands on a rag he had tucked into a hip pocket.

"So, what's up, little lady?" he asked. "That trailer is empty so, with my immensely powerful powers of perception, I'm assuming you are *not* bringing a new horse here." And they both smiled.

"Nope. 'Fraid not," answered Julia. "Something has been in the works for several weeks and it suddenly came to fruition. Without boring you with the details, I'm moving to California. Soon."

"I thought Rance hated California. How does he feel about moving out there?" asked Bryan, almost knowing what the response was going to be.

"Rance isn't going. I've had it with him. It's been coming on for some time now, as I'm sure your 'powerful powers of perception' must have told you. The kids and I put up with too much for too long. Jesus Christ, every day was a daylong argument with him. Hell, he'd start off arguing with himself in the mirror every morning while he was shaving! To say nothing about his other shenanigans and his run-ins with the cops. Enough is enough. Enough is too much. Rance Hurakon will rot in hell, I have no doubt, but I won't be around to endure his shit anymore."

"I'd be lying, little lady, if I told you I was surprised," said Bryan, shaking his head. "Sorry to hear that and I'm sorry that you'll be moving out. I'm assuming," pointing to the trailer, "that you'll be moving Taffy out as well."

"Yes, but the horse isn't moving out west with us. A good friend up in North Georgia bought her. She has a large stable and riding school up there. Taffy is a great schooling horse, especially for young riders. It's a good match." She sighed and looked around. "I really will miss this place. I've had a lot of fun here. Good memories…along with a few sour ones. I'll miss my friends here and I'll *definitely* miss you and Brandy. You two are real sweethearts. The improvements you've made here already are impressive."

"You mean for an old guy?" laughed Bryan.

"You're *not* old, Bryan…just a bit seasoned." And they both laughed. "Sorry about the quick notice, but I'm paid up through this month. If you want me to pay for next month because I didn't give you advance notice, I'd be glad to."

"Don't be silly. You're good. No problem. The only problem is we'll all miss you, Julia. The best of luck to you way out there. Please keep in touch." Although they both knew that that probably would not happen. "Do you need help loading up?"

An older woman, by this time, had gotten out of the pickup truck and was leaning against its side. Waiting patiently.

"No, no, I'm good. Janice over there is waiting to help. She's the one who bought Taffy." Julia and Bryan hugged. "There are still a few bags of feed of mine in the tack room and a couple bales of hay behind Taffy's stall. They're yours now. Janice has plenty at her place. Thanks for everything, Bryan. And please give my warmest regards to Brandy. I hope you both do well here."

Julia collected her grooming bucket, saddles, bridles and riding helmet from the tack room, placing them in the truck. She got her lunge line and halter that was hanging on a hook in front of Taffy's stall and headed toward the pasture gate, calling for her horse. Taffy came galloping up; perhaps thinking it might be feeding time. Julia had stepped inside the gate to hook up her horse, and then led her past the stall and straight to the awaiting trailer. Her horse was an easy loader and walked right up into the open trailer. The rear door was closed and hooked up with chains as Julia turned to take one more look around the place. She looked up at Bryan who, by this time had climbed back up onto the roof. She waved to him and he waved back. She nodded to her friend and they both got into their respective vehicles and drove slowly up the gravel driveway, away from CedarView for the very last time.

Out with the old, in with the new, thought Bryan after getting off the phone with Megan Fairley. She and her husband, Graham, were seeking a new stable for their horse Zanzibar (Zany, for short). Their current stable had just changed to a full-board facility, which, of course, jacked up the monthly fee considerably. As fate and coincidence would have it, Megan was acquainted with Julia Constance. Megan had been a registered medical technologist, working in a local hospital's lab. Julia was in pharmaceutical sales and their paths had crossed a few years ago. While not social friends, their respective love of horses gave them something to talk about whenever they met. Megan had resigned her position and put her career on the back burner when her identical twin boys were born four years ago and was now a stay-at-home-mom. She had lost contact with Julia up until this past month when things changed at the stable.

After meeting with Bryan at the stable later that evening, the Fairley's made arrangements to move Zany to CedarView. The stable was not as fancy as their current facilities, but it looked and sounded like a lot of improvements were in the works. A couple of the boarders were at the stable when they got there and, after meeting them, both Megan and Graham felt good vibes. A woman named Jessie, a perky little thing named Sandi (with an "i") and a tall dark-haired woman named Mary had greeted them like long-lost friends. Evidently this would be a fun-loving group.

Bryan knew that not all of his boarders were originally from the south. Neither he nor Brandy was, for that matter, but had lived below the Mason/Dixon Line longer than they had above it. He had gotten tired of shoveling snow years ago. He loved the south and everything it entailed. He stopped in at the Tack Shack to pick up some Neatsfoot Oil and to shoot the shit with Brenda, the manager. While the two of them were talking, he noticed a rustic-looking hand-painted wooden sign that was for sale. *Holy crap*, he thought, *I'm gonna hang this over at the stable*. And he did. Everybody loved it.

-THE SOUTH –
The place where tea is sweet and accents are sweeter.
Summer starts in April and Macaroni & Cheese is a vegetable.
Front porches are wide and words are long.
Chicken is fried and biscuits come with gravy.
Everyone is Darlin' and someone's heart is always being blessed.

Of course, as anyone from the south knows, that phrase "Bless your heart" has multiple interpretations. It can range from sincere love and affection to genuine concern and sympathy. Then again, there's the ultimate meaning: "You're the biggest dipshit on the planet!"

And then the rains came. And continued. January, oozing toward February, became a dreary, soggy stretch for the next three weeks. Flash flood warnings for low-lying areas were daily occurrences. Bryan's new tin roof would have to wait a while longer. The boarders grumbled about the mess and the horses loved it. Rolling in nice, fresh mud was a horse's delight.

Finally a dawn arrived with nearly cloudless skies. Bryan was ambitious and encouraged by the rare decent weather. With no aches or pains to complain about, he and Brandy enjoyed their morning coffee together and then he was off...heading to the stable and an awaiting ladder.

Progress was being made. Until he slipped and fell off the roof.

FEBRUARY

Stable Affairs – The Musical

"We do on stage things that are supposed to happen off. Which is a kind of integrity, if you look on every exit as being an entrance somewhere else."

Tom Stoppard – Rosencrantz and
Guildenstern Are Dead

Marty Howce was frazzled. And delighted. It had been slightly over a month since he was downsized in a RIF at Compton Paperboard Packaging Company. He had been a popular and successful art director at the company for a number of years, but a sudden turn of financial events at the firm had lead to this situation. He did, however, receive a substantial severance package that ensured his full salary for the coming eight months. On top of that, which thrilled him, many of his clients at Compton followed him into his flourishing freelance business. He was busier than he had been in months and was, in actuality, bringing in *substantially* more money than he had in years. What a problem, right?

He was working frantically in his home studio-office, trying to put the finishing touches on one project before leaving for a client presentation for another project when he grabbed his ringing cell phone. Glancing at the caller ID, he saw that it was his good friend and former co-worker, Max Holliday.

"Hey, Max, my good man, what's up?" he hurriedly blurted.

"Hi, Hemingway...oops, I mean Marty. How's life among the unemployed?" Max responded. Max, who had been the art director in the corrugated carton division of Compton as opposed to Marty being the art director for the folding carton division, had also been affected by the recent RIF.

"Who's unemployed?" Marty laughed. "Hell, I'm busier now than ever. Hey, and thanks to you for sending some of *your* clients in my direction. I'm assuming that you've elected to *not* follow the freelance route?"

"I don't need it, Marty. Too old and too tired for all the bullshit I'd have to put up with. Besides, I've taken up a new hobby. It's called Napping. And I do it very well, thank you very much, every day from about two until four. You should give it a try sometime," and he chuckled, "in your spare time, that is."

Marty shook his head and smiled. His old friend was a force to be reckoned with and could never picture him actually becoming lazy or nap-worthy.

"Seriously, Max, I don't believe a word of it. Really, what's up?"

"I called for two reasons, actually," Max said, pausing briefly. "First, Camellia and I read that manuscript that you foisted upon me at our last luncheon. Basically, we liked it. Very much. It was a fun, easy read."

"*Basically*. Basically?" Marty responded with hesitation. "Basically", he repeated. "Why do I have a feeling there's a 'but' coming somewhere?"

"As I said, we both enjoyed 'Stable Affairs', so here's the down and dirty. We counted at least four typos, some of your punctuation needs... hmmm...refining and I would like to see a bit more character development. Some of your characters were sketchy, at best. Oh, and I was *really* hoping for a murder."

"A murder?" Marty gasped. "I wasn't writing a thriller, you know. Jeeze."

"I know, I know," Max laughed, "but one of your characters was such a freaking asshole. He was a foul-mouthed racist, on top of being homophobic, borderline misogynist and xenophobic. Perhaps one of your other characters could have shot him. *I* wanted to pistol-whip the bastard!"

Marty could hardly control the laughter. He shook his head and grinned broadly. "But, Max, haven't we all met someone just like him? Haven't you?"

"Yes," said Max, "but they'll never find his body." They both chuckled.

"Okay, you made some good points with your critique...*basically*. Four typos aren't all *that* bad, considering my word-count. Spell-Check failed me there. I'll try to correct all the punctuation errors once I find where the hell they are and I'll see what I can do regarding my character development. Not sure, though, when or even *if* I'll ever have the time to get back to it. It's going on the back burner for now. Thanks. I sincerely appreciate both you and your fantastic wife taking the time. Okay, then. You said you had two reasons for the call. What's number two?"

Max hesitated for a moment, and Marty realized that perhaps his friend was lighting a cigarette. He heard Max exhale and envisioned a plume of smoke encircling Max's head.

"Don't have all the details yet, just some sketchy ideas after several meetings. Camellia and I are thinking about making a major investment in the art world," Max finally answered.

"Looking at what's hanging on virtually every wall in your house," Marty remarked, "I'd say you two have made substantial investments in the art world for decades."

"Yes, in that sense, for sure. I know that you know Stet. Stet Brandson. He is a fabulous guy as well as an excellent artist in his own right. Camellia and I...well, Camellia especially...have known him for years. He has the idea that the time might be right to open a major new art gallery here in Buckhead. Galleries had flourished here for years before many of them went belly-up after the bubble burst back in 2008. Looks like things are awakening. He needs some backing. That's where we come in. Hell, Marty, we have more money than we'll ever need. Our damn financial advisors keep things ramped up so much our heads are spinning. We've been damn lucky, that's for sure. Stet's lady friend, Mary, is still over at that stable you're at, right?"

Marty answered in the affirmative.

"She may or may not be moving in with Stet, but that's neither here nor there at the moment. Her son is an architect up in Chicago and, evidently, Mary has spoken to him about doing the design and the build-out when the time comes. And, when that time comes, if it does, indeed, come, we'd like you to design the signage. You know, the logo…the stationery and all the other shit that's needed. Oh, I know…I could do it. I could do it in my sleep, for Christ's sake, but I don't want to. Don't worry, though. We are a long way off from anything being finalized. So you won't have to worry about your current ultra-busy schedule."

"Wow," Marty breathed out heavily, "Interesting. Frightening, too. Damn, that sounds…well…*sounds* great. I see the potential and I also see the pitfalls. Could be a huge success – or it could crash and burn. But go ahead, count me in, of course, but please give me a bit of warning and updates along the way, huh?"

Max agreed, and then Marty glanced at his watch. "Shit! I hate to do this to you, Max, but I should have left five minutes ago for a presentation. Gotta run! Congrats, I think, to all concerned, hugs to Camellia, thanks for the suggestion about a murder and I'm outta here!" He clicked off, grabbed his presentation material and bolted for his car.

Bryan had been lucky. Sort of. When he slipped and fell off the roof at the stable, it had been at the lowest side of the roof. Below him, as he fell, was the large manure pile, mixed with the pine shaving beds from the mucked out stalls. It was much softer than the ground around it, although it was soggy from all the recent rains and had a very pungent aroma, to say the least. He ended up stinking to high heaven and with a twisted wrist and sore ankle. And his pride was wounded. His new roof would have to wait a bit longer.

THE PERSUASION: A lesson in the shameless manipulation of the male ego if ever there was one. Marty never saw this one coming, but he should have.

Jessie wasn't feeling well, having just getting over a touch of bronchitis, so Marty had stable duty this particular night. Dan and Gemmy were happily and noisily munching their sweet feed and were about to shift over to enjoying their flakes of hay. Marty groomed them both while chatting with both Mary and Bryan, who were leaning into the stall. Marty complimented Bryan on all the amazing changes that had taken place so quickly at CedarView. Sandi's little Miata zipped down the driveway and parked with a screech. She went bouncing into the tack room, only to bounce right back out again quickly with Fireball's grooming bucket. She headed to Fireball's stall, which just happened to be next to Gemmy's.

"Watch out, Marty," Mary said with a laugh, "here she comes. Protect yourself. Or hide."

"Oh, stop. She's harmless. If they could bottle her energy it would probably be illegal." Marty continued using the currycomb on Gemmy without pausing.

"Hey, guys!" came Sandi's perky voice as she approached the trio. "How are you enjoying a respite from all the rain? I hated all that soggy stuff. Couldn't put my top down."

The trio acknowledged the unpleasant weather, and then waited for the next topic to pop into Sandi's mind because keeping silent for even the shortest amount of time was just not the norm.

"Oh, I'm just *soooooo* excited!" she exclaimed, bouncing up and down and clapping her hands. *Here it comes*, they all thought. "That little theater that I'm part of just selected their next show. It is *so* ambitious! We normally do simple shows. You know, single set type things but we have set designers who work wonders. Last year we did 'You're a Good Man, Charlie Brown'. I played Snoopy. I don't want to say that I stole the show but…." She shrugged, giggled, and then whispered "but I stole the show!"

The trio laughed politely. But obviously she was not finished. Mary had a feeling that Sandi was leading up to something.

"I can't believe that RockMount Players would even attempt something of this scale. It's considered one of the best musicals in the history of Broadway. Our director, Gus…that's Gus Mansard…said we need to try something big. But he wouldn't even attempt it if Dottie Washington wouldn't star. Dottie Washington...can you believe it?"

All three looked at her with blank faces. Marty shook his head. "I haven't a freakin' clue who this Donny Washington is," he said.

"Dottie," corrected Sandi, "Dottie Washington. She's the absolute best actress and singer in our group. She's done other stuff around town as well, you know, other theater groups. But she doesn't always want to try out. She wouldn't even *have* to try out for this one. She'd be perfect!"

Dan and Gemmy were almost finished with their hay by now and Marty was getting ready to put them back out into the pasture and head for home. That's when the bomb dropped.

"The show is 'Gypsy'," Sandi practically squealed. "Can you freakin' believe it? Dottie, of course would be Momma Rose. She'll be swell. She'll be great! Now all we need is a perfect Herbie, the male lead."

That's when Mary's head swiveled so fast toward Marty that you could hear bones crack. A huge grin came over her face. *I knew it*, she thought, *I just knew this would happen sooner or later.* Well, sooner is now. Marty was oblivious. Bryan had no earthly idea what Sandi was talking about. He and Brandy never went to the movies anymore much less live theater.

"Tryouts for most of the other parts are next week. I'm practically a shoo-in for Dainty June, all ego aside," she laughed. *Here it comes, again* thought Mary. "Marty, you would be *sooooo* perfect for Herbie. You've just got to try out. Please...please...please! I know you're a frustrated actor. I've been talking to Gary Smart and he tells me you always blew everyone out of the water at all those sales meetings at that big company you worked for. He said your presentations are...or were...amazing. Please...please... *please?*"

Marty took a deep breath. "No. Absolutely not. For one thing, I don't have the time. And I certainly do not sing. Can't read music. Don't sing. Period."

"Hel-lo!" Sandi answered. "Jack Klugman created that role on Broadway and he sure as hell was no Michael Bublé! You'd be so perfect opposite Dottie. You're *so* handsome and she's *so* beautiful. And with that deep voice of yours you'd have all the ladies in the audience wanting to sleep with you. Probably a couple of the guys as well."

"Well, *there's* an enticing thought that's difficult to turn down!" Marty laughed.

Sandi gasped. "Then you will? You *will* try out?"

"Hell no, I won't try out. I told you I don't have the time."

"We rehearse only at night. Most of us all have day jobs and our performances are only on the weekends. You know, Friday and Saturday nights and a matinée on Sundays. Also, there are a lot of little kids in this show and most of them will still be in school. We only run for a couple of weekends anyway but we rehearse for about a month before we open. We're not talking Method Acting here…no Stanislavski…no finding your inner motivation. Just fun!"

Bryan had silently slipped away during all of this. He couldn't care less. Mary was leaning up against the stall door, arms folded, slowly shaking her head, laughing hysterically on the inside, and so eager to call Mary Anne and Mary Pat.

"The auditions are next Saturday at the theater, Marty. Would you please consider giving it a try? *Pleeeeease?*"

"I'd consider shooting myself first," laughed Marty. "Now, if you will pleeeeeease excuse me, I've got to get my two big babies back out into the pasture so I can get home to my beautiful wife, my two handsome sons and a well-needed gin and tonic. Thanks for the offer no matter how laughable it is, but, emphatically, no way, José. So, Snoopy, you can climb up onto your Sopwith Camel and try to find another Red Baron…or Herbie…or whoever. And that, as they say, is that!" With that, he hooked Gemmy up to his lead line and ushered him out of the stall past a pouting Sandi, with her arms folded. End of story. For tonight.

Jessie nearly wet herself laughing so uncontrollably when Marty told her about the conversation at the stable an hour before. "Hey, Marty," she said between snorts of laughter, "you know Rex Harrison talked his way through 'My Fair Lady' and won an Oscar for it. I've heard you sing… frankly, I think you might be tone deaf, but you have a pleasant enough voice."

"Oh, *pul-eeeze*," he answered. "Nope. I can assure you the unsuspecting public is *not* waiting to hear my dulcet tones. Flat or otherwise."

The phone lines buzzed with excitement (and raucous laughter) later that evening involving Mary, Mary Anne, Mary Pat, and Gary Smart.

Bryan told Brandy about a show about gypsies that Sandi was going to be in. He couldn't fathom why anyone would want to do a show about a bunch of roaming thieves and crooks. But, that was none of *his* business.

Marty was at the top of his game the next morning. He had finished a series of concepts for one of his favorite clients and was headed off for a luncheon meeting and presentation. He was about to walk out the door when his cell phone chirped. He glanced at it and saw that his former co-worker, Gary Smart, was calling.

"Hey, Smart-ass, what's up?" he laughed. He heard Gary laugh as well.

"Hey, buddy," answered Gary. "Do I hear show tunes playing in the background?" And he continued to laugh.

"Fuck you…and *thank* you very much for insinuating to that mini whirling dervish that I could act…or whatever you said."

"I speaketh the truth, man, forsooth. Do you not have a great calm in front of large audiences? Do you not woo money out of the coffers of gazillion clients? Do you not leave them in awe and clamoring for more? Truth?" responded Gary, who had as much of a talent at sarcasm as Marty does.

"Humility forbids me from agreeing with all you're saying, my friend, but pretending to be someone I'm not and singing about it at the same time is just not for me. Seriously."

"Seriously?" snorted Gary. "You just might uncover a hidden talent. Who knows where that could lead? Hey, word has it that you're writing a book. Send it to Lin-Manuel Miranda…perhaps he could turn *that* into a musical. Be bigger than 'Hamilton', ya never know!"

"Wait. How do *you* know that I'm writing a book? I never told anyone over at the stable."

"Jessie may have slipped up and spilled the beans to Linda one day recently. The two of them were comparing reading material with Megan Fairley as well. They all love to read thrillers, I guess, and this Jack Reacher character has all three of those ladies in a dither. Jessica casually mentioned about your book, but said it wasn't a thriller. Said she really didn't know how to classify it. That's all. It wasn't on the 6 o'clock news or anything. Why? Is it really a great big secret?"

"No, I guess not. Anyway, it's on the back burner. Way back on that burner, for that matter. Definitely not a priority, probably for months to come."

As Marty was talking, he was again getting all of his material together for his client presentation and, with his phone on speaker, walked out to his garage, got into his car and pressed the remote to open the garage door. He hooked the phone up to the hands-free mode and started the engine.

"Gary, I'd love to chat more but the conversation regarding this acting bullshit is finished. The train has left the station."

"What the hell does that even mean?" asked Gary. "The train has left the station. Come on, Marty. For one thing, I was just raggin' you. You know how I am. I won't bring it up again. Promise. But watch out, I think some of the ladies, your precious Jessie among them, might try to persuade you otherwise. Word of caution…just sayin'."

"Okay, then. Thanks for the warning. We still need to talk. I want to hear what's going on with your potential move to Chicago…if it's still on."

"It is and it isn't," answered Gary. "Let's meet for a beer or two later this week, okay?"

"Sounds good, my friend. See ya…oh, and keep smilin'!"

Marty darted in and out of traffic, trying to make up a bit of time he lost while chatting with Gary before he left home. His mind wandered. Yes, he loved being in front of an audience. Yes, he always had whatever audience it was in the palm of his hand. Yes, he loved the sound of applause and laughter after his presentations. But, no, he was *not* going to try out for some ridiculous show. He had taken a stand and, damn it, he was going to keep it!

THE PERSUATION – Part 2: A lesson in the total annihilation of a lone male wolf by a pack of aggressive she-wolves.

Thursday: It was two days before the auditions, Sandi texted Marty. "Pls reconsider!"

Sandi had cornered Jessie at the stable to try to convince her to try to convince Marty to at least go to the audition to see what it was all about. At this point, Jessie thought the whole thing was funny. Although she couldn't picture him singing on stage, she *could* picture how handsome he'd be on stage. Tucked away in the back of a closet, she found a corrugated box with stacks of old CDs. She knew that she had purchased several original cast albums of Broadway shows years ago and was certain she had one with good old Ethel Merman singing her lungs out about everything coming up roses. Sure enough. There it was.

Sandi's energy level had no limits; neither did her amazing powers of persuasion. By this time, with the day of the auditions looming closer and closer, she had Mary, Mary Anne, Mary Pat and Megan working on her behalf. She was certain that, with Jessie also on her side, Marty wouldn't stand a chance. Sandi was smart. She understood about the male ego and how a pack of willful women could work wonders in whittling away its hard shell.

The first thing Marty heard when he stepped back into house after his latest successful presentation was a loud, brassy voice singing *"Have an eggroll, Mr. Goldstone…"*

"What the hell is that?" Marty asked, giving Jessie the squinty-eyed look that he did so well when he knew she was up to something. He knew darn well what "that" was. Although he hadn't heard it in years, Jessie had played it often along with several other show albums seemingly decades ago. Surprisingly, he *did* remember these songs. Jessie walked into the room.

"No." said Marty. "Final answer!"

It was a beautiful day for a ride. Mary called Mary Pat, who in turn called Mary Anne, who then called Sandi. They hadn't been on horseback for a couple of weeks due to the lousy weather and they all agreed that their horses would be full of energy and ready for a good workout.

"I heard one of you mention a few days ago something called Yahoo Hill," Sandi said to the other women as they were saddling their horses. "What's that all about?"

"Oh, that's great!" answered Mary Anne. "'It's a nice little trail ride through some woods to get there, then there is this really steep incline up the trail. We take our turns and go up one at a time. We get our horse set to go, and then we get him galloping up that hill as fast as he will go while we are yelling 'Yahooooo!' Frankly, the first time I did it I was scared shitless. It can be intimidating for some."

Mary Pat had a flashback to last year when Zara had swatted Rance's horse on the rump when Rance was a bit hesitant and sent him flying up that hill, with Rance yelling a very profane word. She chuckled to herself.

"Let's do it, okay?" asked Sandi. "I thrive on excitement."

Tell us something new, thought all three of the other women.

All saddled up and ready to go, they headed off. The air was crisp, filled with the refreshing scent of wet woodlands. There wasn't a lull in the conversation as they walked their horses, then trotted, then walked again, heading toward Yahoo Hill. When they got to the base, Sandi's mouth dropped open.

"Holy crap! When you said 'steep', you weren't just whistlin' Dixie, were you? I can't wait!"

Mary went up the hill first, with Thunder charging like he was going into battle. He had been up this hill several times and seemed to enjoy it more each time.

"Me next, me next!" squealed Sandi, practically bouncing out of her saddle.

"Have at it, little lady," responded Mary Pat. "But be prepared to wet your panties!" And they all laughed.

Sandi positioned Fireball, took a firm grip of her reins, counted to three, then kicked her horse in the ribs and sent him flying up the incline with Sandi yelling "Yahoooooooo!" all the way to the top and into the woods beyond.

After they had all reached the top and got back together, Sandi was breathless.

"Oh! My! God!" she exclaimed. "That was better than sex!"

The three other women just stared at her.

"Then y'all need to find a passel of bettah menfolk, dawlin'" Mary Pat drawled in her southern belle persona.

On the ride back to the stable, their conversation turned to Sandi's theatrical group and the upcoming auditions. Then Marty's name was mentioned.

Friday: It was one day until the auditions. Marty was at the art supply store getting material to make full-sized mock-ups of some packaging designs that were being considered by one of his clients. His cellphone chimed that he had received a text message. Then another…and then another. What the hell, he thought. They were ganging up on him.

Text from Mary: "What could it hurt?"

Text from Mary Anne: "That voice will have them swooning!"

Text from Mary Pat: "Mah po l'il southern haht is fluttering already!"

Text from Sandi: "You'll be swell, you'll be great!"

Text from Sandi again: "2 dorks are trying out for Herbie. One's a little swishy. Please? Please!"

Text from Marty to all of them: "No, damn it!"

THE AUDITION: A lesson in abject surrender.

10:30 on Saturday morning, Marty and Jessica drove away from CedarView after feeding Dan and Gemmy, then putting them back out into the pasture. Five minutes later they pulled into the parking lot of a tired, little, old shopping center, with several stores permanently closed and FOR RENT posters on several windows. Nestled in the corner of the L-shaped center was a tiny theater. Years before it had been a movie theater, the only one around for miles and miles. Progress struck and multi-screen theaters soon began popping up with stadium seating, reclining seats, and stereophonic sound blasting from twenty speakers, deafening everyone over the age of thirty. This poor little theater didn't stand a chance. There was no way it could be upgraded to compete. It shuttered its doors and sat silent, abandoned, for years. A couple of enterprising theater-lovers found it, leased it (the price was dirt-cheap) and converted it. Hence, RockMount Players, a non-profit, almost totally volunteer group, moved from a school gymnasium in Stone Mountain to beautiful downtown Snellville. Although the shows never sold out, it was a popular venue for residents in the area who just enjoyed inexpensive (okay, really cheap) live shows. Sometimes the Players would put on comedies that were old in the 70s; sometimes they would put on intimate musicals. A space had been built off to the right side of the auditorium for a small orchestra…well, a handful of local musicians.

Jessie reached over and touched Marty's arm as they slowed to a stop. "Just relax, Marty," she said with just a touch of sympathy and a bit of irony in her tone. "It'll be over before you know it. We can go home and continue our non-singing lives." She chuckled as he gave her that squinty-eyed look again.

"Thanks a whole hell of a lot," he said, almost resigned to the fact that he had lost. Well, lost *this* battle at least. "You know I'm doing this just to shut all you chattering magpies up once and for all. I should have stood my ground, but there wouldn't have been any peace if I did so. So, here I am, ready to humiliate myself in front of God knows how many people. I shall do as I'm asked. Then I can proudly say I did it and walk away with my head held high. After that, you can all kiss my ass!"

Jessie shook her head and laughed until tears rolled down her cheeks.

"I love you *so* much, Marty. You're a good sport and I appreciate this. Really I do. Hey, I've seen dozens of your presentations. I know you won't have nerves in front of all these folks. Just enjoy the moment. I don't know if I should kiss Sandi for these five minutes of fun or kick her. I've never met anyone as assertive and likeable at the same time."

"Well, you sure didn't feel that way the first time we met her, did you?"

"Agreed," was Jessie's succinct reply.

"We must have driven past this little shopping center hundreds of times over the years, I don't ever remember seeing a theater here," Marty said, boosting his courage to actually go in.

"I guess it's because we were never actually looking for it, were we?" Jessie said, about ready to push Marty out of the car.

As they approached the little theater, almost hidden away in its little corner, they noticed a big sign posted on the door: OPEN AUDITIONS TODAY! Marty sighed. "Okay," he said, "let's get this charade over with.

They opened the door and entered a tiny lobby area. There were children of various ages running around, laughing, squealing and chasing one another. Marty's sphincter clamped shut. Doors were open leading into the auditorium, so they headed in that direction.

"Hold up a second," Marty said, as they were about to pass the restrooms. "I'll be right back out. Better stop in here first."

"Check the toilet for snakes," Jessie teased, referring to his phobia.

Marty glared back at her. "I'm just going to pee, dammit!"

Jessie giggled.

The house lights were up and were bright. Unflattering, to say the least. Theaters have a magical quality about them when the lights are low, in anticipation of something wonderful and entertaining about to commence. Now the theater looked dingy and old. Well, basically it *was* dingy and old, albeit with new seats. The stage was built out into the audience with a new proscenium arch where a movie screen once blazed. An upright piano sat in the middle of the bare stage, surrounded by a few men and, surprise, surprise, Sandi. When she saw Marty, she leaned in and whispered something to one of the men on stage. He turned to look. She had whispered to Gus Mansard, the director, "This is the guy I told you about." She practically flew off the stage like Peter Pan on the way to Neverland and ran, no, bounced, toward Marty, giving him a great big hug.

Jessie had found a seat in the far last row, to remain out of the way. She slouched down in her seat, hoping that Sandi hadn't seen her.

Sandi gave Marty a of couple papers to read and sign. The theater required certain personal information on everyone auditioning and disclaimers regarding personal injuries, etc., etc.

"Personal injuries?" questioned Marty. "I'm here to act like a fool, not be shot out of a cannon. What the hell?"

"Oh, just some simple formalities, Marty," Sandi laughed. "No big deal. They just want to know address, age, and statistics like height, weight, and hair color. No big deal," she repeated.

Marty filled out the paperwork and Sandi hand delivered it to Gus.

A few minutes later, a rotund woman blew a whistle and everything came to a screeching halt. Kids stopped running. Conversations abruptly ended. Dead silence. *This must be the regular routine here*, Marty thought.

It was. Gus Mansard stood and turned to the audience. He was rail-thin, had a shock of thick, startlingly white hair, and a voice two octaves lower than God's. Marty estimated that Gus was probably in his early 60s or thereabouts.

"Okay, folks," Gus bellowed (or, as they say in the theater, projected) from center stage. He walked to the edge of the stage and looked around at the assembled masses. "I have to say, that this show will be the most ambitious we have ever produced here. It's been one of my particular favorites for years. It won't be an easy show, like most of our others have been. It's challenging but should be very rewarding." He stopped to take a breath and clear his throat. "I am thrilled that we have a leading lady to take on the role of a lifetime. I would not agree to direct this show unless she would agree to star." A pregnant pause here, as if he was waiting for applause. "Okay, then. We'll be hearing the children first. We have several roles for them, from age five through the teens. Let's assume that you all know 'Let Me Entertain You', so we don't have to fart around...I mean *fool* around with a multitude of songs. When I call your name, come on up here next to the piano."

If it was at all possible, the lights suddenly seemed to get brighter. One could almost hear the trumpets blare and Aida's triumphal march begin. Dottie Washington had entered the building. She started walking down the center aisle, taking off her coat and gloves as she walked, tossing them into one of the seats.

"That's her. That's Dottie," said Sandi, leaning in to whisper to Marty.

"So that's the goddess herself, eh," snickered Marty. "Where's her sedan chair and Nubian slaves carrying her?" Marty whispered back.

Sandi swatted him on the shoulder.

Dottie Washington *was* attractive in an offbeat way. No one would ever call her beautiful (as Sandi had), but she exuded a sensuality that was hard to miss. She was neither tall nor short, had dark brown hair cut into a bob, large pouty lips and just a hint of a bump on the bridge of her nose. By the way she sauntered down the aisle, it was apparent, at least to Marty, that this diva thought her shit didn't stink.

The first child's name was called and the auditions began. *Well, damn,* thought Marty, *this is going to be a very long day.* In actuality, the kids' tryouts went by smoothly and swiftly. Dottie chatted with many of them as they left the stage. Obviously she knew many of them from previous shows. A lunch break was called. Sandi hastened to get Marty and Dottie together. She did the introductions. Jessie, who had fallen asleep several kids ago, suddenly sat up straight and peered up front.

"Nice meeting you, Marty," Dottie purred. "It's nice to see fresh meat come join our little troupe of players. What have you done before?"

"What do you mean? Acting wise?" Marty responded. "Nothing. Absolutely nothing. I'm not an actor. I'm not a singer. I'm here practically on a dare."

Dottie looked askance; Sandi cringed. "Well," said Dottie. "Well. Well. Well." She turned to walk away. "Break a leg, then, dear."

Jessie slid back down into her seat, laughing harder than she should have.

An hour later, they were back at it. Gus's voice once again boomed across the auditorium…and was probably heard three towns away. "Well, we all know who our 'Rose' will be, now let's see who her handsome leading man will be, shall we?" A name was called and a middle-aged, balding guy approached the piano. Marty couldn't believe that guys still did horrendous comb-overs, especially like this one.

"Okay, Jerry," said Gus to the man, "I know that 'Wherever We Go' is, basically, Rose's song but it's a good one to hear a voice and how you handle a melody. I want to hear you solo it at first, then Dottie can sing with you as a duet. I want to hear your voices together. Okay?"

"Sure thing, Gus. Let's do it!"

The piano began. Jerry came in a bit late but picked it up.

"A little louder, Jerry. I can't hear you," called Gus who was sitting in the front row of the theater.

Marty actually knew this song and was humming along, very, very quietly.

Jerry finished, and then Dottie joined him for the duet. When they finished, there was a smattering of applause.

"Jeff Pringle, I know you're out there somewhere. Jeff? Come on up, you're next, my friend," called Gus.

Marty assumed it was Jeff Pringle who loped up onto the stage. He was tall; perhaps six feet, bearded, and grinned like the Cheshire cat. Not unattractive, but one would not ever call him handsome. He had been the male lead in just about every musical the Players had produced within the past several years. He bowed to the audience before heading to the piano. He got a small round of applause and some laughter.

He began to sing. "A little less swishy, there, Jeff," called Gus. "We're not doing 'La Cage'."

"Swishy? What the hell? I'm *not* doing swishy." He started over from the beginning. No hint of swish.

Solo, then duet…over and done. A nice round of applause. There were several moments of discussion up at the piano. Gus turned to look out into the audience.

"Marty Howce? Is Marty Howce still out there?" Gus asked. Marty rose and stepped forward. "Well, then, come on up here. Don't be shy. Let's see what you can do, man."

Marty stood up and headed for the stage. "Wait a second, young man," said Gus. "Sandi has told me great things about you but I don't know you from Adam. I have no idea about what you can or can't do. Tell me a little bit about yourself. What *do* you do aside from coming to auditions on a dare?"

Marty sort of chuckled inside. *Well,* he thought to himself, *I've pissed off the director as well as the leading lady, so it's a cinch I'll be outta here in a heartbeat.* Marty told Gus about his profession, what he did, about the presentations he gave, and about his family.

"Sandi was right," said Gus, looking Marty up and down. "You do have an incredible voice. Speaking voice, that is. Haven't a clue about your singing abilities. Of course Jack Klugman couldn't carry a tune in a bucket and look where that got *him.*"

Gus then gave Marty the same instructions as the other two men and he walked up onto the stage and stood next to the piano. Marty took a deep breath. Jessie held *her* breath. And Sandi crossed her fingers.

The piano began and so did Marty.

"Slow down just a bit, Marty," Gus said. "You're getting ahead of the piano."

He surprised Jessie. He surprised Sandi. He surprised himself.

Dottie gazed into his eyes when they sang the duet.

When the song ended, there was silence. Total silence.

The audition continued well into afternoon, and then segued into early evening. The children had been dismissed earlier while all the adult characters could be auditioned. Some of the actors would be cast in multiple roles, if at all. Gus thanked everyone, with a nod from the rotund lady who Marty never got to meet, and a bow from the piano player. "We'll let you know who's doing what, if at all," said Gus. "I appreciate all of your time and your respective talents…or lack thereof," he joked. A few nervous laughs followed. "Good night, everyone. Drive safely. Perhaps we'll all be rehearsing again sometime soon. I'll be in touch. Or not."

One by one, everyone got their coats and meandered, chatting, toward the exit. Marty turned to look back at the stage as he and Jessie walked up the center aisle. Dottie and Gus were sitting at the piano, side by side, her head leaning gently on his shoulder. He played softly and she sang as the theater lights slowly dimmed.

Jessie and Marty drove straight to the stable following the audition. It was beyond feeding time and they knew Dan and Gemmy would be pissed. Horses and senior citizens get grumpy when they're not fed on time.

"Marty, I'm proud of you. I think you did a great job. Surprised the hell out of me," Jessie said, almost in a whisper, as they slowly pulled down the driveway to CedarView.

"I'm just glad it's over and now you ladies can leave me the hell alone about all this crap. I flubbed it, I can tell. That poor piano player just couldn't keep up with me. We were all over the place. Nobody said anything afterwards. They didn't have to."

"But, they…" Jessie started.

"End of discussion, please, Jessie. It's over now."

They fed and groomed their two horses and then put them back out into the pasture. There were snow flurries in the air and Marty felt them brush his face softly as he walked back to the car. Jessie was looking forward to dinner and then a cup of hot chocolate after telling the boys about their father's big day. Marty was looking forward to a gin and tonic. Period.

The following week was an extremely busy one for Marty. If he was not in his little home studio working on the several projects he had going, he was out giving a couple presentations to his clients. Revisions were required on a few of his concepts and a few more were accepted as final artwork moved to the production stages. Every time his cellphone chirped, he winced, hoping it wouldn't be from the RockMount Players. Sandi had told him that the rotund lady who he never met was actually Gus's very loyal assistant, Gladys Floy. She had been taking extremely judicious notes throughout the audition and both she and Gus would be the ones making the casting decisions.

One of the phone calls this week was from Stet Brandson. He was, indeed, moving ahead with his art gallery and wanted to spend some time with Marty regarding potential names and logo development. Marty was actually very excited about this prospect and set an appointment time for them to get together. Stet had become one of Marty's favorite people and this would be a fun project.

Early Saturday morning Marty's phone chirped. It was Sandi. She was seemingly breathless, if that was possible. She had gotten the call from the Players a few minutes ago and, yes, she had gotten the part of Dainty June. It was so obvious during the audition that she was perfect for the role that Marty wasn't surprised.

"I can't wait!" she squealed into the phone. Marty had to hold the phone away from his head. Her voice was so piercing. "The rehearsals will start next Monday. It's an elaborate show, so we'll have six weeks of rehearsals. We'll open on March the fifteenth. Yikes, the ides of March!" and she laughed. Did you hear from them yet?"

"Nope, nada, zip…not a word," Marty answered. "I'm sure that I won't. That Jeff guy seemed like he'd be perfect for the part. Isn't he always the lead in all your shows?"

"Yeah, he is," answered Sandi, sounding a bit dejected. "Everybody thinks he's hot shit, including himself. But I don't get it. He's not…well, I don't want to say anything disparaging about anybody. I guess he'd do okay."

"Good luck, Sandi, you'll be outstanding, I have no doubt. Jessie and I will come to every performance and cheer you from the front row."

"Thanks. You guys are the greatest. See ya at the stable later. Bye!"

Thirty minutes later Marty's phone chirped again. Unknown Caller was on the screen. *I hate these damn robocalls*, thought Marty; *there must be a way to block them.* But he answered anyway before it went to voice mail.

"Marty?" asked a deep male voice.

"Yes, good morning," Marty responded.

"Hey, this is Gus Mansard. I wanted to thank you for coming to the audition. I should have taken a bit of time afterwards to chat with you a bit more. Dottie and I did a *lot* of chatting afterwards."

Marty tensed up. *Where the hell is this going? Please don't let this be what I think it is*, he thought.

"Marty, Dottie and I would love to have you be our 'Herbie'. You two would be so perfect together. Please say yes!"

Marty said "Oh, for shit's sake!"

MARCH

One Eggroll Too Many

"Curtain Up! Light the lights!"

Stephen Sondheim

Jeff Pringle was seething. He was seated in the second row, behind all the actors selected for the leading, or more important roles. He had been cast in dual roles: Uncle Jocko, a buffoon of a host for a kiddie talent show, and Mr. Goldstone, a booking agent for the Orpheum Circuit (a big deal during the heyday of vaudeville). Uncle Jocko has, at best, three dozen lines of dialogue; Mr. Goldstone is a non-speaking part. Both roles are early in the first act, and then they never appear again in the show. His mind was racing, with excruciating, demeaning thoughts. *What the hell?* he thought. *I've always been the lead. Audiences love me. What the hell? In strides this… this nobody out of nowhere. I hate open auditions. It's not fair. What the hell? Yeah, sure, he's good looking. Sure, he has a great voice. Couldn't really tell from what little singing he did if he can really sing. What the hell? And who knows if he can even act, for Christ's sake! I'm pissed, for damn sure. I hate him already! What the hell? I wonder what he looks like naked?*

It was the first night of rehearsal. Scripts had been distributed along with yellow highlighters. This was going to be a read-through, where the actors would read and highlight their lines of dialogue. No acting required, just straightforward reading aloud. Gus Mansard had introduced himself first (as if he really needed it but, his ego being what it was…well, you know), and then asked everyone to introduce themselves to the rest of the cast and tell what role, or roles, they'd be playing. Several actors were playing dual roles…except the leads, of course. Jeff Pringle grimaced when his turn to speak was approaching. Gus then described what would be happening over the next six weeks. A lot of hard work ahead for such a monumental show, but he promised, it would be well worth it. He introduced the crew who would be designing the sets and indicated that they would be simple moveable flat panels with various painted scenes. "We're definitely *not* Broadway here, folks," he joked. His assistant, Gladys Floy was taking notes. The musicians would be introduced later in the week.

"We'll do our read-through tonight," Gus continued, "then go home and start memorizing your lines. I know most of you and I know that you're quick learners. I expect to be off-book by the middle of next week. Two weeks, tops. Tomorrow we'll start to do the blocking, scene by scene."

The term "blocking" meant that the director would instruct and place the actors in their various positions and movements for the best interest and dramatic effect throughout a scene. Entrances, exits, and everything in between. In essence, it is a form of choreography. The term "off-book" means that the actors have memorized their lines and will no longer need to rely on their scripts.

The children involved in the show, and there were many, would be rehearsed early every evening so they could get home to bed. Their rehearsal call-time was 6 P.M. and they would be finished by 8. The adults' call-time was 7 P.M. and would go until 10…or perhaps beyond, if needed. The weekends would be strenuous, with rehearsal from 9:30 A.M. until, possibly, 6 P.M., with a lunch break in between.

Marty's head was swimming. Why, oh, why had he ever agreed to even audition? His workload at home was daunting and now this! Then, one more element was added to the mix. Gus remembered that Marty had told him, during their little chat at the audition, he was a graphic designer. Gus pulled Marty aside after the read-through (which went very well, by the way) and asked if perhaps, just perhaps, if he had the time, could Marty design the show posters? Oh, and the program cover as well? In his mind, Marty closed his eyes, put a pistol to his head and pulled the trigger.

"Sure, Gus, I'd love to," Marty lied. "I'll come up with a few concepts and bring them with me tomorrow night." *Yay, like I need one more thing to add to my plate!*

Gus put his two palms together and clapped them silently in a tiny motion. Then he gave Marty a theatrical bow. *Oh dear God,* Marty *thought, what a freakin' ham.*

The cast was dismissed, and they all scurried off to their respective cars, drove to their respective homes and dove into their respective scripts. Marty slammed the door as he entered his house, startling Jessica who had fallen asleep in front of the television. "Well, here's another nice mess you've gotten me into, Stanley," he said as he strode into his office, slamming *that* door as well.

Stet was due for a brief meeting with him around 10 o'clock the morning following the first rehearsal, so Marty was frantically making early morning phone calls to clients, putting some finishing touches on concepts that he would be presenting later in the day to another client and beginning to think about some potential theater posters for The RockMount Players' grand production. Three cups of coffee and a quick shower later, Marty sat in front of his computer tapping furiously as he awaited Stet. Baillie, Marty's beautiful collie, announced Stet's arrival by running to the window and barking. Marty greeted his friend at the door with a hearty handshake.

"Can I get a you a cup of coffee, Stet?" asked Marty.

"Nah, I'm good, thanks. I stopped by Mary's place on the way here and had a couple of cups."

Judging by that silly look on your face, Marty thought, *you had a bit more than just coffee.*

Stet was almost afraid to bring up this topic, but he asked Marty about the show.

"Don't even go there, my friend," he said, shaking his head and rolling his eyes. "Never in a million years did I ever imagine such a thing. Shit, I barely sing in the shower, much less in front of a theater full of strangers. Jessie and her partners in crime...including your beloved Mary...are to blame for this impending disaster. One way or the other, I'll get even!" And both men laughed. "Okay, Stet, what's up with *your* new adventure?"

Stet had brought a large notebook and a printout, which he handed to Marty.

"Mary's son, Greg, is flying in from Chicago this afternoon. He and his college roommate have their own little architectural firm outside of the city. He may or may not be helping me in selecting, then building-out a gallery. He and I haven't met in-person yet, but all three of us have Skyped like crazy the past few weeks. I'm excited about this and, honestly, scared shitless as well. Maybe you and I are in somewhat the same boat, eh?" Marty just slowly shook his head.

"Who knows where either of us will end up," Marty said with a sigh. "Both of us could be naively boarding the Titanic. Whatcha got there? What's this printout?"

"I started playing with some potential names for the gallery. You're the expert, so I want an opinion or two...or three," answered Stet. "Please be honest. I can take it."

Marty glanced down the list of names and immediately had opinions about all of them. *Frankly,* he thought *they all stank,* but he would go down, one by one, and explain to Stet exactly *why* they stank. He would ease into it, though.

"These are good beginnings," Marty sort of lied. "I know you're looking for something distinctive and memorable. A name that will look great when all the art critics review your shows," and he winked at Stet. Stet nodded.

"Okay, here we go," Marty began. "You seem to want to get across that you're a southern gallery, hence the Southern Creations, Southern Inspirations, Southern Perceptions, Vision South, Southern Images, Inspire South. I get your thinking here, but a couple of them sound like churches. Southern Creations and Creations Unlimited both sound like a fashion house. A couple of the others...well, Creation Plus sounds like something out of Genesis on steroids. And Terminus Gallery. Look, I know that's the original name for Atlanta but, frankly, it sounds like the end of the line."

Stet's shoulders drooped and Marty could tell that he was deflated.

"Yeah…I see your point, Marty. I guess I came up with these too quickly."

"Now, wait a minute, Stet. I'm just giving *my* opinion. If you are in love, really in love with any of these names, then go with it. This is *your* gallery. *Your* business. Hey, Mary Anne didn't listen to me when she started *her* little catering business for the kids. I hated the name Cater-Tots and hated, even more, the stupid tag line she came up with to put on her van. She insisted…I designed her damn logo…and she's thriving like crazy these days. So, just because I've been in this business for twenty some-odd years, and won countless awards, doesn't mean I have all the answers. I didn't mean that in a flippant way, understand. I'm just being honest."

"I *do* understand, Marty and I *do* appreciate your honesty. Damn, you were fast. You just glanced at my list and made some very valid points about each and every one of them. I'm impressed. You *do* know your stuff and I sincerely respect that. It took me all of two seconds to relook at my list and absolutely agree with every critique you made. Back to the proverbial drawing board, I guess."

"Don't be too dejected, my friend," Marty said, trying to console Stet. "This is merely a beginning. Yes, a name is very important, for sure. As I said a few minutes ago, you want it distinctive, memorable, recognizable and so forth. If you think coming up with a name is tough, just wait until you and whomever you get to design the place get going. There will be some knock-down, drag-'em-out fights, for sure. You all will be squabbling about every damn thing, right down to the light switches, believe me."

Stet slid back in his chair and sighed.

"Don't worry, Stet. You have the balls to do this. It won't be any easy process, but it *will* be a rewarding one. Trust me. I know. Just takes time. Listen to others and listen well but, by no means, refuse to speak up about *your* musts and wants. This time next year your shows will be opening to critical accolades and your gallery will be a crowning jewel down there in Buckhead. Just wait…you'll see!"

"Thanks, Marty. You can certainly take me from low to high again in a heartbeat. It might be pure bullshit but, hell, I'm believing it!"

"Granted, Stet, in my profession there *is* a lot of bullshit. I have to schmooze unlikeable clients at times and soothe the ruffled feathers of likeable ones. I can design great things and, by the same token, have to almost prostitute myself by changing some of those great designs into shitty ones because of a client's horrid taste. I can argue, cajole, and plead until the cows come home or, in my case, until the horses come home. Some things end up in my portfolio for me to boast about. Some things will never end up in my portfolio, but they have made a client very happy. Win some, lose some. Quote me if you'd like." Both men laughed.

"You're good, Marty," Stet laughed. "You're good."

"You're a great guy, Stet. I shall enjoy working with you…and Mary and her son. Oh, and I promise that I won't sing a note when we're together."

"Just let me know, Marty, when those tickets go on sale. Mary and I will be there on opening night, sitting in the front row!"

"Oh, for shit's sake!" Marty exclaimed.

Stet and Mary stood side by side, holding hands, in the large lobby area separating the north and south terminals at the Hartsfield-Jackson Atlanta International Airport. They were behind the roped off area designated for people waiting for deplaning passengers as they rode up the long escalators from the transporting trains down below. They had seen by the monitors behind them that her son's plane had landed ten minutes earlier so, depending how quickly he had gotten off the plane and into the train coming from his particular concourse, he could be coming into view momentarily. Mary was excited. Although they communicated via Skype and Facetime often, she hadn't actually seen him in-person in over two years. Stet had been introduced to Greg via Skype as well, so they were not going to be total strangers when they met.

"There he is!" Mary said, dropping Stet's hand and jumping up and down like a schoolgirl. Greg saw her immediately and came running toward her. Boyishly handsome, with a roguish grin, he embraced his mom as they rocked back and forth. Mary kissed him repeatedly on the cheek, then pulled back to look at him. He was shorter than Stet had expected (but what can you tell when you Skype with someone?), perhaps 5' 9" at most, ruffled dark brown hair and with the now fashionable prerequisite of a day's growth of stubble on his face. Stet waited patiently for Mary to release her firm embrace, then formally greeted Greg.

"Hey, Greg, it's great to finally get to meet you face to face instead of screen to screen," said Stet.

"Same here, man," responded Greg with a very deep voice and a very firm handshake.

"Let's head into the baggage area for your stuff and then we can head for home," Mary said.

"Nope, this is it, Mom," answered Greg, indicating the small backpack over his shoulder. "I travel light. Always do. We can head out now!"

"But you might be here for a week or so, you know," Mary said, looking at Greg's backpack.

Greg laughed. "Mom, I backpacked through Europe for a month with just about what I have in there now. Like I said, I travel light. Come on, let's go."

He and Stet exchanged glances and smiled. Stet was the exact same way. Stet had backpacked up and down the Appalachian Trail with a small backpack as well. And travelling throughout Europe? That was the only way to go! Stet had no doubt that he and Greg would hit it off just perfectly.

Although Mary hadn't accepted Stet's invitation to move in with him (yet), she and her son *would* be staying with him while Greg was in town. Stet's place would be their base of operations. The drive from the airport to the little town of Between would take about two hours, depending upon traffic, which was always bad. The three of them chattered, non-stop, from the minute they got into Stet's pickup. Stet told them about his early morning meeting with Marty, where all the names he had come up with were shot down in flames. He told them a few of the names.

Greg laughed. "I don't know this Marty guy, but I agree…totally, with him. No offense, man, but…well, no offense."

Stet gave him the stink-eye and they all laughed.

Almost three hours later they turned off the road heading toward Stet's place and pulled down his long driveway. His ultra-contemporary house came into view.

"Holy fuck, man! I love your freakin' house," exclaimed Greg. "I just may stay here forever!"

Meanwhile, back at the Howce house…

Marty had just enough time to put the finishing touches on half a dozen poster concepts for the theater, print them out, grab a quick bite to eat, kiss the boys and Jessie and then head out to rehearsal. He was tired already. He pulled into the parking spaces behind the theater, grabbed his concepts and script and entered the door marked, strangely enough, STAGE DOOR. He heard the tinkling of a piano and the young voices of children singing "Let Me Entertain You". *Kids are quick learners,* Marty thought. Their rehearsal time for today was running down and the adults' time was about to begin. He walked through the back room area, passing what had become a large prop and costume room, a tiny restroom and a couple other very small rooms that Marty assumed must be dressing rooms. He peered out from around thick curtains to see the kids still frolicking about on the stage. The piano had been rolled off to the side. He looked out into the audience and saw that several of the other adults had arrived and were studying their scripts. Gus was watching the kids on stage and nodding his head in tune to the music. He applauded, the kids stopped.

"Great job, boys and girls," he boomed, "A very nice beginning. You should all be very pleased. Can't wait to see what happens with real choreography there."

The kids looked at one another and smiled, some giving each other a high-five.

"Okay," Gus continued, "now git home and get some rest. You guys are gonna be great. See you all tomorrow. Pleasant dreams!" Aside from being a very good director, Gus was an excellent actor: he absolutely hated children. But, with this particular show, children played a very important part, if only early in act one.

Marty stepped down quietly into the auditorium and sat next to Dottie and Sandi, acknowledging all the other adults with a nod and a wave. Jeff Pringle nodded back and, in his imagination, shot Marty the bird.

The children and their parents departed. Gus called for the actors who would now be a part of act one, scene one…which included Marty, Dottie and Jeff Pringle.

"Okay, folks," Gus began. "We'll pretend that the kids are still here doing their stuff and we'll block what you'll be doing."

Dottie already knew that her first entrance, as Momma Rose, in the show would be the classic, traditional one for this show: from the back of the house, she would come striding down the center aisle toward the stage with brass and bravado. Gus later had the idea that perhaps when Marty (Herbie) makes *his* first entrance it should be in the same manner. At that point in the show, Herbie had been watching Rose's two daughters perform on a vaudeville stage.

The rest of the evening's rehearsal went fairly well, with blocking being assigned and rehearsed a few times. It was a beginning. Marty was actually beginning to enjoy this. Things were winding down. Gus was pleased with this night's work and he announced that everyone could call it a night. Marty pulled him aside and got his poster concepts from a large envelope. At first, Marty thought Gus was having a heart attack by the way he staggered back and clutched at his chest.

"Good God, Marty!" Gus exclaimed loudly. "You amaze me. These are fucking brilliant. Better than the ones used on Broadway, I swear."

Marty wondered who would ever have the guts to tell the director that he was over-acting.

"We'll put these up for a vote with everyone tomorrow. We run a democratic ship here," Gus said excitedly, "but I already have my favorite. It needs just a little tweaking. Don't get concerned…just a little tweaking, Marty. But these are great. Thank you, thank you, thank you." Again with a theatrical bow.

Jeff Pringle had overheard the conversation…well, who *couldn't*, with Gus's booming voice…from across the auditorium. He put on his coat and headed for the exit. "Fuck him," he muttered under his breath. "I hope he *does* break a leg!"

Stet, Mary, and Greg had enjoyed a delicious steak dinner and then round after round of after-dinner shots of fine tequila. Greg was as impressed by the interior of Stet's house as he had been when he first saw the exterior when they drove up earlier that afternoon. It hadn't taken Greg very long to take to Stet like an older brother rather than his mother's lover. After all, only three years separated them. And Stet had immediately liked Greg as well. This was going to be a fun week. The prospect of touring potential gallery locations thrilled both of the guys and they chattered away into the night like long-lost friends. Their conversation was punctuated, from time to time, by shrieks of boyish laughter. Mary was very happy, watching her two "boys" getting acquainted.

Greg had gotten his architectural degree from the prestigious Cooper Union in New York City. It was an intensive five-year course, which Greg had breezed through with an insatiable hunger for more and more knowledge. His classmate, roommate and best friend, Ashton DuRand, was from Chicago and Greg visited that city a few times during holiday breaks. He fell in love with the excitement and history of that city by the lake. Ashton, Ash for short, and Greg moved to Chicago upon graduation and immediately set up their own little shop. Ash's Dad, a stockbroker working and residing on Chicago's Magnificent Mile, had been a staunch backer and it didn't take too long before the two guys were doing renovation work on older buildings and homes in the area. Greg's girlfriend throughout his Cooper Union years, an art student, was a beautiful young lady from Ireland. Doolin, Ireland to be exact. Greg had spent several trips across the pond to the Emerald Isle snuggled in Aideen's arms while flying First Class. Aideen was loaded! Well, her parents were anyway. Her parents owned two of the best B&Bs in Doolin and one of the most popular pubs, where tourists clamored every single night of the week, year-round, for authentic Irish music while downing pint after pint of Guinness. Aideen had refused to move to Chicago with Greg and Ash but it appeared that things were beginning to cool down between them anyway.

Stet had printed out several potential locations that the three of them would explore this coming week. They also checked them out via the realtors' websites. He had set up several appointments with realtors for the tours. None of them knew what to expect, but Greg had had some experience, obviously, with renovating and reconfiguring old buildings. Ash was holding down the fort in Chicago for the week that Greg would be in Atlanta as their workload had slowed down during the cold foreboding Illinois winter weather.

Stet glanced at his watch. "Hey, guys," he said, "it's almost midnight and we have a long day ahead of us tomorrow. Time to call it a night?"

"Oh, come on," said Greg, "it's only 11 by my time. It's still the shank of the evening."

"Shank of the evening?" laughed Stet. "What the fuck? I haven't heard that expression in ages. You're a throw-back, young man," laughing again.

"Who're you calling 'young man', young man?" Greg slurred. Tequila has that effect, you know. "You're what? Six months older than me?"

"Three years, you young whippersnapper!" joked Stet, also beginning to slur his words.

The guys started playfully poking and jabbing at each other like little kids. In a flash, the two of them got into a fake wrestling match, rolling around on the floor, tossing and turning, each one trying to pin the other one down. Luger, Stet's Doberman, started barking and bouncing around the two men, almost joining them in the roughhousing.

"Jesus H. Crist," shouted Mary. "What are you, five-year-olds? Stop acting so ridiculous. Grow up!" Then she, too, laughed.

The two men rolled off one another and lay flat on their backs, breathing heavily, with their arms outstretched. Greg stared straight up at the ceiling. Luger quickly curled up next to Stet.

"Shit, I haven't had this much fun in years. I love you guys. I know I just met you Stet but, dammit, I love you already," Greg said wistfully. "Mom, I've missed you *so* much. I don't want this week to end."

By the end of the week, after being shown a half-dozen different sites and rejecting all but one, Stet, Greg and Mary had agreed on a particular location in the heart of Buckhead, on Pharr Road, two blocks off of Peachtree Street. Stet wanted his two backers, the Hollidays, to tour it, too, before any final decisions would be made. All the parties concerned made appointments for the weekend to do just that.

By the end of the week, rehearsals had proceeded beautifully. All the actors had really gotten familiar with each other and lines were beginning to be learned. The entire first act had been blocked. Marty, having listened, by now, to the original cast album, realized that Herbie really didn't have all that much singing to do. A couple lines in a couple songs, part of a duet with Rose and a song involving him, Rose and Louise (the soon-to-be Gypsy Rose Lee). However, during this time came the part in the show where Momma Rose and Herbie have their first kiss. Uh, oh! Marty was uncomfortable. He had never kissed another woman on the lips since he and Jessica got married. Years ago! The scene was set, the lines were spoken and he and Dottie leaned into each other. Their lips touched. Marty's heart started pounding...he was feeling guilty. Like he was cheating on Jessie. Wait, this is only acting. He started to pull back, finishing the kiss. Dottie held on for five seconds longer. When he opened his eyes, she was staring at him.

"Whoa," sighed Dottie, "your wife is one lucky-ass lady!"

Gus came up to them. "You know," he said looking at them both. "I've seen dozens of productions of this show and this is the only goddamn time where I can honestly believe that Rose and Herbie actually do sleep with one another!"

The weekend proved eventful...and successful...for Stet's vision of an art gallery. He, Mary and Greg met with Max and Camellia Holliday at the selected site. The flamboyant and completely loveable older couple fascinated Greg. Max was wearing a burgundy sport coat, black slacks and a paisley ascot tucked into his white shirt. Camellia's head was topped with a large, flouncy hat that would put any Kentucky Derby attendee to shame. An extraordinarily long double strand of pearls set off her dark navy blue dress and matching coat. She tottered on dark navy blue high heels. Stet's trio was dressed in scruffy jeans, denim shirts and sneakers.

The place was dusty and smelled musty. Greg took lots of photos with his smartphone all around the site, including the ceiling, the back entryway from the parking lot behind the building and the loading dock. He wrote copious notes in a large pad, took measurements of the entire place and quickly drew rough sketches of some random thoughts. He wanted to know the structural integrity of certain walls before tearing them down, if necessary. He and the agent chatted constantly as they moved throughout the space, Greg asking question after question. The overall space was large, square-foot wise, but there were too many rooms that broke it up. Greg envisioned a more open space. The agent who had accompanied them to the site provided a couple sets of blueprints. Greg had several ideas already about the potential layout, as did Stet.

Greg called Stet and Max over to what would become the larger part of the gallery. They stood side-by-side as Greg started talking, facing the back wall. He extended his right arm straight out with his hand bent at the wrist, facing upwards toward the ceiling, and made a very broad sweep, from left to right. He then quickly drew a very rough sketch in his note pad to illustrate his concept. Max was impressed. Stet got a look on his face that said "WOW!" Mary and Camellia stood aside and chatted while the men did their surveying and note taking.

"What do you think, guys?" Stet asked the two men.

"Great possibilities here, man," answered Greg.

"It could work," added Max.

"Sign the damn papers and let's go to lunch!" chimed Camellia from across the room. And everybody laughed.

The price, per square foot, had seemed a tad high to Max but Stet assured him that that seemed to be the going rate in this part of tony Buckhead. Greg had done a little research on his smartphone beforehand, quickly and quietly, as they were roaming through the building. He slowly wandered over to Stet.

Greg, leaning shoulder to shoulder, whispered into Stet's ear: "I know that I'm telling you something that you should already know. Negotiate. Remember that *everything* is negotiable. Going rate or not, I repeat, negotiate. Don't seem too eager. The agent is hungry. Play it cool, man. This place has been vacant for some time. A long time."

In the days that would follow, a lot of paperwork and more meetings were scheduled with the realtor, Stet, Max and a lawyer friend of the Hollidays. All the legalities would make Stet's head spin…insurance, property taxes, maintenance costs, security deposit, rental (and allowable escalations in the future), and who pays for the modifications and new fixtures (that involves a TIA…Tenant Improvement Allowance), etc., etc. Wait, there's more! Rentable Square Feet vs. Usable Square Feet. Say what? Don't ask. A certain amount of negotiating that was accomplished seemed satisfactory to Stet, the lawyer, and the Hollidays, so it seemed apparent that Stet's dream was becoming a reality.

Greg's flight back to Chicago was at 5 that afternoon. After an hours-long, laugh-filled lunch with the Hollidays at the nearby Fish Market, Stet and Mary drove Greg back to the airport, with nary a lull in the conversation as they sped down I-85. They pulled up to the departure drop-off entry and jostled for a space. Greg grabbed his backpack and hopped out of the truck. Mary and Stet joined him on the sidewalk. Mother and son hugged each other and said their goodbyes. Mary kissed Greg repeatedly on both cheeks. The two men shook hands vigorously, and then embraced.

"This has been an awesome week, guys," said Greg. "It's been a fucking blast. I'll start doodling on the plane, no doubt, and I'll zip off some sketchy ideas to you in a of couple days, Stet. Then we can get down to some serious business. I guess you'll have to run these concepts past the landlord for approval. Facetime, Skype, whatever. This is going to be a fun project. Great for our portfolio. I can't wait for Ash to come out here, too. He will be impressed, for sure. He's a real cool guy and you'll hit it off right away, I can tell. Hey, gotta go! Love you guys!"

Greg turned and disappeared among a throng of a gazillion people heading off to God knows where.

The weekend proved eventful…and successful for the cast of "Gypsy". The long days were exhausting but fun, as the show slowly began coming together. Gus had made several alterations to his blocking, but they all seemed to be for the best. Sandi was ecstatic as she watched Marty run through his lines and scenes like a pro. She was *so* glad she had persuaded him to audition. She chuckled inwardly as she observed loopy Jeff Pringle glare at Marty.

Just in time for the lunch break on Saturday, Marty noticed a man enter from the back of the theater and look around. Nobody but Marty was left in the room. He didn't recognize him from the audition or the preceding week of rehearsals. There was an arrogant saunter about this man. For some reason, Marty instantly had an image of a Mafia Don pop into his head. The guy was short, middle-aged, fairly good-looking in a rough around the edges way and was dangling a set of car keys in his hand.

"I'm looking for Dottie Washington," said the man abruptly. "Seen her? She here?"

"Yes," answered Marty. "I think she may have just gone to the restroom. Does she know you?"

"Yeah, kinda," was the smug answer. "I'm her husband."

"Oh, damn! I'm so sorry. I didn't realize that," apologized Marty. "I'm sure she'll be right back out."

"No problem," came the reply…and no smile either. This man did *not* exude warmth.

Marty tried to add a little levity to this icy beginning. "Hi, I'm Marty Howce," he said, extending his hand. "I play Herbie. I'm the guy who kisses your wife."

"Good. Thanks. Takes the pressure off *me*." And the wiseguy turned away, still looking, waiting for Dottie. Marty's arm was still extended for a handshake, which was totally ignored.

Oooooh-kay, then, thought Marty. *Nice to meet you, too, Mister Shithead!*

A few seconds later, Dottie returned to the stage area, saw her husband and then got her purse. She withdrew a set of car keys and exchanged them for the ones in her husband's hand.

"Thanks for getting my car serviced," she said coldly to her husband. "I took good care of yours on the way here this morning. Not a scratch on it."

He nodded, turned around and locked eyes with Marty for a brief moment, and then exited the building without a word to Dottie. Not even a smile.

"Don't mind him," Dottie said as she saw Marty watching, "he's not always such a grump. Once or twice a year he smiles."

Marty shrugged, as if to say no big deal…not my problem…who the hell cares.

The next couple of weeks zipped by, with the show taking shape perfectly. The musicians joined the rehearsals, choreography was addressed (Marty had a very brief dance sequence with Dottie to accompany one of their duets), costumes were made and fitted and the sets were painted. Marty was very impressed. Their moms made most of the kids' costumes. The rolling, moveable panels were painted with various scenes, from an old vaudeville theater, apartment room, Chinese restaurant, office, and an old burlesque dressing room. The one scene that Marty thought was especially effective was an old deserted railway platform, with train tracks disappearing off in the distance. Pretty cool, he thought! Lighting effects were created by a couple of older guys who really knew what they were doing. This show was going to be beautiful.

Oh, and then there were the three strippers! Always a musical number to get the loudest round of applause, this song, "You Gotta Get A Gimmick", was a classic showstopper if ever there was one. The three actresses who had been selected for these roles were absolute perfection. Marty loved watching them rehearse this number, over and over. He knew they were sure to bring down the house.

The final weekend before opening, they ran through the show from beginning to end a couple times each day. Both Rose and Herbie were going to have a very fast (15 seconds) costume change backstage. Dottie had a dresser to help her; Marty would be on his own. He had to get out of one suit and put on another. He was a little uncomfortable about it at first, but then he realized that everyone was going to be so busy elsewhere, nobody would even notice him standing there in his boxer-briefs for all of five seconds.

The night before opening: full dress rehearsal. There were just a couple of minor glitches and a dropped line by a minor player but, other than that, it went well. Gus was pleased and let the group know when the curtain came down. Everyone was excited…yes, even Marty. They were scheduled to run for two weekends. Friday and Saturday nights with a matinee on each of the Sundays. Marty was eager to get back to normal, however, because his workload had not let up and his days had been frantic.

Opening Night! Cue the soundtrack: "Another Op'nin', Another Show"…okay, okay, I know that's from "Kiss Me, Kate", but it sure applies here. Parking in the lot behind the theater, none of the actors would see the notice that had been taped to the front door leading into the lobby: SOLD OUT. Never in the history of this little group had any of their shows been a sell-out.

The house lights dimmed. The overture began, played by a keyboard, a trumpet, one violin, a bass, and a set of drums. Excitement grew. Curtain up…light the lights! It's show time, folks! Momma Rose made her classic entrance down the center aisle, shouting out her directions to her two daughters on stage. Not too long afterwards, Herbie, a travelling salesman selling candy to vaudeville theaters, made *his* entrance down the aisle as well. Sitting in the audience, Mary Anne gave Mary Pat a nudge. "There he is!" she whispered, "There he is!"

Act one sped by, fast costume change and all. As Marty slipped off his pants backstage he glanced up and saw Jeff Pringle peeking at him from around a corner of a curtain. What the fuck? Herbie and Rose are now an item, he becoming their agent. Baby June grows up to be Dainty June; Louise is still awkward; Mr. Goldstone is offered an eggroll (and much more); Rose pisses off the Orpheum Circuit and rips up a contract; June runs away to get married and Rose still thinks everything is coming up roses. Act one ended to great applause.

A fifteen-minute intermission and the theater was abuzz with conversation and laughter. The house lights dimmed again.

Act two began. A lot happens. Rose, Herbie and Louise bounce from town to town, ending up (by accident) getting booked into a burlesque hall. The strippers sing and gyrate, bringing down the house and generating an encore. It always does and Gus had planned for it. Louise is asked to fill in for a missing-in-action stripper; Rose thinks it's a great idea. Louise is nervous. Herbie and Rose have a huge, loud argument and Herbie walks out of Rose's life forever. And then the awkward caterpillar Louise becomes the famous butterfly Miss Gypsy Rose Lee! Then Rose sings her 11'oclock number, "Rose's Turn", which is a stunner and requires a strong set of pipes. Curtain comes down. Thunderous applause, with the audience rising to its feet. Atlanta audiences will give standing ovations if a mouse farts onstage, so why should this audience be any different.

And then the cast got to mingle with the enthusiastic audience in the auditorium. The whole gang from CedarView was there…including Remy Major, to everyone's surprise. Mary and Stet had, indeed, been in the very front row. Marty had seen them when he made his first entrance. Sandi came bouncing over to the group, clapping her hands and jumping up and down. "See?" she squealed with glee, "I told you so! I told you so! Wasn't he fantastic?" Marty shook his head and blushed as they all gushed. From the back of the house came the Hollidays. "Holy crap!" exclaimed Marty. "I never expected to see you guys here, too!"

"Wouldn't miss it for the world," extolled Max. "Now I'm confused. I don't know whether I should call you Hemingway or Olivier!"

Camellia planted a juicy kiss on Marty's cheek, leaving a big red smear of lipstick. Some things never change. "Gracious, Marty!" she blurted, "You took me totally by surprise. Wonderful performance. I just may consider hiring you to be our guest performer at this year's New Years party!"

Max and Camellia had sat in the very last row, so no one behind Camellia would have to ask her to remove her enormous hat.

Slowly but surely the hubbub began to subside as cast members and audience alike drifted away, some to go back stage, some to go home…or out to celebrate.

"Come on, Max," Camellia said as she tugged on her husband's sleeve. "We'd better get going before the parking lot gets emptied out. I don't want us to be the only ones left out there to get mugged in this god-forsaken place. Never been to Snailville before."

"Snellville, dear," answered Max. "Snellville."

The Hollidays got very nervous if they ever had to set foot outside the Atlanta Perimeter.

The weeks had sped by for Stet, as well. Greg had sent several rounds of concepts for the gallery space, with various configurations. They dickered back and forth with revisions and changes until they agreed on a workable layout. The discussions had gotten a little heated on a couple occasions but Greg, in his wisdom, always seemed to prevail. This was followed up with small mockups made of Foamcore, which they both reviewed and discussed via Skype. There would be several moveable panels, which could change the interior layout from show to show. There would be a small reception area at the front of the gallery and a very large, long area behind closed doors at the back of the main space for storage and shipping. Greg had a computer program that enabled him to recreate his concepts as almost walk-through visuals, making it look real. The computer applications included the latest two-dimensional drafting and three-dimensional modeling and animation programs.

He placed several pieces of artwork on his virtual walls…a Picasso here…a Magritte there…and Stet loved it!

"Oh, Greg," Mary told him via Facetime after looking at the walk-through. "You put those guys on HGTV to shame, for sure."

"Who?" was Greg's confused-sounding response. Mary and Stet laughed.

"Never mind. Just take our word for it. This is *so* great. Can't wait to see it come to life."

Greg scheduled a return trip to Atlanta to secure a working crew recommended by the landlord and to take care of all the required permits. Ash, his working partner, would join him for this visit. Mary and Stet were extremely excited about the time they would spend with these guys. They had "met" Ash via Skype during one of their working sessions recently and were eager to meet him in-person. Ash, a tall African-American with skin the color of coffee with just a splash of cream, was just as eager to meet Mary and Stet. Greg had told him about his fun week and he was looking forward to fun, as well as some serious business. This would be their first long-distance project and a great one to add to their portfolio. The one thing that Ash would *not* bring up, however, was the fact that he and Aideen (Greg's soon-to-be ex-girlfriend) had begun a steamy long-distance correspondence. Ah, sweet mystery of life…and love.

The show at RockMount Players was a record-breaking smash hit. Every night had been a sellout; even the sometimes sparsely attended Sunday matinees had been sold out. The show was extended for one more, final performance on the Friday following what would have been the concluding weekend. And then a cast party would follow the next night. Marty was surprised to learn that Dottie and her husband, Nathaniel, would host.

The show's successful run ended, finally, and everyone hugged, kissed, cried and laughed. Makeup came off (yes, Marty had learned how to apply theatrical makeup so his facial features would show up from the back of the house.) and costumes put away. Tired performers drove off into the night, looking forward to a bash the next night.

The next night, Marty and Jessie drove up to a McMansion in the tony Smoke Rise section of Tucker. Marty had told Jessie about Dottie's "friendly" husband; so neither one knew what to expect here. The party was in full swing when they entered and Dottie rushed to greet them as soon as she saw them, kissing Marty on the cheek. She turned to Jessie, "He's a fabulous kisser, you know," she winked at Jessie. "It's been fun, hasn't it?" she gushed. Gus came up to greet them both as well, pumping Marty's hand and patting him on the back.

"You were fabulous, Marty," he oozed charm. "You shouldn't keep your talents hidden. My 90-year-old mother just loved you. She told me that I should have given Herbie a solo, even if it wasn't really in the show. How about *that*, eh?"

"Hell, I'm just glad you didn't," Marty laughed.

(Theater Trivia: Actually, a solo had been written for Herbie, "Nice She Ain't". It was given to Jack Klugman one week prior to opening on its pre-Broadway tryout tour. But he couldn't memorize the keys and the staging in time, so it was cut.)

Another guest, the wife of one of the musicians, came up to Marty. "I thought your Herbie was terrific. You did such a great job. When you got mad at Rose, yelled at her and then left her…well, I cried. I just cried."

"Well, thanks," Marty said, beginning to blush.

Sandi came running up to them and threw her arms around Marty. "Oh. My. God! You were so freakin' amazing. Surprised the hell outta me, frankly. You need to do more shows with us, huh?"

"Not a chance, kiddo," Marty exclaimed with a shake of his head. "Done, finito, nada, over and out! Curtain down…lights out." And all three of them laughed.

The evening went on, no sign of Mister Shithead. Evidently Dottie's husband had better places to be. Maybe he was out dumping a cement-encased body into the Chattahoochee. The group grew louder and drunker, Marty and Jessie included. This was, indeed, a fun little crowd. Marty, taking a little breather from all the drinking and chatting, found a comfortable seat on a small sofa in the corner. Not a minute later, Jeff

Pringle, drunk as a skunk, sidled up next to him, putting one hand on Marty's thigh. Marty thought that if anyone lit a match near him right now, Jeff's head would burst into flame and explode.

"You know, Marty," Jeff slurred big time, "I was watching that quick change that you had to do backstage. Every performance. Nice legs, by the way. I kept hoping that one night you might forget and go commando and I'd get a little surprise, you get my drift?" And he winked.

Marty got up abruptly. "You're barking up the wrong eggroll, Mr. Goldstone!"

APRIL

A Lesson in Seduction

"The tragedy is all right there...in the very beginning, when he smiles at her. When she instantly forgets. Forgets how dangerous he is.

Jane Austin

It was a quiet tree-lined street, ending in a cul-de-sac, with simple, craftsman style houses sitting on well cared for three quarter-acre lots. The French *cul de sac* was originally an anatomical term "vessel or tube with only one opening." How appropriate. All the houses backed up to a densely wooded area, with paths snaking through the trees, sometimes frequented by joggers, hikers and nature lovers often photographing the various native plants. On this beautiful spring afternoon, the leaves on the trees still had that fresh, chartreuse green following their awakening from winter. Ferns had recently unfolded their long fronds and were gently swaying in a soft breeze. The almost daily rains earlier this month had the wooded area looking lush with new growth. The scent of honeysuckle hung in the air.

Various birds were chirping loudly, fluttering from tree to tree. There could also be heard, from time to time, the soft bleating of goats.

The young man slowly walked through the woods, glancing from side to side, and front to back, often, to make sure he wasn't seen…or heard. He had parked his car at the Kroger Shopping Center four short blocks away. Standing just over six feet, his well-muscled arms and chest stretched his tight dark charcoal gray T-shirt. It was late in the afternoon and the sun, piercing through the overhead foliage, seemed to set his closely cropped red hair aflame.

He slowed his pace as he neared the second house from the end of the street. He smiled. He felt a rush. He felt a hard-on beginning. He was also nervous as he cut through the back yard. Tall Leyland Cypress trees bordered each side of the yard, shielding the views from either neighbor. He slowly approached the back door, after climbing the four steps up onto the porch. There were several potted plants, in full bloom, surrounding the porch. *Well kept,* he thought to himself. He hesitated for a few seconds, took a deep breath and rapped lightly on the door's window.

He heard footsteps approaching the door and then her face appeared. *Oh, God, she's gorgeous,* he thought, his heart beginning to race. She smiled at him as she unlocked the door and swept it open wide.

"I wasn't sure you'd actually come," she said with a big grin. "I am so glad that you did, Aaron. Come on in, silly…don't just stand there."

She, too, was tall. Possibly nearly six feet, with raven-dark hair, vivid blue eyes (which may or may not have been contacts) and a toned body from daily workouts. She wore a thin black tank top and short…very short…cutoff jeans. It was obvious that she was braless. He could tell by her protruding nipples. Her hair, which she normally had done up in a ponytail, hung loosely around her shoulders. He liked the look and imagined that, with luck, he'd soon be burying his face in…well, perhaps in everything.

She coyly reached out, hooked her fingers into the top of his jeans and pulled him into the house, closing, and then locking the back door.

"Do you want something to drink? Coke? Beer?" she asked, tilting her head slightly. He continued to stare at her and slowly, ever so slowly, he shook his head. A grin appeared on his handsome face. She reached up with her right hand and took hold of his chin. A bit of ginger stubble; she leaned in close, their lips just a breath apart. His heart nearly leaped from his chest. He had gone commando and he was certain that his erection would soon burst through his button-fly jeans.

She turned around and motioned for him to follow, which he did gladly. He was excited, but nervous. Apprehensive. This was dangerous. This was *so* wrong. But she had initiated it. *Am I being a fool,* he thought? *Shit, I'd be a fool to turn this down!*

Her bedroom was small but the bed was large. He stood in the doorway, almost afraid to enter this den of sin. She was still in her tank top and shorts as she sprawled back against the headboard. He kicked off his sandals but stayed, barefoot, where he was, nerves beginning to show just a bit. She giggled and indicated with her forefinger to come closer. *Here goes,* he thought! He pulled off his T-shirt, revealing his ripped, smooth, freckled chest.

"I just love that flaming red hair of yours, Aaron. It turns me on so much I can't stand it," she said, as she hungrily eyed his torso. "Are you a redhead all over?"

He hastily unbuttoned his jeans, slid them down his legs, and kicked them into the corner.

"Ooooh, my God, you are!" she squealed with delight. "Jesus, I've never seen such luscious red pubic hair and, good lord, young man, you're hung like a fucking horse! It's certainly obvious that you live up to your name, Aaron Hardin. Somehow I just *knew* that you would."

He glanced down proudly at himself and saw that a few drops of pre-ejaculate were glistening on the head of his ramrod erect cock. She noticed it also.

"Come here, Aaron, let me lick that off for a while," she laughed. He was afraid that if she *did* lick it, he would come all over the place.

"Can we take this a bit slow?" he sheepishly questioned.

"Is this the first time for you, Aaron?" she asked with a big grin.

"Oh, hell, no, ma'am," he responded quickly. "Well, in a manner of speaking, yes, I guess it is." And then they both laughed.

"You can call me Josie here, Aaron. Considering what we are about to be doing."

Before he even realized what had happened, Josie was naked and had her hand firmly grabbing his balls. She lay back on the bed and guided his cock up to her face, still holding his balls. She licked it, tasting the sweet-salty pre-ejaculate. He shuddered and tensed up. He did not want to explode…not yet, anyway. His eyes roamed her body…*perfect, perky tits,* he thought. *How did I luck into something like this?* He pulled away, then slid his own face down to her very wet vagina and drove his tongue deeply into it. She moaned, ecstasy an understatement, and wrapped her legs around his now-sweating body. His tongue explored and he loved her taste. In a flash, he moved upwards, swiftly, expertly replacing his tongue with his throbbing cock. She grabbed his firm ass and pulled him in closer, tighter. The bedsprings vibrated and squeaked with each thrust. He was breathing faster and faster. He was trying to fight the building urge of release. It was a losing battle. She kissed him; she squeezed his ass tighter; she wouldn't let him slide his cock out of her. BAM! He came like he had never come before. He screamed; she screamed; his cock felt like it would never stop pulsing, sending load after load of hot semen into her. And he collapsed onto her.

They lay there, side-by-side, naked and dripping with sweat, smelling of sex, for five minutes. Then they did it all again.

We shall leave this torrid little scene for now. Yeah, yeah, I know. Sorta like coitus interruptus, right? But don't worry, we shall hear of this couple later on. It's not what you might think.

MAY

Current Events

"Whatever you want to do, do it now. There are only so many tomorrows."

Michael Landon

April showers bring May flowers. Or so goes the trite old expression. But when April showers linger into May, and linger, and linger…well, they bring sour equestrians. The weather had not been very conducive for riding and the boarders at CedarView grumbled about it every day. Not that there was anything anyone could do about it. Mark Twain was absolutely correct when he said, "In the Spring, I have counted 136 different kinds of weather inside of 24 hours." Seriously. Especially in the South.

Mary Anne was concerned that the inclement weather would ruin her annual Derby Day party. Amber was concerned that the annual horseshow at Double D Stables would be a washout. Or that her trip to St. Simons Island with Raymond would be a soggy, dreary one. Bryan was concerned that the progress on his renovations and repair of the stable would come to a screeching halt, even if temporarily, until those days when the sun actually did shine. The horses weren't concerned at all. They got fed, put out in the pasture, brought back in, fed again with no strenuous riding or workouts to interfere. Happiness, to them, was a flake of hay and a few pounds of sweet feed twice a day. Being that most of the horses also enjoyed rolling in the mud, their owners would forgo the daily grooming. Why bother?

Bryan felt sorry for the new boarders who had moved in at the end of April. *A nice enough couple,* he thought, but after a few conversations with the wife, Bryan (never one to judge), considered her all foam and no beer. Their horse, Machu, a smallish Peruvian Paso, hadn't been saddled since they arrived. Not that Machu really minded.

Charles Tallman had heard about CedarView from a friend of a friend and needed to move their horse from their current stable to make way for a new subdivision. Yes, the developers were on the move again.

"Yeah, I hate progress, sometimes," had said Charles on the phone to Bryan. "Anyway, that's life I suppose. I've lived here in Georgia all my life but my wife is from Yankee-land," he laughed. "Anyway, she's originally from a small town in Massachusetts. Chicopee (which Bryan heard as Chicken Pee) out west of Boston. Anyway, she's been down here long enough for her to say 'y'all' and 'bless your heart' like a good ol' southern gal. Anyway, we'd like to swing by your place, take a look and move on in if it looks good. Anyway, we've heard good things about your place."

"Well, that's just fine, Charles, looking forward to meeting you," Bryan responded, eager to fill up another stall.

"Hey," answered Charles, "Call me Chips. That's my nickname. Hardly ever go by Charles anymore. Got the nickname from my friends when I was a kid. Remember that company that delivered potato chips to your house? The ones in those big cans? Anyway, we used to get them every week and I loved 'em. My friends used to tease me by calling me Charles "Chips" but they eventually dropped the Charles part. And it stuck. Anyway…" and he let the topic just wander away.

Charles…oops, "Chips" was in his late thirties, maybe early forties. He was just shy of 6', with sandy brown hair, very expressive eyes and had a soft speaking voice with just a hint of an accent. He worked in the accounting department at the corporate offices of Home Depot. His wife, Felicity, was mid-thirties, shorter than her husband by a few inches, hair color somewhere between light brown and her next application of Clairol, and was also, very obviously, pregnant. It would be their first child.

Machu fascinated the other boarders. None of them had even heard of that breed. Known for their temperament and comfortable ride, he was a beautiful specimen – solid gray, with a luxurious mane and forelock – although he was short, standing just barely over 14 hands. "Hell," exclaimed Mary when she first saw him, "he could walk right under Thunder without stooping!" Well, not really, but the size difference was laughable. Both Felicity and Chips rode but it was just for pleasure, mainly short trail rides and workouts in the ring. Machu's gait was unusual… well, not for his breed…but it intrigued Mary especially. Chips explained that this particular movement was referred to as "termino", an outward swinging leg action. A few days after moving in, the sun was shining and the temperature was pleasant, so Chips and Felicity gave the boarders a demonstration in the riding ring. They were all impressed and showed it with a hearty round of applause when Machu finished. Several of the other horses that had been put out had trotted up to the edge of the riding ring, which bordered their pasture. Their heads bobbed and there were nickers and snorts as they watched this new arrival. New horse scents for all concerned.

Brandy Dennison finished cleaning up the breakfast dishes, then told Bryan to be careful today (he was going to be up on the roof at CedarView finally getting the chance to replace it) before she headed off to visit her parents. After months of gentle pleading and consoling, Cliff Ambridge, Brandy's father, had still not relented to admit his wife, Sara, to the assisted living facility that Brandy had researched. Not wanting to admit her without patient, tearful conversations (even if she was confused about the entire situation) Sara said she would not go quietly, insisting that nothing was wrong with her and that she would much prefer to go live with her son, Bud. Brandy's older brother, Bud, had died suddenly of a massive heart attack years before. Sara's dementia had progressed within the past year to the degree that, while lucid for great stretches of time, she no longer had a sense of time or place. To her, current events involved the war in Vietnam and what that "awful" President Johnson was doing to this country. And, at times, she lost bladder control. Although he was resisting as long as possible, Cliff began thinking about selling their large house. He maintained it beautifully, but now what was the point of this huge house for only him if, indeed, Sara was put in a…well, how can you really call it a home? He was healthy now but how many tomorrows did *he* have remaining?

"Time speeds up, Brandy," Cliff said sadly. "Days are tumbling together. Bumping into one another. Each morning I awake to a numbing, nameless day. I have to stop and think what day of the week it is. People often use that tired old trite metaphor for life. You know, it's like a roller coaster ride? Well, they got it all wrong. They think it's up, down, and all around faster and faster. With a mixture of screams and laughs, ending with a slow stop. It's *not* like that ride that you and Bud loved so much up at that lake. What was it…the Lost River? *That* ride ended with a laugh-filled splash in the water as your boat came down that big drop. But it's really just one very long, very slow and frightening incline. You reach the top and just sort of hang there for a second or so. Then comes that awful drop…that seemingly endless drop. Faster and faster until the ride comes to an abrupt, sudden stop. Darkness. It's over. I used to enjoy the ride, Brandy, and didn't want it to end. I'm not so sure anymore. But it sure was fun while it lasted…up to a point."

Sara wandered into the room, dressed to go out. "Oh, hello, dear," she said, looking at Brandy. "Will you be coming with us, too? Bud's coming for us soon. I think we're going out to lunch."

Brandy turned to her father, confused look on her face.

"She heard me on the phone earlier this morning. I was talking to a painter. I want to start getting this house in good shape before I think about selling it. If I *do* sell it, that is. She must have heard me mention lunchtime…when he would be here…and made an assumption. For some reason, every time the damn phone rings, she thinks it's Bud calling. And those irritating robocalls from telemarketers drive me bats. We got twelve of them yesterday. I've hit *61 and used call-blocking so many times that the damn thing is full and I can't use it any more. If I don't recognize the number, I simply don't pick up. I don't need someone with an accent I can hardly understand tell me about a brace that I *don't* need or how they can help fix a problem with my PC computer which I don't have."

Brandy chuckled at that one. She and Bryan have the exact same complaint.

"Dad, I am so sorry about this whole situation. I'm not talking about the phone calls. I'm talking about Mother. And I hate to hear you sound so despondent and down. That's not like you. Please, for your own sake and your own health, listen to what I'm saying about that assisted living facility. Or some other facility, for that matter. Something with more care attached to it, if you know what I mean."

"Not yet, Brandy, not yet. The ride might not be fun anymore. The thrill might be gone. But I'm not ready to say goodbye to Sally." He had called his wife Sally since the day he first met her. "This has gotten here way too quickly. I want to get right back on that roller coaster with sweet, young, beautiful Sally by my side, and start the ride all over again."

"That would be great if we all had that choice, wouldn't it? Sorry to say, Dad, but this is one ride where you get only one time around the track. Some of us would gladly stay on and go around again. Others are grateful and relieved when the ride is over and they can get off. But wasn't that view from the top of that first long incline wonderful?"

Cliff sighed and shook his head as he watched Sara walk over to a front window, looking up and down the street, apparently waiting for Bud to come for her and take her out to lunch.

Brandy was exasperated, as usual, upon leaving her parents' house. More days. More tears. More battles ahead.

Derby Day dawned to a brilliant blue sky and blazing sun. Mary Anne was buoyant as she made all the final preparations for her big party. Her rose garden was in full bloom, looking lusher than ever, thanks to the wet springtime. The aroma of her classic burgoo wafted through the house and out into the surrounding yard. Her big bear of a lover, Don Edwards, would again be her bartender, handling the making of dozens of those once-a-year Mint Juleps. The potato salad was made, the derby pies were baked, the bourbon balls were rolled, and the tables throughout the yard were set and decorated. She glanced at her watch. The guests should start arriving in forty-five minutes!

Amber Givings was glad that the annual horseshow at Double D did not interfere, this year, with Mary Anne's party. She and Raymond Futtz were still together, surprise, surprise. She had not had a relationship last this long. Ever. They were very fond of each other although neither one had uttered the "L" word yet. A lot had changed within this past year. She and Raymond were no longer virgins. The weekend following Mary Anne's party would be spent visiting Raymond's parents on St. Simons and then the following weekend would be the horse show at Double D. Busy, busy, busy!

Following the rip-roaring success of "Gypsy", the RockMount Players put on a modest little Neil Simon comedy. The show running currently was a musical about Annie Oakley. Sandi had hopes that her persuasive wiles could woo Marty to try out for the role of Frank Butler. But, like Homer's Odysseus, he was able to resist this sweet Siren's song once and for all. Sandi pouted but she got over it. For the record, Marty would never set foot on the musical comedy stage again and was even able to curb so much as a feeble warbling in the shower. Also, for the record, from time to time, Jeff Pringle still fantasized about Marty's…ummm…"eggroll".

Mary Anne's spacious front lawn was already filling up with cars as Remy Major slowly pulled down her bumpy driveway. He had resisted coming to her Derby Party for years and he had a slight tinge of apprehension now, but he had missed seeing all of his former boarders. And he missed Zara. He took a deep breath, got out of the car and slowly meandered toward the backyard where he knew all the action would be. Mary Anne reacted with delight when she saw him round the corner and come into view.

"Remy, Remy, Remy!" she squealed as she wrapped her arms around him and hugged him tightly. "I am *sooo* glad you came. Everybody over at the stable has been asking about you. You'll probably be bruised black and blue tonight from all the hugs you're going to get today. Come on, I'll walk you to the bar for your first mint julep of the day." She linked arms with him and then called out, "Look who's here, guys!" It was at least fifteen minutes later before Remy was able to sip that drink because of all the hand shaking, cheek kissing, back slapping and hugging from the gang from CedarView.

"Good lawd," Mary Pat exclaimed in her very best faux southern accent when she caught sight of Remy. "Ah am truly et up with the vapors!" she continued, fanning her face with both hands. "Give this po li'l lady a squeeze," as she air kissed both of his cheeks. They both laughed then hugged for real.

By the time Remy was on his second mint julep, he had greeted all his former boarders and was introduced to several new ones. Extending his hand for a shake, Chips Tallman then introduced his wife.

"Hello, Mister Major," Chips started, "Nice to make your acquaintance. Anyway, this is my wife Felicity."

"Remy, please…call me Remy," Remy replied, shaking Chips hand and nodding at Felicity.

"Anyway, it's a pleasure. We love it over at the stable. The folks there are so nice. We moved in, when, honey? Seems like a couple days ago, anyway. It was so nice of Mary Anne to invite us to this little shindig. She hardly even knows us yet, anyway, but we appreciate the hospitality."

"Do you have horses?" asked Felicity, seemingly in a daze. Chips gave her a quick look and almost imperceptivity shook his head. Had she forgotten about Remy and his wife?

"No. Not any more," was Remy's succinct reply.

"Oh, I had assumed being that you owned the stable…" and she was cut off by her husband.

"Anyway, it sure is a nice stable. I understand that Bryan is making a lot of changes. Have you been over there to visit? Anyway, you should. It's real nice."

By the time Remy politely finished the conversation and wandered away, he was ready for a third julep.

One after the other, Remy chatted with so many of the folks he had known for years. The years they had all thought of him as the grump of the century. He searched for Bryan and Brandy Dennison. Finding them, they all settled into a long conversation about the stable and the new boarders.

"I just met your latest additions," Remy mentioned, "the Tallmans."

"Yeah, well," answered Bryan, "What did you think?" looking around first to make sure the new boarders weren't near. "The guy's nice enough. Oh, his wife is too, I suppose, just a bit on the ditzy, dippy side if you ask me. Actually," Bryan said, again looking around to make sure the coast was clear, "when Brandy and I talk about them at home we refer to them as Chips and Dip."

"You're terrible, Bryan!" Remy exclaimed, shaking his head but still laughing.

Bets were placed, with Mary Anne's now live-in beau, Don Edwards, functioning as both bartender and bookie. A five-dollar pool and the guests drew horses' names from a hat. Excitement was mounting as post time drew nearer.

"Riders up!" shouted Mary Anne. "Head for the nearest TV."

All this excitement for the merely two minutes or less that it takes twenty horses to run a mile and a quarter. It takes much longer for all the female attendees to put on a damn hat than it takes the horses to complete the course. The final horse barely made it into the gate when the bell sounded and they were off! Then came the cheering and hoots and hollers from Mary Anne's guests.

The race ended, the bets paid off and dinner was served. The guests lined up along the various tables of food that Mary Anne had placed out, collected plates and silverware (okay, plastic-ware) and searched for places to park themselves and eat. And talk some more. There were never lulls in conversation at this party.

"Don't tell me the infamous Remy Major has honored us with his presence this evening?" came a soft voice with a mild German accent from behind Remy. He turned to greet someone he hadn't seen in years.

"Ingrid, wow, how nice to see you again," he answered. "How have you been?"

"Fine, dear, just fine," she said, turning her head to blow her cigarette smoke away from him. "Come, let's find a place to sit. We can eat and catch up."

Ingrid Schumacher, a neighbor of Mary Anne's, was in her late fifties, a natural blonde with sky-blue eyes and a quick wit. She and her family had come to the United States from Munich (or München, as she called it) when Ingrid was ten years old. Her English was impeccable. She wore form-fitting white slacks and an untucked pale blue blouse that seemed to match her eyes. Small diamond studs sparkled from her earlobes and a tight strand of pearls clung to her firm neck.

"Is Pete here?" Remy asked, looking around. "I haven't seen *him* yet tonight."

Ingrid turned her head to blow smoke away from Remy once again, then looked down. She answered quietly.

"Peter passed away last year," was her response. Remy would have known that if Zara were still alive. "Complications from surgery. Long before his time, yes?"

"Oh, my God, I am so sorry, Ingrid. I'm sorry, I didn't know."

"No worries," she shrugged. "You can't be sorry for something you didn't know, right? At least he didn't linger for a long time. And, *I* am so sorry about Zara. I miss her…as I'm sure you do."

It was Remy's turn to look down and turn his head away for a moment.

"Yes. Yes, I do. I still hear her voice at times."

"Ah," sighed Ingrid, "as I hear my beloved Peter call to me at times. Life can play such cruel tricks, yes? It's a grim reminder that we have fewer miles ahead of us than we've traveled thus far."

Mary and Stet stopped by the table to chat with Remy and Mary introduced her handsome lover to Ingrid. The four of them conversed and laughed for several minutes before moving on to get some of Mary Anne's famous derby pie.

"Beautiful couple," Ingrid commented wistfully as she watched them saunter away. "Beautiful couple."

The sun had gone down and the moon had come up. Stars were slowly making their appearance as the sky darkened. Some guests had departed but the ones remaining chatted and laughed raucously well into the evening.

"Hey, Raymond," teased Amber Givings, giggling, "want to go smell Mary Anne's chocolate mint out there in her garden?" That was just about the last thing Amber had remembered from last year's party.

"Nah, I think I'll pass!" And they both laughed.

Another successful party was now in the books. Aside from Jimmy Buffett singing about changes in latitudes on the stereo, the house was quiet. Mary Anne found Don sprawled out on a chaise lounge on the back deck. Finding the remnants of margaritas in a pitcher, she poured herself a glass and cuddled up next to her lover. He was smoking a cigar and let out a large trail of smoke. They watched as it slowly drifted upwards, disappearing into a cloudless sky.

The weather had remained sunny and pleasant the days following Mary Anne's party. Dusk was falling and Felicity Tallman heard a commotion from way behind their backyard. Their house sat on the top of a long slope that dropped down to railroad tracks and a dirt access road along the tracks. Beyond the railroad tracks was a wide embankment along the Yellow River. Due to all the recent rains, the current in the river was swift. There were signs posted all along the river, tacked to trees: DANGER and NO SWIMMING. Felicity knew that she had seen young teenagers ignore those warnings, from time to time, and dive in, swimming out into the river.

There were several men at the river's edge and a rowboat had been launched. There were hand-held floodlights bouncing all around the scene, flashing up into the low-hanging branches of the large trees along the bank and bouncing off the water's surface. It became an eerie sight. It was getting darker and Felicity could barely make out silhouettes at this point. It looked like a man from the rowboat had dived into the river, searching for something…or someone. Chips hadn't come home from the stable yet and she wanted to hold someone's hand, knowing that a potential tragedy was playing out a few yards away. Neighbors, who had heard the commotion as well, joined her in her back yard, wondering what really was going on down there in the river. One of the neighbor's sons ran down to ask about the situation. He came scurrying back up the slope in a matter of minutes.

"Two kids from down the block decided to go for a swim," the young man reported. "They both jumped in but only one kid came back up to the surface. His friend called for him and dove under a couple times but couldn't find him. He ran home to tell his parents and now this is happening," he said, as he pointed down to the riverbank. "Oh, God," he said, "I hope it's not Bobby." Bobby was a friend from two blocks away and was known to be a bit of a daredevil.

The people standing in Felicity's backyard could barely see, now that it was really getting dark, but they saw a lot more activity and heard a lot of shouting going on. No more than two seconds later they could hear a siren as an ambulance raced down the access road toward the group at the river. That was closely followed by a police car, blue light bar flashing, which came to a sudden halt. A silhouette leaped from the back seat.

Felicity had never heard a more frightening, ear-piercing scream as had just split the nighttime into a million pieces. The anguished cry of a mother seeing her dead son lying on a riverbank.

Almost instinctively, Felicity embraced her pregnant belly, as if to protect her unborn child. Tears flowed down her cheeks, turning her head, not wanting to intrude upon an unknown mother's grief.

The unfortunate and reckless young man had dived in with his buddy. The current was swift and he had had to fight. But apparently his T-shirt had gotten snagged on several of the roots from the large trees along the bank that extended, unseen, underwater. He was not able to get himself free in time before his lungs gave out. His name was Bobby.

The current temperature on St. Simons Island is 86°. That's what Amber read to Raymond from her iPhone as they zipped down I-95 heading to his hometown. He had not been back to visit his parents in over a year and he was eager to show Amber around the place. He couldn't believe that she had never been to the "Golden Isles". He turned off the interstate and picked up little Route 17, just before crossing the marshland and over the causeway to that beautiful little island.

"I see the ocean! I see the ocean!" he exclaimed with excitement as he glanced to his left, over some sand dunes, still on route 17. Even growing up on the island, the first sight of the ocean whenever he returned gave him a thrill and he reacted like a little kid. He cracked open the window and took a deep breath of the refreshing salt air.

Raymond's parents lived in a small house on a narrow street a few blocks away from McKinnon Airport. The tiny airport received no large, major commercial flights, only smaller, private aircraft. Actually, at one time, Raymond considered getting his pilot's license and working from here. He turned the car onto his parents' heavily shaded street and drove slowly past huge, old Live Oak trees with Spanish moss hanging from every limb. These magnificent trees created a unique visual, with their twisting and turning branches and limbs. TRIVIA: The name *live oak* comes from the fact that these evergreen oaks remain green and "live" throughout winter, when other oaks are dormant and leafless.

The car tires made a soft crunching sound as they rode across the crushed shell driveway of the Futtz residence. The front door to the house opened and out raced an energetic brindle Boxer, heading straight toward the car, barking as he ran. Raymond's mother soon followed out onto the front stoop.

"Rocky!" Raymond called to the dog as he stepped from the car. The dog bounced up and down, barking and wagging his stump of a tail. Raymond bent down and was soon smothered in the slobbering kisses and licks from the dog. "I think he's glad to see me!" he said to Amber as she got out of the car. Raymond's mother was soon joined by her husband as they approached the car to greet their weekend guests.

As Amber stepped from the air-conditioned car, the humidity enrobed her like a dripping wetsuit. The aromas that wafted into her nostrils combined those of the salt marsh with the various musty scents of the local vegetation. It wasn't an unpleasant sensation…she actually liked it…but it *was* different, to say the least.

"Hi, I assume you must be Amber," Raymond's mother said as she reached out her hand to Amber. "I'm Jeannie and this is Tom," as she introduced Raymond's father.

Amber wasn't sure if she should hug them (she's a hugger), but settled for a handshake from both of them. Strong handshakes, at that. Raymond *did* exchange hugs with both parents, and Amber picked up that there was a lot of warmth and tenderness there. Jeannie was slender and youthful in appearance, wearing white shorts and a pink blouse. No jewelry. Tom looked to be a few years older than his wife but in good shape. He was wearing a light blue polo shirt and slightly darker blue golf slacks. *Perhaps he had been out on the course before they arrived,* thought Amber.

"Come on in and get settled," Jeannie said, turning to go back into the house. "You've had, what, a five-hour drive?"

"Yup," blurted Raymond, "but we're still up for a run on the beach."

"Well, bring in your luggage and put it in your rooms," answered Tom, "and you can head to the beach in a little bit."

Rooms? Amber thought. *Rooms, plural? Does that mean...?*

Rocky the Boxer raced toward the house, beating the others to the front door, and then turned to look, waiting for them. Raymond carried the two small overnight cases that they had brought with them. Amber stepped into the house and was instantly overwhelmed by pastels. Every wall, every piece of furniture, every lamp shade, every rug or carpet was a pastel color. Her immediate impression of the living room, with framed Thomas Kinkade prints on every wall and one, two...no, wait, three crucifixes, was one of trepidation. She hadn't realized until just then that the exterior of the house was a pastel blue with pastel green shutters. Based upon the color palette, obviously Raymond's mother had a cotton candy fixation.

"What a lovely home, you have here," she lied to Jeannie. "It looks so... serene." She couldn't think of another word offhand.

"Thank you, Amber," answered Jeannie, looking around the room with pride. "We just love the peacefulness of it all. It's our decompression chamber, so to speak. Ray, you know where *your* room is, come on Amber and I'll show you to yours."

Amber wondered if Jeannie would be handing her a chastity belt before sundown.

Amber was led down the narrow hallway leading to the bedrooms. There were three of them in the small house. Kinkade prints lined the hallway and Amber spotted a couple more crucifixes. Rosemary's baby wouldn't stand a chance in this place!

"Here you go, Amber," Jeannie said as she ushered Amber into her tiny bedroom. "Please make yourself comfortable. Come join us out on the back deck when you're ready."

The room was mauve. Totally mauve, in various tones. Walls, curtains, bedspread, even the sheets as Amber found out later that evening.

Sweet baby Jesus, thought Amber, *my head might explode the next bright color I see.*

Rocky padded up behind Amber and gave her a cursory sniff before turning and walking away again. *Damn,* Amber again thought to herself, *Rocky's the brightest color in the whole damn place and he's brown.* She wondered if Raymond might be able to sneak into her room during the night…or if Tom will guard her door with a shotgun.

She unpacked what little she brought, changed into shorts and wandered out of her room in search of the back deck. She followed the laughter and found them. Raymond, also now in shorts, and his parents were out there, reminiscing. The deck was shaded by the huge limbs of Live Oaks dripping with Spanish moss that was gently swaying in the afternoon breeze. A tall privacy fence enclosed the spacious backyard and Amber could see the tops of other houses in back and on both sides. Birds were chirping from every tree (there were tiny bird houses all around the yard) and Rocky was in a corner chewing on a bone. The whoosh of a small jet taking off from the airport broke the serenity for a brief moment before it trailed off into the distance. Amber looked around at the deck chairs and chaise lounge…all pastel, of course…and sat in a comfortable chair next to Raymond.

"Would you like something to drink?" asked Jeannie. "Ginger ale, Coke, water? We have fruit juices, too, if you prefer. Oh, I think we might also have a bottle of root beer."

"What are all of *you* drinking?" asked Amber. She saw that Raymond's parents had tall glasses of a sparkling beverage with lime slices. Could that be gin and tonics…or, better yet, vodka? Amber got her hopes up.

"Oh, I'm sorry. I forgot to mention this," Jeannie said laughingly, holding up her glass. "This is seltzer with a twist of lime. Would you like one?"

"Sure. Why not?" Amber shrugged. "I like to live dangerously." And she laughed. She was the only one doing so.

"I'll go get it," said Tom as he rose from his chair. "I'll bring some snacks too…so all of us can live dangerously," and he winked at Amber.

He was back out on the deck in a few minutes, carrying a tray with Amber's drink and a bowl of various crackers and a large block of Muenster cheese. There was also a small bag of goldfish-shaped crackers. He set the tray down on a small table in front of them and they all seemed to reach for the snacks at the same time. They all laughed and waited their turns. Rocky sniffed the air and came running up onto the deck and stared at Raymond.

"Ha! I know what *you* want, you little devil, you," laughed Raymond. "Haven't outgrown this, have you?"

Raymond reached into the bag of goldfish and withdrew a handful. One by one he tossed them into the air. Rocky caught each one in his jaws, swallowing them with hardly chewing and waited for more.

"Dang, you spoil that poor dog, Ray," said Tom, shaking his head and chuckling. "He only starts begging when you're around. Good thing you don't come back home too often or he'd be overweight and lazier than he is now!"

"Well, dang, yourself, Dad," laughed Raymond right back. "You're the one who brought out those crackers. You *know* he loves 'em."

Dang. Twice. Amber remembered that when she first started dating Raymond he never swore… "dang" being the strongest word he would utter. And he didn't drink alcohol either. After more than a few mint juleps at Mary Anne's Derby Party last year that had changed. A few other things had changed. *But,* thought Amber, *I have no doubt that Raymond will be on his best behavior this weekend.*

They all chatted about the past year's events and both Jeannie and Tom brought Raymond up on all of the current goings on around the island. Who had died. Who had moved away. Who had moved back. They remarked about Raymond's fear of horses and how Amber must have helped ease him away from that.

"Oh, Raymond's been great with my horse, Flapjack. He hasn't gotten on to ride yet, but I keep trying. He helps groom him and next week is a big annual show at Double D Stables. We're looking forward to that, right, Raymond?"

"Absolutely!" he responded with just the barest hint of sarcasm. He quickly glanced at his watch.

"Hey, Amber, let's walk over to East Beach. It's only a few blocks away. I want to get my feet in that great water before the sun sets."

Jeannie then glanced at *her* watch. "Okay," she said, "It's 4 o'clock now. Be sure you're back no later than 6. I'm having your favorite for dinner tonight. Take Rocky with you, but keep him on leash until you get to the beach. There are way too many squirrels around here and you'll never catch him if he goes chasing after them."

Rocky heard the leash being picked up and came running toward Raymond and sat, looking up at him with eager anticipation, tongue hanging out of his mouth.

"No squirrel hunting, ya hear?" Raymond said, looking down at his furry friend. "Your chance to run will be on the beach."

Amber and Raymond, with Rocky pulling on his leash, meandered slowly through the narrow, shaded streets toward the beach. There were other people strolling along the streets as well and several bicyclists rode by and waved.

"Dang, I love this place," uttered Raymond, almost to himself. Suddenly remembering that Amber was by his side he added "Sorry I left, sometimes. But I'm *so* glad I met you, Amber."

"Well, why *did* you leave, you big lug, if you love it here so much?"

"No decent jobs around here, I guess. I wasn't really putting too much effort into looking, though. Most of my friends had all moved away. My Mom's sister and her husband own Cousins Feed and Seed, as you well know, and they suggested that I come up there to work for them. I thought I'd give it a try, not that loading feed and stuff into folks' trucks is any great shakes, but it's fairly good money. I suppose." And he let out a big sigh.

"What do your parents do? Are they retired? They sure don't look old enough for that, or anything…just asking. You never, ever told me anything about them, Raymond."

"They own five or six rental homes here on the island. I lost count. You'd be surprised at how much money there is in that! Their houses are usually booked months in advance. Return guests even book a year in advance during the on-season. Even during the off-season they do well. Not bragging or anything, but my parents are loaded."

Amber was taken aback by this revelation and was very hesitant about her next question. "Does your mom do all the decorating for those other houses?"

"Nah, she hires a decorator for that." He laughed, and then turned to look directly at Amber. "You mean because of all that pastel crap in their house? And those god-awful pictures on the walls?"

Amber blushed and stammered, "Well…I was just…well, you know…I…"

Raymond laughed until he cried.

"Hey, my mom realizes that she might have overdone it with those colors, but she loves them. Always has, since she was a little girl. And my dad doesn't give a hoot what colors are on the walls as long as my mom is happy. Yeah, those paintings…well…" and he chuckled. "She has a couple hanging in a few of the other houses and, believe it or not, someone *always* asks if they are for sale. So she hesitates, on purpose, hems and haws, then says a price. Sold! She has a bunch more in a closet back at the house. Oh, and about all those crucifixes?" He stopped, shook his head and laughed again. "She saw 'The Exorcist' on TV years ago and it scared her witless, so she started hanging those things all over the place hoping to protect us all. Yeah, crazy, huh? But, hey…it worked! None of us is possessed yet!"

Amber giggled and asked, "Out of idle curiosity, what color is *your* bedroom?"

"Purple. Dark purple. You want to believe I used to be a huge Prince fan?"

They reached the beach and stood there, staring out into the beautiful, calm ocean. They both took in deep breaths and Amber held her head up, letting the breeze blow through her hair. The tide was out and the sand extended far out into the water. There was practically no surf, with little waves rolling lazily onto the sand. Sandpipers scurried along the water's edge, scampering away as the small waves approached their feet. Raymond reached into his pocket and pulled out a tennis ball.

"Hey, boy," he said to Rocky, "looky here!" The dog's head popped up, eyeing the ball, and he started to prance. The three of them walked down, now barefoot, to the water's edge. Raymond unhooked the leash and tossed the ball far out into the water. Rocky was off like a shot, bouncing through the water and barking with glee. He was back, ball in mouth, in a heartbeat, waiting for another toss. Amber and Raymond walked down the beach, tossing the ball to Rocky as they strolled. The dog never got tired of that effort. A small crab scampered out of their way as Amber bent over to pick up a couple shells.

"Hey, look, look, look! Out there!" Raymond exclaimed, pointing out into the ocean.

A small pod of dolphins was surfacing and diving back under the water not too far from the shoreline. Up and down they went, with the late afternoon sun glistening on their backs. A large pelican flew low over them, as if escorting them along the way.

"Oh, my God, that's so cool!" squealed Amber, jumping up and down clapping her hands. "I love that! Wow, this place is gorgeous."

Sea gulls swooped overhead and their calls made Amber smile. Cue the soundtrack. How about a jazzy version of "La Mer" for this walk on the beach?

They strolled up the beach, Rocky with tennis ball clenched tightly in his jaws, and Raymond pointed out Jekyll Island across the sound and told Amber about beautiful Driftwood Beach that they might visit during the weekend if they had the time. They leisurely strolled past the old, venerable King and Prince Hotel. A wedding was taking place on the back lawn, facing the ocean, and the three of them stopped to look up at the black tie affair.

"Ooooh, that's *so* romantic," swooned Amber. And she sighed. They turned to each other and locked lips in a passionate embrace.

"Hey, look at the time!" Raymond said abruptly. "We need to get back, pronto!" He called to Rocky, hooked him up on leash again and they headed back to his house.

A table was set on the deck. Amber hadn't noticed before, but there was a string of tiny lights strung along the posts, casting a romantic glow as dusk began to set in. As soon as they had come back into the house, Raymond sniffed the air.

"I know what you're cooking, Mom, and it's been way too long since I've had that! My absolute favorite."

"Go sit, you two. Your dad and I will be right out there. Sweet tea is already poured and out there on the table."

They were sitting at the table, Amber leaned back and watched the gentle swaying of the Spanish moss overhead and nearly cried at the serene beauty of it all. A couple small candles in glass jars flickered in the center of the table. Cue that damn soundtrack again. Let's do Sarah Vaughan, "Make Yourself Comfortable". Jeannie came out onto the deck carrying a large platter of plump fried shrimp and Tom followed closely with a large casserole of macaroni and cheese. Raymond's eyes bulged and he almost started to salivate.

"Don't tell me you actually make that," Amber said, indicating the shrimp. "I didn't think anyone really made fried shrimp except at restaurants." Jeannie, Tom and Raymond guffawed.

"Dang, my Mom's is the best ever. Better'n the ones you can get up at the Crab Trap. Seriously."

The platter of shrimp was passed around, along with three kinds of sauces: the traditional cocktail sauce, tartar sauce and remoulade sauce. Amber scooped out a huge helping of the casserole and took a whiff. Raymond noticed the smile on her face.

"And you won't get mac and cheese like this outta any old blue box, neither," he said.

Amber took a bite and turned to look at Jeannie.

"This is amazing! I've never tasted mac and cheese like this before. What's your secret?"

Jeannie smiled. "Thanks, Amber. I appreciate that. My mom used to make this decades ago. I'll share the recipe if you'd like. I use three different kinds of cheese and I put a *lot* of love into it," as she turned to smile at Raymond.

Dinner was followed by fresh cherry pie, another of Raymond's favorites, and then a couple hours of idle chatting still at the table. Rocky, smelling of salt water, fell asleep at Raymond's feet. Amber, also, began to drift asleep sitting there and Jeannie laughed.

"Looks like you tired that poor girl out, Ray. All this fresh salt air will do that. Why don't you both head off to bed. Your dad and I will clean up."

Amber eyes popped open suddenly. "Oh, I'm so sorry. Did I just doze off? That's so rude. But this air is so relaxing. Raymond, we'd better head off to our respective rooms before I embarrass myself and fall face first into what's left of this delicious cherry pie."

Jeannie smiled at them both. "Don't think, Ray, that your dad and I are so naïve to think that one of you won't try sneaking into the other one's bedroom during the night. When you do, just don't make so much noise going at it that you'll get Rocky howling. I don't want the neighbors calling to complain."

Amber stood there, mouth agape.

"Oh, don't look so surprised, Amber,' Jeannie laughed. "Tom and I were young once, too, you know. Pleasant dreams, kids."

Back at CedarView Monday evening after her fun-filled weekend away, Amber was chatting excitedly with Sandi, Mary and Megan. The weather had been perfect and Amber had a hint of a tan beginning.

"Oh, his parents are so nice," Amber said, "and his mom is a fabulous cook. Not so great at decorating, however," and she giggled, and then explained about the color pallet in their house. "The island is so beautiful and romantic. We went to Fort Frederica and Raymond surprised me by knowing so much of the history of that place. It blew me away. I was so impressed. Yesterday we went over to Jekyll Island before we headed for home and walked along Driftwood Beach. Oh, my god, those weird, twisted trees and branches were like works of art."

"Oh, I've been there, too, and love that place," exclaimed Megan. "It's almost surreal with all that fantastic driftwood, isn't it?"

"Did you get a chance to see the stables on St. Simons?" asked Sandi. "They are super."

"Yes! Yes, we did," squealed Amber, almost breathlessly, "They are fantastic, aren't they? Holy crap, they have like, what, thirty stalls? And they have miles of trails through the woods…oh, and even out onto the beach. I hope we go back again soon. Damn, Flapjack would love it!"

"I was down there last summer and met the owner." Megan said, "Oh, my god, she is *soooo* nice. And pretty, too. She studied up here at Emory. That's *my* alma mater. We had a nice chat. And those trail rides *are* spectacular, just so ya know!"

"Well, it sounds like you had a terrific weekend, young lady," Mary interjected. "Now, are you up for the show at Double D on Saturday? You and Flap need to be practicing. I don't know who they have judging the English classes this year, but the current scuttlebutt is that there were so many complaints about Veronika Snapp last year, and at some other shows, that she won't be back this year. And, by the way, I'm taking Thunder and will be riding, too. Don't worry, my friend, we aren't in the same classes, age-wise, so we won't be competing with each other." And they all laughed. "The only problem might be the weather," Mary continued. "Things aren't looking too promising for a sunny day on Saturday. We just may be getting wet…and muddy."

As it turned out, the weather wasn't all that bad, considering the wet spring so far. It had rained earlier in the week and, yes, the rings were a bit on the muddy, messy side, but nothing to be concerned about. Saturday dawned with thick cloud cover, but the sun tried to break through at times. There was a pleasant breeze that would make the riding enjoyable. Mary and Stet had gotten there very early and parked in a prime spot. Although he wouldn't be riding in the show, Stet swung up into Thunder's saddle and trotted him around in one of the rings. Sandi, who was there just to cheer on her stable mates, ambled up to Mary as she watched Stet.

"Who's *that* tasty-looking piece of hunkness?" joked Sandi. Mary gave her the stink eye.

"Watch it, lady!" and they both giggled like schoolgirls.

Amber, filled with excitement and enthusiasm as always, walked Flapjack over beside Mary and Sandi before going into the ring to warm him up.

"Where's Raymond?" asked Mary, looking around.

"Well, he couldn't get off two weekends in a row, so he's at the feed and seed loading trucks today. I'll probably be seeing him later, though."

Cut to the chase. Well, to the end of the show, anyway. Amber and Flapjack had entered four events: two western and two English. They were going home with two blue ribbons (first place, naturally), one red (second place) and one yellow (third place). Mary and her horse, Welcome Thunder, had also entered four classes, all English. They were heading home with four blue ribbons. Judges could not be anything other than impressed by Mary's imposing and well-trained steed. And why not? He was a horse to be reckoned with.

JUNE

Black and White

"Learn to see what you are looking at."

Christopher Paolini

Megan Fairley's eyes fluttered open slowly. After an early morning ride up Yahoo Hill with Mary Anne and Mary Pat, she had decided to curl up with the latest Jack Reacher thriller while her twin sons napped. She noticed that on page 6, there was a small, pale brown circle, about ¼" in diameter, in the center of the page. On page 7, it was a bit darker. She knew immediately what it was. She flipped the pages ahead to page 14 and the dot now had a black center. *Well, damn,* she thought to herself (it was a library book). *Obviously some asshole that was reading this was a smoker and dropped a damn spark or ash.* It pissed her off, the audacity of someone being so callous and careless. She shook her head and started reading again. Within five minutes, she had fallen asleep, leaving Jack in a very precarious situation. She suddenly jerked wide-awake fifteen minutes later and glanced at her watch, 3:30. The boys would be stirring soon, too early for dinner and her husband, Graham, was in Boston on business until tomorrow. *We'll go for a nice walk,* she thought to herself.

Not two minutes later, Lucas stumbled into view followed by Mason, still rubbing his sleepy eyes. The towheaded identical twins yawned, one after the other, and came running to crawl up into Megan's lap. They were big for their four years and fought taking naps, claiming they were too old for baby stuff. Nevertheless, they napped daily.

"Hey," said Megan, "shall we take a bit of a walk down the hill to say hello to Miss JaNelle? We haven't fed her goats in a while. Would you like to do that?"

Each boy nodded his head so quickly it looked as though they might be yanked loose from their necks. Megan got the boys dressed, washed their faces and cut up several carrots into little pieces putting them into a baggie. She called to their English Cocker Spaniel, Chelsea, and hooked her up on leash. They all set off on their little adventure for the afternoon.

JaNelle White, a stunningly beautiful African-American woman in her late forties, and her husband Bernard (Bernie to everyone), a handsome white man in his early fifties, lived down the hill and around the corner from the Fairleys. Their house was the last one in a cul-de-sac, which backed up to a densely wooded area. Most people had dogs or cats as pets. JaNelle had 3 goats. Their property was just outside the city limits, so certain rules regarding farm animals didn't apply. The Whites had a very attractive and very popular daughter who was a senior at Georgia Tech. She shared an apartment in Atlanta with two friends and JaNelle missed having her around. She loved kids and welcomed the chance to spoil them, especially when Megan brought her two boys around to see the goats. She almost always had freshly baked cookies, just in case.

Megan and the boys, hand in hand…and Chelsea…slowly made their way down the hill and turned the corner, heading toward the "goat house", as the boys called it. The weather was perfect, not too hot yet and with a slight breeze. *The houses along this street were all so well kept,* Megan thought. She stopped, from time to time, to admire the landscaping and plants and flowers along the way. Birds were chattering and squirrels were scampering, causing Chelsea to tug at her leash. They were approaching the second house from the end when Megan heard what she thought must be a car backfiring. Somewhere a dog started barking but Chelsea ignored it. Then came a tinkling of bells and tinny-sounding music. She knew what it was. She turned and smiled as the ice cream truck pulled into view. She glanced at her watch. Yep, right on time. Mr. Frosty hit this neighborhood, faithfully, every day at four. Fortunately her boys had yet to discover what the ice cream truck was all about. *That old vehicle must have been the one that backfired,* she thought. As she and the boys reached JaNelle's house, Megan hesitated and looked back at the ice cream truck, now surrounded by kids jumping up and down in anticipation of something that would probably spoil their suppers. Megan laughed.

JaNelle had seen them approaching and came out onto her front porch with arms outstretched. The boys saw her and took off running straight for her, almost knocking her over with their exuberance. They hugged her around her legs…she was tall and they couldn't yet reach her waist…and she kissed each on the tops of their heads. She and Megan hugged as well.

"You smell gooood, Miss 'Nelle," said Lucas as he continued to hug her legs.

JaNelle, laughed and shook her head. "Well, thanks, little darlin', aren't you sweet. It's Bibliotheque, probably mixed with a dab or two of linseed oil," she said to Megan as she winked. JaNelle had skin as smooth as silk, always seemed to be beautifully dressed no matter what she was doing and had a melodious voice that could charm the wildest beast. Her hair was kept closely cropped and she reminded Megan of that famed bust of Queen Nefertiti. She had been standing in front of her large easel, deep in concentration with her recent painting in progress as she saw the trio approaching. It was a portrait of a goat. One of her prized Nubian goats. Obviously this was her theme at this time. Megan glanced around the room and noticed several goat portraits in various sizes and totally different, sometimes weird color combinations and styles.

"Haven't seen you guys in ages," JaNelle said, eyeing the boys, "where y'all been hiding? Looks like you've grown a might, too, since I saw you last. Growing like kudzu, I swear. Ya'll will be taller than me before you know it." And the boys smiled sheepishly. "Come on back through the house to the back. The goats have been waiting on y'all. Nearly starved since you haven't been here in forever," she laughed.

Megan loved visiting the Whites. The house was filled with gorgeous paintings, all done by JaNelle, with various themes. She might select flowers as a theme of the month and paint large canvases of blooms of all types. She also liked to paint dead flowers in vases. They had such interesting shapes too, she thought. The paintings in the house were changed on a regular basis…plants, flowers, animals, old houses, railroad scenes, old cars, etc., and Megan was always delighted with this private gallery. They headed through the house, stopping briefly in the kitchen so the boys could select a chocolate chip cookie or two from a plate.

The four of them went out the back door and three goat heads immediately popped up and, if that was even possible, seemed to smile. They quickly came prancing over to the boys, probably remembering from past experiences about the treats they were about to receive. Yes, goats have great memories. Lucas and Mason giggled with glee and hugged each goat around the neck. It almost sounded as though the goats were giggling, too. Megan pulled the plastic baggie containing the carrot chunks out of her pocket. The goats suddenly changed allegiance.

"Hey, calm down, kids," Megan laughed. "Be patient, there's enough for everyone. I still can't really believe their names, JaNelle. I think you're pulling our legs."

"Nope. Seriously. Look, my hubby might be a high-powered lawyer but his roots are…well…sometimes *so* plebeian." And she rolled her eyes.

Bernard (Bernie) White was, indeed, a high-powered lawyer. He worked at a prestigious law firm in midtown Atlanta. A law firm that constantly ranked in the top ten places to work in Atlanta by the *Atlanta Journal/Constitution* newspaper. Yes, he was the one to name the goats. Larry, Curly and Moe enjoyed this beautiful back yard paradise. Needless to say, the Whites could afford to live in a far tonier part of town, in a much larger house and property but, for all their wealth, they enjoyed the simpler, more conservative lifestyle that this little suburb offered.

The boys were slowly feeding the carrots to the goats. Chelsea always ignored these creatures, never sure what to expect from their sounds or antics, so she remained sitting on the back steps as an observer. JaNelle's cell phone chirped and she reached into her pocket to retrieve it. Taking a quick glance at the caller ID, she answered, lowering her voice to a sexy, husky purr.

"Hey, good lookin', don't tell me you're gonna be stuck downtown again tonight?"

"Hell, no, Mrs. White," answered Bernie with a chuckle. "I'm heading home to your beautiful self right now but I *do* seem to be stuck on 78. Apparently some asshole thought he was Bubba Wallace and tried to race an eighteen-wheeler to an exit. Neither of them ended well."

"Well, that's horrible, sweetie. Now who the hell is Bubba Wallace?"

"Ha! Never mind, sweet cakes. No matter. We're still on for our date night tonight but it just might be a tad later, okay?"

"Sho 'nuf," JaNelle responded in her best faux southern accent, "drive carefully, ya heah? An' tell that Bubba guy to stay clear of you!" She clicked off and replaced the phone into her pocket.

The two women chatted briefly as the boys ran around the back yard, either chasing the goats or being chased *by* the goats. All of them squealing with delight.

"Come on, boys, time to tell your long-eared friends goodbye for now. It's been a long day and Mommy is pooped!" She had told JaNelle about her day at CedarView Stable and the fun ride up Yahoo Hill while the boys had a play date with some other neighborhood boys. "Almost time for dinner and Daddy said he'd call before you guys went to bed." The boys made no attempt at stopping. "Boys!" she called loudly and emphatically with hands planted firmly on hips. All three goats responded with a few weird sounds and everybody laughed.

Five minutes later, the three of them and Chelsea were walking back up the hill toward their house. Noticing a few garbage cans along the side of the curbs reminded Megan that tomorrow would be collection day and that she should put their own garbage cans out tonight before going to bed. It was Graham's "job" to do so as a rule but the situation now lay at Megan's feet being that he wouldn't be back home until late tomorrow evening. She hoped that she would remember before falling asleep with Jack Reacher again tonight.

Two days later Megan's cell phone buzzed and she hoped it would be Graham. As fate would have it, his business situation in Boston had turned sour and he didn't return home as planned. Negotiations would extend for days and he hated it. Megan saw that it was JaNelle calling.

"Good morning, neighbor, what's up?" Megan cheerfully said.

"I assume you know what's been going on down here," responded JaNelle succinctly. "All this hubbub and activity that's driving the goats bonkers."

"What? No. What are you talking about?"

"Girl, don't you watch the news? Have you left the planet? Haven't you even heard all the noise or seen the TV news vans around?"

"No, I'm sorry, JaNelle, I have no idea what you're talking about. I stopped watching the news years ago, too depressing. I know I should keep up with current events…or what's happening around town but, frankly, I have grown very callous and don't really give a shit any more."

JaNelle let out a little laugh. "Well, then, sit down, darlin', before you fall down. There's been a murder in ye olde neighborhood. Well, *my* old neighborhood. Right next door, for that matter."

"Whaaaat?" stammered Megan. "Holy shit, I can't believe that. When? Oh, my god, I'm hyperventilating, I think. That's horrible."

"Well, then" started JaNelle again, "if you're *not* sitting, dearie, grab something because you're about to fall down. The cops estimate that it was two days ago. Guess when? Here comes! At the time you were here with Larry, Curly and Moe." There was silence. A long silence. "Megan? Are you still with me?"

"Yes," Megan answered meekly. "Still here. I read too many thrillers and now something like this in my own back yard…practically. Damn!"

"I hope you don't mind, but I gave the police officer your name. He asked what I was doing at the time and I told him about you and the boys. He might be contacting you."

"Oh, that's fine, JaNelle, I certainly don't mind but I don't know what I could tell him that would be of any help. What does Bernie think about all this?"

"Oh, please. Bernie is a 'Criminal Minds' addict and he's getting his rocks off with all the excitement. As for me, it just scares me to think a murder happened right next door, in broad daylight. I really didn't even know the lady. Wouldn't know her if I fell over her. Well, I suppose *now* I would…if I fell over her. That's cruel. Sorry I said that. Well, thought I'd give you heads-up regarding Inspector Columbo, or whoever."

"Sure, JaNelle, thanks for the warning, if that's even the correct term to use. I'm sure I'll be useless to him but at least I might find out a bit more about that poor woman. I'll call you and keep you posted. Just don't look for me on the 6 o'clock news."

There she was, a mere few hours later, Megan Fairley being interviewed on the 6 o'clock news. It was taped and severely edited, having been recorded at 2:30 that afternoon. Inspector Harold Black had contacted Megan before noon, asked permission to come to her home for an interview and hinted that he may be bringing a cameraman with him.

Harold Black was as far removed from Peter Falk's Columbo as you could get. He was lanky and young, perhaps in his early thirties and so pale white he looked like alabaster. He neither wore a rumpled trench coat, nor carried a small note pad and pen. His soothing voice put Megan at ease immediately. After introducing himself, showing his badge and credentials and gaining permission for the cameraman to video the interview, they positioned themselves in a very photogenic part of Megan's back yard.

"I understand that you were in the vicinity when the crime allegedly took place, is that correct Mrs. Fairley?"

"Yes, apparently," responded Megan, almost afraid to look into the camera. "My sons and I were on the way to visit our friend JaNelle…I mean Mrs. White… and feed her goats. We hadn't been down there to see her in weeks. I felt guilty about that and…oh, wait, I'm starting to ramble. Sorry. I do that when I'm nervous."

Inspector Black smiled. "Nothing to be nervous about, Mrs. Fairley. Okay, so what time, approximately, were you in the vicinity?"

"Oh, I know exactly what time it was. It was 4 o'clock. I heard and saw the ice cream truck come into the neighborhood. Mr. Frosty is always on time, you can count on him. Same time every day all during the summer. Sometimes he extends his route into the fall months as well, after school has started again and…well, sorry. I'm rambling again. What did you just ask?"

Inspector Black rolled his eyes. "Did you see or hear anything unusual as you were walking toward Mrs. White's house?"

Megan scrunched up her face, trying to remember something. Anything.

"No, I don't think so. When I heard the car backfire, then saw Mr. Frosty's truck…well, I figured it was his old rattletrap of a truck that had backfired and of course the bells and music was a dead giveaway. Oh, didn't mean to say 'dead', that's awful considering what happened. Well, I mean, it's just a manner of speech and all the kids looked so happy to see him and they were jumping all around waiting their turns…"

"Okay, Mrs. Fairley," Inspector Black interrupted this verbal barrage, trying to reel her back in, "was there anyone else in the vicinity? Aside from Mr. Frosty and the children?"

"No, there wasn't," she said abruptly. Then she paused. "Oh, wait. Now that I think about it, I saw a guy come from between a couple houses down the block to put something into a trashcan. It was garbage day the next day and some folks already had their trashcans out along the curb. That's all. I didn't see anyone else."

"Can you describe this man? You said he came from *between* the houses. You didn't see him come *from* either house?"

"Well, I figured he must have lived in one of them and was coming from his backyard or garage or something. I didn't think anything about it. Describe him? Hmmm…no, he was too far away, I couldn't even begin to describe him. I wasn't really paying that much attention. Oh, but I *could* see that he had red hair. You know, like Prince Harry. And then we went to feed the goats."

"Could you see what he put into the trashcan?"

"Looked like a regular plastic garbage bag, to me. But it was just a quick glance."

"You've actually been very helpful. Mrs. Fairley. Thank you so much for your time. But I will say this. Considering where you were at the time of this crime, *you* may not have seen the perpetrator but there is the distinct possibility that he or she saw *you*."

Well, thanks a whole hell of a lot, thought Megan. *That sure puts my mind at ease.*

Megan's slot on the 6 o'clock news regarding the tragic event was edited down to 5 seconds, with her only line of dialogue being "And then we went to feed the goats." JaNelle had a brief showing on the news as well, with her segment lasting about 8 seconds.

In actuality, Megan's brief interview with Harold Black was more helpful than she realized. That's why the drastic editing for TV. The police had interviewed all the surrounding neighbors, most of whom had not been home at the time but there had been nary a redhead among them.

Mr. Frosty (real name, Alphons Lapinski) had also been interviewed. His truck, despite Megan's description, was in very decent condition and didn't appear to be one that would ever backfire. The murder victim, who had been shot in the back of her head at close range, Josephine Thales, was a very popular English teacher at the high school. She was 32, single, never married, no boyfriend, but apparently sexually active. Evidence of semen was found on her rumpled bed. Along with a red pubic hair. Everyone these days has a cell phone…but hers was not found. Perhaps that was why it pinged in the vicinity of the Lawrenceville landfill.

It didn't take long. At precisely 6:17 Megan's cell phone went crazy. First one call, then a few more. Mary Anne from CedarView was the first, followed by Marty Howce and then Mary Pat. "Mah, word," Mary Pat fluttered into the phone, using her very best faux Scarlett O'Hara voice. "Mah po' li'l ol' haht just stood still when I saw your beautiful face pop up there on the screen between all those pharmaceutical commercials! What in the world?"

For the third time, so far, Megan went through the story. She related how she hadn't even heard about the murder until her neighbor called two days afterwards. Neither Megan nor Graham watched much television any more. They had both gotten into the habit of reading every evening after playing with the boys and putting them into bed. Megan had her thrillers and her husband loved historical novels. Now there was a real-life thriller happening right around the corner. Was crime encroaching on their quiet little neighborhood or was this an isolated incident?

"I heard that a friend of hers found her dead, right?" Megan asked of Mary Pat, who seemed to know what had happened.

"Yay-us," answered Miss O'Hara once again, "shockin', to be sure." She then dropped the accent and continued. "The dead lady and her friend were going to go see Bon Jovi but the dead lady never showed up. She had been excited about it for weeks…evidently she's a sort of groupie and follows Bon Jovi wherever he's playing. Her friend texted her when she didn't show up at the concert. No response. Her friend was too high after the show but stopped by the dead lady's house the next morning. That's when the shit hit the fan."

"How awful for her friend to find her like that. And they haven't a clue who or why at this point?" asked Megan.

"Well, evidently not. The press hasn't released too much info aside from the dead lady's name and occupation. I gotta stop saying 'dead lady', don't I? Sounds kinda cold. No pun intended."

"I guess it was somebody she knew though, right? Because from what the police inspector told me there was no forced entry and it didn't look like a robbery...or burglary or whatever you call it. But..." Megan stopped. She *was* reading far too many thrillers and now she was trying to solve it along with Jack Reacher...or Myron Bolitar. She didn't even know the victim so how the hell could she even hope to figure out the perpetrator's identity? So, what actually happened? What was the motive? Why did it happen?

"Hey, I gotta go, Mary Pat," Megan finally said after coming out of her 30-second reverie. "Graham's flight landed two hours ago and, barring the usual rush hour traffic, he should be home soon. I have a nice meal planned. The boys and I sure missed him and I'm eager to hear how things went in Boston. He's had a tough week but he missed my 5 seconds of fame on CBS just now." They both laughed.

"I'll be over at the stable in the morning," Mary Pat said. "Interested in going for a short ride? Not up Yahoo Hill this time, though. I don't want to find any bodies back there in the woods!"

"Thanks for asking, Mary Pat, but Graham is taking tomorrow off and we'll just spend a lot of time around here, the four of us, relaxing and playing catch-up."

"Well, then, behave yourselves you two love birds...the twins just might end up with a new brother or sister," then Mary Pat giggled like a schoolgirl.

"You're incorrigible, Mary Pat. But I love ya anyway. Say 'hi' to everyone over at the stable for me if you *do* go in the morning. We'll probably all stop over later in the day to care for our big baby, though. I just spoke with Marty before you called and Jessie will take care of Zany in the morning. Hey, Graham's pulling up the driveway now. Gotta go... see ya. Bye!" And she clicked off without hearing Mary Pat's response.

The boys chattered endlessly throughout their leisurely dinner of grilled steak and steamed asparagus. Believe it or not, the twins *loved* their veggies. They eagerly told their dad about Miss 'Nelle and her goats and the long (to them) walk down the hill and back up again from her house to theirs. Megan told Graham about her thrilling ride up Yahoo Hill (he had seen it once…never daring to try it) and Graham filled her in on the negotiations in Boston. She tried not to yawn. Graham had built a solid reputation as a labor arbitrator, which took him around the country from time to time. It paid well, but wasn't consistent. He might go weeks without a case. Then the four hundred pound gorilla in the room woke up. The "incident", as it would henceforth be referred to, was approached. Completely out of touch with the media, Graham was flabbergasted about the local murder. It also frightened him. Although it appeared that it was some sort of domestic situation, he was concerned about his family's safety, especially since he often travelled out of state. He had a gun, which Megan hated, and it was always safely locked away to prevent the boys from accidently finding it. Megan, too, knew how to use it but she didn't like the thought of having to actually use it on anything but a paper target.

Megan mentioned during dinner that she was negligent the last time she went grocery shopping and poor Chelsea had only one scant meal left. Graham said that he would run down to PetSmart and pick up some more dog food. He also said that he'd take his car and gas it up. He hadn't wanted to stop on the way home from the airport, even though it was running on fumes. The twins, of course, wanted to go with Daddy, but Megan elected to stay back home, clean up from dinner and get back, at last, to reading the book she had started last night.

Graham and the still-chattering boys departed. She quickly finished putting everything into the dish washer, started it going and grabbed her book, heading into the living room and her comfy favorite reading chair. She flipped the book open to her bookmark. It felt good to relax. She leaned back, took a couple of deep breaths and started reading. Myron Bolitar and his good friend Win were being pursued by some horrendous evildoers in a large, black SUV and were just about to be run off the road, over a cliff, when her front doorbell rang. Without thinking she swiftly opened the door.

"Hello, Megan," said the stranger.

Standing before her was the handsomest redheaded man she had ever seen.

At the store, Graham encountered a neighbor, also shopping for pet supplies. Obviously the discussion regarding the "incident" came up. Neither man knew anything about the victim but felt a sense of sorrow that something so tragic and drastic happened practically within earshot of their respective homes. The two men chatted as Graham kept his eye on the boys who had run off to stare up at the tropical fish tanks. The conversation eventually segued into a discussion about the Atlanta Braves (the Fairleys had season tickets) and their great start to the season. *That* topic segued into the neighbor, Adam Grant, boasting about his son's talent for Lacrosse and how *his* team was excelling, heading for the state playoffs. Graham had lost sight of the twins, so he quickly and politely ended Adam's rambling and went in search. The boys had simply changed their interest from looking at fish to watching the large cage of parakeets squawking and flying from perch to perch.

"Come on, boys. We gotta go. It's getting close to bath time and your Momma will be mad at me for keeping you out."

"Can we get one of those?" squeaked Mason, as he pointed up at the birds.

"Mmmm, I don't think so. They're too noisy and too messy. The noise would drive poor Chelsea crazy. Come on, gotta go!" answered Graham, with a big smile. The boys had also wanted goats after visiting with JaNelle, and a zebra after visiting the zoo.

He paid for the dog food, got the boys strapped into their car seats and headed off to the gas station.

Fifteen minutes later Graham pulled the car into the garage, pressed the remote to shut the door, unhooked the boys, grabbed the bag of dog food and entered the house. He called out to Megan alerting her to their return home. There was no response. He poked his head into the living room, expecting to see her curled up in her reading chair. The book she had been reading was lying upturned on the floor, in the middle of the room.

"Mommy, Mommy!" called Lucas. "Can we getta 'keet?" No response.

Graham ran upstairs to their bedroom, calling Megan's name. He was feeling a little rattled now. Perhaps a bit too paranoid…but still, with the recent events he was concerned. Water was running in their bathroom. The shower.

"Megan?" he shouted as ran into the bathroom.

Megan screamed. She was in the shower. "Damn, Graham! You scared the crap outta me. What the hell?"

She *had* been reading in her favorite reading chair, fully engrossed in the adventures of two of her favorite characters when fatigue had overcome her. By now, Megan had stepped out of the shower, wrapped herself in a big, fluffy towel and started running a comb through her dripping hair.

"Oh, honey, I'm so sorry. Didn't mean to frighten you," she said. "I was reading and fell asleep. I dreamed about a good-looking redheaded guy coming to our front door. You know, perhaps the killer? He mentioned my name and I screamed. It scared me so much I wet myself, so I had to get a shower before you guys got back home."

Graham shook his head, and then smiled a relieved smile. Obviously the situation down the hill and around the corner had them all a bit too much on edge.

"That's cool," he said, "sorry that I probably over-reacted. But just remember to keep all the doors locked from now on. You know, just in case."

Two excited boys burst into the room, nearly bumping into their dad.

"Mommy," shouted Lucas, "Can we getta 'keet? Daddy said we could."

"Wait, wait, wait, young man. I said no such thing!" responded Graham. "Don't be telling a fib, now." Both Mason and Lucas looked crestfallen.

"A what?" asked Megan?

Graham chuckled. "The boys seemed to be fascinated by the parakeets at PetSmart. And, just for the record, I already said no. Emphatically."

Just for the record, two weeks later there were two parakeets flapping happily around in a large cage in the Fairley's bright sunroom. One green, one blue...Snowflake and Joker. Chelsea was not impressed.

The weeks went by and news of the still-unsolved murder appeared only sporadically on the evening news. The obligatory interviews with Josephine Thale's fellow teachers and friends had come and gone. As in almost all of these cases, the victim was described as friendly, cheerful, always up-beat, wouldn't hurt a fly, ambitious...oh, and could walk on water. The only new revelation was that the victim was slightly over one month pregnant at the time of her death. According to Georgia law, it was now considered a double homicide.

The twins were enjoying their day care so Megan called one of her riding companions. Following a few days of gray skies and rainy weather, it was another one of those absolutely glorious late June mornings in the south. As it turned out, luckily, Mary Anne didn't have a party scheduled so the Cater-Tots lady was free to ride. She, in turn, called Sandi Prescott who was also available, who, in turn, then called Mary Pat. Just plain Mary was going to be spending the day with Stet, so she was unavailable for anything other than, probably, a wild, sexy, sweat-drenched afternoon of naked abandonment.

"Let's head out to that big pond, whadya say?" asked Mary Anne as the ladies were grooming and saddling their horses. "It's a nice, pleasant ride and, as far as I know, they've never found any dead bodies along the trail." Megan gave her *The Look* and shot her the bird. They all laughed. Neither Megan nor Sandi had ridden this trail before, but they had heard the story (repeated several times) about Mary Anne's horse getting stuck in deep mud the year before. It had been a frightening experience but the description of beautiful Mary covered from head to boots in mud had brought tears of laughter on several occasions. Mary had been the one to jump off her horse, Thunder, and wallow in the mud, pushing Mary Anne's horse from behind. Literally.

When they weren't trotting, they walked their horses lazily, some side by side, through the lush wooded area leading to the pond. Dragonflies flitted around, landing here and there on the tall reeds surrounding the pond. They could hear the call of a hawk as it swooped high overhead and buzzing cicadas calling out to potential mates echoed from tree to tree. Did you know that only the male cicadas make that sound? Well, now you know.

Sandi, astride Fireball, looked a little apprehensive as they approached the pond.

"Hey," she called out to the other riders. "Are there alligators in there?"

"Dawlin'," Mary Pat drawled, "They're so big they can swallow yo li'l ol' ass whole if you don't watch out!"

"Stop that, Mary Pat!" called out Mary Anne, as she stifled a laugh. "No, Sandi, don't worry. Alligators aren't this far north. It's those twenty-foot anacondas that live in there that'll get ya!"

Sandi pulled up her horse abruptly. "Why do I have the feeling that you're both full of shit?" laughed Sandi. "I was only trying to be funny when I asked that about the alligators, you know."

Due to the rainy weather recently, the pond had grown in size since last year. Every once in a while the horses had to step over tiny rivulets that trickled from the pond and flowed onto the trail and then into the weeds beyond. Fireball stopped at one and stomped his right front hoof into it, sending a spray of water and a splattering of mud into the air.

"Oh," said Sandi, "I think my horse might like to play in the water. Either that or he's trying to frighten those mean anacondas."

They all chuckled and moved their horses out at a trot. The women chatted almost non-stop, their conversation punctuated often by raucous laughter. Their topics actually revolved around the "menfolk" with whom they were all involved. Comparisons and critiques, with an occasional compliment. They laughed at all the male foibles and shenanigans.

"Poor Amber," said Mary Pat, shaking her head. "Raymond is sweet as they come and he's as cute as a teddy bear. I think she seems to love him dearly. But, frankly, I get the impression that he's dumb as dirt. From what Amber tells me, Raymond's idea of great humor is repeatedly watching 'Cats vs. Cucumbers' on YouTube."

"Hey, I *love* that!" shouted Sandi. "I don't have a boyfriend or a husband, but my dog Rufus the doofus sleeps up on the bed with me every night. He farts up a storm, let me tell you!"

Mary Pat started in with her comments. "Derrick scratches himself while he's out in the field coaching the boys. He says he's readjusting." Air-quotes there. "He doesn't do it constantly, like he has crotch rot or anything, but I think it's disgusting."

"I'm still having trouble with Don and a couple words," said Mary Anne, notorious for correcting peoples' grammar and pronunciations in her head. "The one that irritates me the most is 'mischievous'. He keeps pronouncing it miss-chee-vee-us. Drives me up the wall. Aside from that he's perfect. Well, he could stand to lose about ten pounds. Oh, and his snoring sounds like a freight train." Mary Pat rolled her eyes.

"Well, Graham likes to frighten me while I'm sitting on the toilet," Megan began. "When I forget to shut the damn door. I told him I hate it, but he still does it from time to time. Usually I take a book in there with me to read. He'll get nekid as a jaybird. Then he'll jump into the bathroom, arms high in the air, his little willy just-a waggin' away and yell 'Oogga-Boogga!' at the top of his lungs."

The women all snorted at that one, and Mary Pat just about choked. They all agreed that they would never be able to look at Graham Fairley the same way again.

The four critics, perfection personified all of them, continued to talk and laugh all the way back to the stable. The one topic that was *not* discussed throughout the entire ride was the one about a very recent, too-close-for-comfort murder. And a redheaded man.

JULY

Kicking at Raindrops

"People who think they know everything are a great annoyance to those of us who do."

Isaac Asimov

What a difference a year makes. Last year at this time Georgia was suffering from a three-year drought. This year, the ground was so saturated that large trees might uproot and tumble over if someone in the vicinity so much as sneezed.

Sandi had just brought Fireball in from a torrential rain to feed him. As she poured his feed into his bucket, he forcefully stomped his hind hoof.

"Hey, be patient," she admonished him, "Holy moly, you act like you're starving!"

Marty, in the next stall taking care of Gemmy, laughed and called out. "He's probably just kicking at raindrops, Sandi. He's sopping wet, right? And, no doubt, a great big stream of water ran off of his back and down his leg. He thinks it's a fly or something, so he stomped to get it off. Nothing there. Just a big raindrop. They do it all the time. Just watch out, he might shake in a minute just like a big wet dog. Then *you'll* be kicking at raindrops!"

The boarders, old and new, at CedarView were looking forward to a 4ᵗʰ of July day of celebration, riding, eating, drinking, playing games, gossiping...riding, eating, drinking and so forth. The ones who remembered last year's bash were grateful that rancid Rance was now out of the picture and it might actually be a fun event from start to finish. Their main concern, needless to say, was the weather. Each day, from the middle of June onward, was blessed with severe weather warnings almost on a daily basis. Go ahead, cue the soundtrack: "Stormy Weather" sung by the inimitable Lena Horne, of course. People with swimming pools or swim clubs at...

BREAKING NEWS: After an exhaustive search at the Lawrenceville landfill, police indicate that they have located the weapon thought to have been used in the alleged murder of local teacher, Josephine Thales. Wrapped in a black plastic garbage bag, along with a gun, was the alleged victim's cell phone and laptop. A person of interest is being sought.

...all the best subdivisions had hardly been able to take advantage of the warmer days. Those people who normally brandished enviable tan lines by now skulked about with dour expressions of despair. Hopes were up, therefore, with a 5-day forecast of partly to mostly sunny skies starting on July 3ʳᵈ.

As predicted, and hoped for, July 4ᵗʰ dawned under cloudless skies and rising temperatures. By mid afternoon, the parking area at CedarView was packed solid. The Crepe Myrtles that lined the fence along the driveway were fully laden with their deep fuchsia blooms. The trees swayed gently in the soft summer zephyr. Folding tables and chairs were abundant and a couple of charcoal grills would soon to be sizzling with burgers, hot dogs and bratwursts. Coolers were loaded with beer, wine and soft drinks for the kids. And the kids were racing around chasing one another, seemingly oblivious to the rising temperatures. Marty and Jessie's two sons were there, along with Bryan and Brandy's two grandsons. Megan and Graham Fairley would soon arrive with their two little twin boys. Gary and Linda Smart, who had still not moved to Chicago (if, indeed, they would ever), had their little son, Alex, who would turn one year old in a few months, in tow.

Stet and Mary pulled down the driveway just ahead of Amber Givings and lover boy Raymond. Mary Anne and Don had stopped off to pick up Sandi Prescott, who lived nearby. Mary Pat and Derrick would not be in attendance. They were preparing for a visit (an almost dreaded visit, at that) from Derrick's brother and sister-in-law. Soon music would be blaring, burgers burning and endless conversations and laughter would be competing with the cicadas singing throughout the surrounding trees. Even the horses in the pasture were in a holiday mode, despite the rising heat. They nickered, snorted and pranced around playing their "come chase me" game.

Earlier that morning, Mary Anne and Sandi were laughing and talking about a couple of the older men in their Zumba class as they walked from the parking lot into the gym. Sandi's Zumba class would be the last one this morning before the gym closed at noon for the holiday.

"I can't remember when Barry started doing it, but it's beginning to freak me out a bit," said Mary Anne. "He flirts something awful. He knows I have a boyfriend. I've told him about Don. He winks at me during the class sometimes, too."

"I, for one," replied Sandi, "find it kinda cute. I've watched him do that. It's not just you, you know. He flirts with practically woman, old or young, in the class. Yes, even me. You know he's probably just lonely. I think his wife died a few years ago. He also tries to say and do silly little stuff during class. He just wants…maybe *needs* attention, that's all. I have no doubt he probably was the class clown in school and he must have been the most annoying kid in fourth grade. Obviously he's trying to relive his childhood. In a way, it's sort of sweet. Well, maybe *sweet* isn't the right word but nobody else has said anything to me about it."

"And just when you think it's over, it's not," continued Mary Anne. "Every time that other guy, Walter, brays 'One! More! Time!' at the top of his lungs I want to scream."

"He doesn't really bother me either," shrugged Sandi. "I'm sure some psychologist could have a field day with his obsessive need for attention and his daily 'look at me…look at me!' antics. I simply don't let those guys get to me. They're harmless. Or, at least I *think* they're harmless. Barry's not a dirty old man. He's just a lonely old man. It certainly isn't full-blown sexual harassment now, is it? He's not a groper. He's not like that guy in Hollywood, what's his name. And Walter? I think he's just trying to compete with Barry for attention. Don't you think it's a silly little thing? It's nothing to get worked up into a dither over. Just kicking at raindrops, as Marty says. Nothing there. And, frankly, we *all* have our own little peccadillos, now, don't we?" And Mary Anne had to agree. Reluctantly, but she agreed nonetheless.

The class was smaller than usual, obviously due to the holiday. Barry wasn't there…but Walter was. The music began and the room began to vibrate with a dozen bodies getting worked up into a lather. By the time "La Bamba" finished, halfway through the hour, the group was dripping with sweat.

"Grab some water when you need it. Be sure to keep hydrated," Sandi announced. "Wow, Tanya," she called out to an over-ebullient, over-energetic buxom silver-haired woman in the front row. "You sure are loaded with energy this morning, aren't you? Sure that's water you got in there and not a gin and tonic?" She and the group laughed.

"You never know, sugar," Tanya laughed hysterically, raising her Yeti high as if giving a toast. "You never know. Perhaps I'm starting to celebrate early. Cheers!"

It was nearing the end of the rousing "Gangnam Style" routine and Mary Anne was just waiting. Would he? Yes, he would. And he did.

"One! More! Time!" brayed Walter.

Mary Anne just rolled here eyes as Sandi glanced over at her, smiled and winked. *Yes, I guess,* Mary Anne thought, *just kicking at raindrops. Nothing there. Nothing at all.* Okay, so what if it *was* annoying? It was just a minor, momentary irritating distraction, after all. We all encounter them every day, in some way or another. Perhaps we even do them ourselves.

When the class finished, Mary Anne and Sandi headed to their respective homes to shower, then change and get ready to party at CedarView.

The boarders almost passed out from shock when, later in the afternoon, Remy Major's car came down the gravel driveway. After he got out, he walked around to the passenger side and opened the door. Ingrid Schumacher stepped out and Mary Anne gasped.

"What the hell?" She gulped as her next-door neighbor walked toward the group.

"What?" asked Ingrid in her soft German accent, looking at her neighbor, "You always invite me to your Derby parties, but don't include me in these other horsey functions? Shame on you, pussycat," she laughed, "Shame on you. Well, Remy was a gentleman enough to do so. So there." And she playfully stuck out her tongue at Mary Anne.

Perhaps Ingrid had seen some of the boarders only once a year on Derby Day, but she fit right in…although she was the only smoker in the group.

Chips and Felicity Tallman and their month-old son, Adam, intended to make a brief appearance. They wanted to stop by and say "hi", have a drink or two and get back home out of the heat. And Chips wanted to proudly show off a colorful new T-shirt. But they were enjoying all the friendly chatter so much that they stayed well into the evening.

"Damn," exclaimed Mary Anne, "Isn't he the cutest thing?" as she leaned down to the little carrier to see Adam. "*Adorable* just doesn't cut it, guys. He is going to be so handsome, I can tell!" The Tallmans blushed and thanked her for the compliments. Mary Anne, stepping back, took a look at Chips's T-shirt.

"Don't tell me you ran the Peachtree this morning!" she asked. "It was stifling, wasn't it?"

"Yeah, I ran it. Anyway, my Dad and I ran it together. He's been running it every year since it started way back in 1970. Hate to say it, but he always pulls out in front of me during that last mile. Anyway, he sure is fast for 73. And, yes, it was hot, hot, hot, for sure. I think they said this was the hottest temperature at starting time ever. Global warming, I guess. Anyway, I got another shirt to add to my collection."

He got a round of applause from everyone on the deck and was handed a cold beer. He downed it quickly…Felicity politely refused one. She was nursing. All the women gathered around the baby, ooohing and aaahing, while the guys all complimented Chips and his run earlier in the day.

A few beers later, Remy and Bryan were walking side by side as Bryan proudly showed off many of the improvements he had made to the place. Remy was impressed, complimenting Bryan as they walked.

"Yeah, well…you know that big storm that blew through here a couple nights ago?" Bryan asked, "Knocked down a tree across the fence out there in the woods. Had to crank up that trusty chain saw and fix the damn fence before the horses got out. I sort of have a love/hate relationship with chain saws. I love 'em when they start quickly but I hate it when I actually have to use one. I remember you grumbling about that a few times." Remy chuckled about that.

"I do *not* miss walking the fence line," answered Remy, "Don't miss that one little bit. And I *hate* chainsaws! I don't think they like me, either." And both men chuckled at that as well.

"I'm tellin' ya, though, one of the unexpected side benefits to all this activity," Bryan continued, "is that I've lost fifteen pounds and feel ten years younger. Brandy has been after me for years to lose weight. She got her wish! Still love my biscuits and gravy, though."

"I could tell about the weight-loss," said Remy. "You're looking great."

"So," Bryan whispered, glancing over his shoulder back at the crowd of boarders chattering away, "are you and Ingrid an item, now?"

Remy laughed. "No, we're not an *item*," using air quotes for 'item', "We're just getting reacquainted, that's all. She's lonely…and I'm lonely. She and Zara used to talk a lot and, needless to say, we both miss her. We've talked on the phone and I've been over to her place a few times. She has the cutest little Schnauzer."

Bryan snickered. "Hehehehe. Is that what they call it in German? You old devil, you. Just be careful now, at your age…"

Remy cut him off. "It's her dog, Bryan. She has a cute little Schnauzer named Schnitzel."

"Oh," Bryan answered with an embarrassed grin, "I thought…well, never mind what I thought. That's great, Remy! Life is great and surprising at times, right? Just when you think it's over, it's not."

Remy wasn't totally sure he knew what Bryan meant, but he laughed and nodded anyway.

Periodically, the children would end up back on the deck to rest from all their running around. They'd be breathing heavily, dripping with sweat and looking for something cold to drink. The big old oak tree next to the deck offered shade but little respite from the heat of summer.

"You know what my beloved Grandma once told me, boys?" Bryan said as he called the boys over. "I was just a little bit of a thing, if you can believe that, and I'd get all hot and sweaty too, running around like a maniac just like you kids. She told me to hold my wrists…the underside of my wrists," and he demonstrated, "under the tap. Cold water, of course. She said it would cool me off in a heartbeat. I have done just that ever since. And, trust me, it works. Y'all go on up there and turn on one of those hoses and let the water run over your wrists. You'll be cool as a cucumber before you know it. Scoot!"

They looked at him, and then slowly headed off to the hose outside the tack room door. Megan and Graham's 4-year-old twin boys scampered after the older boys, trying to catch up. They all took their turns letting the water run over their wrists, but then it wasn't too long before they began squirting each with the hose, laughing and giggling as they did so.

"Well, then there's *that* way to cool off, too," said Bryan, shaking his head.

The sun went down, and a full moon would soon come up. Fireworks were blasting all around in the distance, with glowing bursts of color from every direction in the nighttime sky. Interspersed with the distant bursts were the summer sounds of crickets and katydids, calling to each other from tree to tree. It sounded as though one group of katydids nearer to the deck would call out, only to be echoed by another group further away. The rhythm was almost hypnotic. Bryan had added additional floodlights along the tops of the stalls facing out into the riding ring illuminating it for nighttime riding. Dozens of moths and other smaller insects swirled around the lights, buzzing into and out of the brightness.

The conversations jumped from topic to topic, from humorous to deadly serious, from laughter and accolades about Marty's foray into theatrics and grumbles and gripes about current politics. Remy had plenty to say about the current administration in Washington and he got very few disagreements or rebuttals.

"Oh, my gosh, Sandi," blurted out Mary Anne almost as an afterthought. "I totally forgot to ask you about last Saturday. I haven't seen you since then. I forgot to ask you after class this morning. Didn't you mention that you had a date? Who was he?"

"Ah…yeah…well…" Sandi stammered. "It was okay. In a strange way, I guess. It was with Trevor, a member over at the gym. He isn't in any of my Zumba classes, he's always working out on all the other equipment. He's that guy who's always wearing that Georgia Tech tank top, the one with the big yellow jacket on the front. Did you ever notice him?"

"You mean that tall, well-built, good-looking blond guy with the hairy chest and those nice muscular hairy legs, a great ass, that gorgeous tan and the cleft in his chin? Nope, haven't noticed him at all." Don turned and shot her a look.

"Yeah, well," continued Sandi, "That's him. He's a nice enough guy, don't get me wrong. We started chatting a few weeks ago and I had the feeling he was going to ask me out eventually. And he finally did. He lives in a real swanky apartment complex with a fantastic pool. He invited me over for a swim on Saturday afternoon and then he grilled some steaks out on his balcony. He has a great body, by the way, without that tank top and workout stuff. I mean, in his bathing suit. That's *all* I meant…in his bathing suit. Seriously!"

"Do we really need to hear what might be coming next, young lady?" laughed Ingrid with her beautiful soft German accent. "Shall we shoo all these other guys away, yes? And then we can hear the details." And she laughed again, leaning in closer to Sandi.

"No, no, no…" laughed Sandi in response, tossing her head from side to side. "Nothing like that. Honest! Well, to begin with, he's a collector and from now on I shall have to call him Lego Man." And she covered her face with her hands she was laughing so hard.

"Say what?" asked Mary, looking confused.

"He collects Legos. A *lot* of Legos. And he's obviously a 'Star Wars' nut as well. I think he must have every freakin' thing about 'Star Wars' that Legos ever produced. Boxes of them stacked everywhere. Legos 'Star Wars' characters are lined up on all his shelves. Hundreds of them were staring at me everywhere I turned. Okay, yes…we *did* make it into his bedroom. Yep, you guessed it, a 'Star Wars' bedspread. And there's a huge Legos Millennium Falcon hanging over his bed."

"Hey," interjected Marty. "Is this going to turn into an X-rated story, or what? I'm telling you that the visuals I'm getting right now are a bit dicey."

"Ha! I wish," snorted Sandi. "Right next to his bed, on his night stand, was this huge Lego bust of Darth Vader. Life-sized, I'd guess. You think I'm going to get frisky and start sounding like a Wookiee in heat with Vader staring at me? I was so hoping I'd get to play with his light saber, if you get my drift, but…yeah…well, *that's* not gonna to happen."

"What is it, this Wookiee thing you mentioned?" asked Ingrid.

At this point the entire deck was in hysterics.

"You've probably noticed, Mary Anne, that he hasn't been back to the gym since then. Well, not while I'm there anyway. I hope I didn't embarrass him but I lost it. I just broke down and laughed like a crazy woman in his bedroom. I thanked him for a great time…the swim and the fantastic steaks and all. But I just could *not* proceed any further. I gave him a quick peck on the cheek and left. Okay, so maybe I dreamed about Harrison Ford that night…but, end of story."

"I'm almost sorry I asked," laughed Mary Anne, shaking her head, "but that was a great story. Did you embellish that at all? You can be *so* melodramatic. Are you making any of that up?"

"Would this face lie to you?" Sandi giggled in response, pointing to her face with both hands.

After all the laughter finally died down, and Ingrid was informed about Wookiees, the topics turned, again, to more serious subject matters, although images of floating Legos stayed in their thoughts for a while longer. The immigration problem along the Mexican border was touched upon but quickly sidestepped. Global warming got its share of the conversation as well, with record heat waves in Europe to horrendous flooding in our own Midwest. Are we still, basically, coming out of our last Ice Age or are we headed toward oblivion? Everyone agreed that it's too cold in the winter and too hot during the summer. Was it Mark Twain or someone else who said, "Everyone talks about the weather, but nobody does anything about it"? Eventually Stet was asked about the progress of his art gallery and he gladly filled everyone in on what was happening.

"I know that Mary is too shy…or too proud, to boast." said Stet, "But I will. Her son Greg is not only a fantastic guy, but his architectural talents blow me away. That kid knows his stuff, that's for damn sure. I hope that you'll all get the chance to meet him sometime soon. I don't want to sound all mushy and maudlin but, hell, I really love that kid already." He paused for a moment of reflection. "But, you know what?" he continued. "This could have gone in a totally different direction. Greg could have reacted in the most negative of ways. His dad was killed serving his country and here I come, a few years later and replace him in his mother's affection. Greg could hate me or, at least, resent me and I probably wouldn't blame him. I guess I'd understand. Sort of."

"First of all," Mary started, "You and Greg are so similar in so many ways I'm astounded. The same temperaments, the same attitudes and, worst of all, the same goofy sense of humor. And you seem to have the same ideals. Honestly, you two act more like brothers. Yes, Greg and Frank had a fantastic father-son relationship. Hell, we traveled all over together and had great times. And, yes, Greg was totally devastated by Frank's death. Of course, we both were. For a very long time. We did a lot of crying together. A *lot*. But Greg does *not* regard you as a replacement, Stet. He regards you as an addition. Frank will always be in Greg's heart. Now you are, too."

There were sighs all around and Brandy dabbed at the corners of her eyes with a tissue.

The story of Frank Gordon reminding her about someone in the military, Megan began talking about the latest Jack Reacher thriller she was reading. But then the thoughts about the recent real-life murder sent chills down her back. Graham got a chuckle from everyone when he related the story regarding Megan's dream about a redheaded man coming to their front door.

All the while, in the background, Raymond had been strumming his guitar and singing softly to Amber.

Marty looked over at the two lovebirds, and then he glanced up at the full moon rising over the treetops. "Jessie," he said with a big smile on his face. "Remember our long-distance connection from the moon?" Jessica thought for a moment and then it dawned on her.

"Oh, yeah…I do, now. I had totally forgotten about that. That was so sweet and romantic, wasn't it?"

"Wait. What?" piped up Felicity Tallman as if from a daze. "A long-distance connection from the moon? Were you an astronaut or something? Do you and Lance Armstrong have something in common?"

Yep, all foam and no beer, thought Bryan.

"No, no…nothing like that," answered Marty, smiling. "And I think you probably mean *Neil* Armstrong. But, no, I wasn't an astronaut or something. When I was working for Compton, a few years ago, we had a working relationship with a sister packaging company in Trinidad and Tobago. I was sent down there for a week to educate their sales group about the benefits of marketing and good packaging design. I knew that on one of those nights there would be the full moon. So, before I left home, Jessie and I made a 'date' to both be looking up at that full moon at 11 o'clock on that particular night, when the moon would be high in the sky. So, there we stood, a thousand miles apart but with a cosmic connection. At that moment, I actually felt as though we were standing side-by-side. *'I'll be looking at the moon, but I'll be seeing you'*," he crooned softly. "Okay, that's it. No more singing from me. Ever!"

"Oh, Marty," sighed Mary, "that is so romantic." And she leaned a bit closer into Stet's shoulder.

"Sounds pretty sappy to me," joked Gary Smart, shaking his head. "So, in essence, you mooned each other, right?" Linda swatted him on the shoulder. "What?" he said to her, "I was just joking, for Pete's sake!"

"Talking about the moon, anyway," Chips Tallman spoke up, "there are still some idiots who think that moon landing fifty years ago was faked."

"Pathetic, isn't it?" responded Stet. "And there are still countless idiots who think the Earth is flat…and that The Holocaust was a hoax."

"That's worse than pathetic," answered Brandy. "Those morons drive amongst us…and breed…and, maybe worst off all, they vote!"

"Yeah, well," said Bryan, shaking his head, "take a look at our current Congress. There's the result."

"Wait, wait, wait," said Gary, "you mean the Earth *isn't* flat?"

Linda swatted him again.

The evening was slowly winding down. One by one, the couples began to pack up and share their goodbyes. Bryan and Brandy's two grandsons and Marty and Jessie's two boys came up on the deck to say goodnight to everyone.

"Boys," said Bryan, beckoning them to come closer. "Before you go, I have to ask you something. You all are animal lovers, aren't ya?" he asked.

"Yes, sir," answered his grandson Jason and the others all nodded in agreement.

"So you should know a lot about animals, right?" he continued.

"Well...sorta. I guess," answered one of Marty's sons, with a little bit of hesitation. He wasn't sure where this was going.

"Well, then" started Bryan. "Do you know why horse poop looks like little brown golf balls in a pile?"

"No, sir," answered Terry, Bryan's other grandson. The other boys shook their heads.

"Well," Bryan continued, "Do you know why cow poop looks like flat patties?"

"No," answered Terry again. The other boys looked confused and tried not to laugh at the word "poop".

"Hmmm, well, do you know why rabbit poop looks like teeny, tiny little pellets?"

"Nope," answered Jason once again.

"Aw, hell...you boys don't know *shit,* do ya?" laughed Bryan.

"Bryan!" scolded Brandy loudly, as the boys ran off the deck giggling.

It had been an exceptional, fun-filled event, even though they had all missed Zara. She would have enjoyed the day immensely. The horses, long since fed and put back out into the pasture, were still meandering around the fences along the riding ring, hoping for another slice of watermelon or two. Spoiled horses! They, too, seemed to enjoy these gatherings. The boarders had failed to notice that, with Rance Hurakon out of the picture forever, not one "Fuck you!" "Fuck off!" or "Fuck everybody!" had been uttered the whole day.

The lights were turned off, the tack room doors were locked and the goodbyes said. As the cars, one after the other, drove up the driveway heading home, there were still bursts of fireworks from the surrounding towns coloring the sky. Interspersed with these were flickers of lightning and the soft rolling sound of distant thunder. Someone, somewhere was getting rained on, but the folks at CedarView had just had a perfect day.

Mary Pat didn't know how she would ever be able to get through a long weekend without lapsing into her faux southern accent. All of her friends came to expect it and to accept it as second nature. For the most part, it was used satirically and to the delight of those around her. Except, of course, those who had a *real* southern drawl who thought she was mocking them. She wasn't. She was just being Mary Pat.

Derrick's brother, Allen, and his wife, Karen lived, along with their two daughters, in Dallas, Texas. Allen had been a professor of history, having earned a doctorate, and also lectured at various locales throughout the United States and Europe. Karen, also in possession of a doctorate degree, was a speech therapist. Mary Pat was grateful that they visited with these relatives rarely. In fact, it had been twelve years since they were last together. It had been Derrick and Mary Pat who had travelled to Texas. The Phillipses, up until this fast-approaching visit, had never set foot in Georgia before. She considered Dr. A. Phillips and Dr. K. Phillips supercilious to the nth degree. Allen was so full of himself that he would probably be starting to relate an amusing anecdote (about him) as he stepped out of the car upon arrival and conclude the story (about him) as he was getting into the car to depart three days later. Mary Pat was concerned that Karen was judging her speech patterns and grading them on a scale of one to ten. Their two daughters, Karen and Bitsy, were so tethered to their parents' apron strings that Mary Pat was convinced that neither girl knew how to wipe her own ass.

"Oh, please. I'm sure you're exaggerating, Mary Pat," Mary Anne said after hearing about the upcoming visit and what it might entail. "Derrick is so nice, I just can't imagine his brother would be that much different."

"Mah deah," Mary Pat drawled, fanning her face with her hand, "y'all have no idea. Mah panties'll be in a wad fo three fuckin' days before they arrive and fo a frickin' week afterwards. What in the *hell* we'll do with 'em fo three days is anybody's guess. They are *not* outdoors people at all but we'll probably drag their sorry asses over to the stable at least once. The boys have elected to lay off the sports for the summer, so there won't be any games to go to, or practices that Derrick will have to coach. At least their two daughters won't be with them. I think they're on some sort of trip overseas. And what the hell kind of name is Bitsy anyway?"

Mary Anne couldn't keep from laughing. Her friend's plight seemed humorous at worst, negligible at best. But the visit was sure to be fuel for Mary Pat's fiery, exaggerated story telling for months to come.

The soon-to-arrive guests were driving to Georgia from Texas. Following their visit with his brother, Allen and Karen would then drive down to Florida to visit Karen's mother who lives on St. George Island (population 641). Then, the three of them will take one of their multitudes of cruises, which seem to take place every other month. They are all retired. Allen, fifteen years older than Derrick, had elected to take a lucrative early retirement package and, along with that, live off the royalties from his multiple books and lecture fees.

At 4:15 on Friday afternoon, Derrick's cellphone started playing "Take me out to the ballgame"…his favorite ringtone. He glanced at caller ID and sighed. "Guess who?" he asked Mary Pat before answering.

"Hey, Allen!" he said in as chipper a voice that he could muster.

"Hey, yourself, Derrick!" came Allen's reply. "GPS says we're ten minutes away. Get ready for Hurricane Allen, bro, we have a lot of catching up to do! See you soon." And just like that he clicked off.

"Get ready, dear heart,' Derrick said to Mary Pat, with a hangdog face.

"Get ready yourself," Mary Pat shot back. "Get ready to help me hide the bodies if need be!"

Ten minutes later a Midnight Blue Cadillac Escalade came to a stop in Mary Pat's driveway. She and Derrick had watched as the car had turned into their subdivision and had slowly driven up the street. Allen Phillips got out first and stretched, arching his back after a long drive. They had spent the previous night just outside of New Orleans. He was tall, slightly over 6', with a salt-and-pepper beard and a very shiny, hairless head. He was wearing light tan linen slacks, a pale pink oxford button-down shirt and Dockers. Slowly, the passenger side front door opened and Karen slinked to a standing position. She was wearing sleek black slacks, black pumps, a silk black and white polka-dot blouse, the brightest red lipstick and nail polish that's available on this planet, with a large beaded necklace to match. She stood about 5'5" or so, in very good shape for her age (she and her husband were both 61) and hair cut into a short bob. Hair so white that it was almost blinding.

Nobody has hair that white, thought Mary Pat (she would be doing a lot of thinking to herself this weekend). *What does she do, wash it with Clorox?*

Both Mary Pat and her husband were wearing shorts, polo shirts and sandals. Thankfully Derrick was not wearing his favorite Atlanta Braves T-shirt.

Derrick rushed out to greet them and to help carry in their luggage. A three-night visit and five suitcases? They all came up the front steps, across the wide front porch and into the foyer. Allen had led the way and stopped abruptly as he entered the foyer, looking into the expansive living room. The living room with vaulted ceilings, original artwork on every wall, furniture right out of HGTV (Mary Pat had exquisite taste), recessed lighting and floor-to-ceiling bookcases on either side of the marble fireplace.

"Oh," said Allen, matter-of-factly. "Nice little place you have here."

Yeah, thought Mary Pat. *All 4,200 square feet of it. Small place, my ass.*

"Point us to the guest room," the male Dr. Phillips said, "and then we can get this weekend going!"

Up to this point, the female Dr. Phillips had said nothing.

"Well, damn," exclaimed Mary Pat. "Don't I get at least a hello or a hug or back slap or something?" Then she laughed as though she really was trying to be funny instead of being the smart-ass sarcastic bitch that she really felt.

"I am *so* rude," responded Allen, "You are so right, Mary Pat. I apologize profusely," he said as he bowed from the waist and took her hand, giving her the same kind of hug you might give a leper.

The female Dr. Phillips had *still* said nothing.

"Don't mind him, dear," the previously mute white-haired lady said, a bit on the haughty side. "He's probably just tired."

Well, damn, Mary Pat thought, *Cruella de Vil can speak!*

The visiting Phillipses were shown the guest room and in a matter of minutes headed back to the living room.

"I'm glad to see that you like books," Allen remarked as he pointed to the bookcases. "I brought you a little gift for graciously hosting us this weekend. It's my latest," he said as he handed Derrick a book that must weigh three pounds. "It's signed," he grinned proudly.

Derrick took the book, "The History of Economics & Society During the Renaissance: A Guide to Enlightenment", and thanked his brother profusely.

"Wow, I'm impressed," Derrick lied, "look at this, honey, isn't it great?" as he handed the weighty tome to Mary Pat. "This will have a prized location up there in our bookcases." Collecting dust, no doubt. Or used to squash a tarantula should one attack.

"The temperature has dropped down a bit after the sun went behind the trees and it's comfortable outside. It's not so humid today, either. I thought we could have cocktails out on the deck," Derrick suggested, after placing the new book on their coffee table.

"Are there bugs out there?" asked Nancy.

"Well…yeah," Mary Pat answered slowly. "But after they take a couple sips out of my wine they get drowsy and just doze off on the railings. They won't bother us, though."

"Oh," was the simple reply.

"What?" asked Mary Pat trying not to sound *too* sarcastic. "You don't have bugs in Texas? I thought you could practically saddle-break your cockroaches out there. Was I misinformed?"

Derrick gave her *that* look. This was going to be a looooong weekend.

Cocktail hour, with a couple pitchers of Margaritas, crackers and a Mexican Corn Dip, was enjoyed inside…in the living room. Mary Pat had planned and prepared meals ahead of time. Simple meals that could be heated quickly with little or no preparation required so she would be able to spend more time with her guests. A decision she now regretted. She had prepared the most time-consuming one, lasagna, earlier in the afternoon and it would be popped into the oven momentarily. Actually, it was a very elaborate recipe gotten from Jessica Howce, who had gotten it from Camellia Holliday, a friend of Marty's.

An hour had gone by since their arrival and Allen had not stopped talking since. Nor had he even asked how his hosts were. That query would not pass his lips, nor Nancy's, for the entire weekend. As luck would have it (and the boys thanked them profusely upon their arrival back home), Mary Pat and Derrick's sons were all away, spending a couple weeks at a friend's house on Hilton Head after a last-minute invitation.

"And your two daughters are where?" asked Derrick. "Did you tell me, what, London, or something?"

"No," jumped Nancy at the chance, "Nancy and Bitsy…she's my gifted child, are doing a study program in Paris for four weeks, language skills, and then they'll be moving on to Athens for two weeks."

So, thought Mary Pat, *how nice. We can categorize them: there's a Nancy 1 and a Nancy 2, and a gifted child named Bitsy.*

"Do your daughters get involved with any sports when they are back here and in school?" asked Derrick.

"Oh, my heavens, no," responded Nancy 1 very quickly, almost spilling her third margarita. "No…no…no…no, not at all. No tomboys in *our* family thank you very much. We're simply not outdoor people at all. The girls have gone to cooking schools from a tender age and ballet…they're both wonderful dancers…oh, and creative writing classes. Bitsy, my gifted child, is turning out to be quite a writer, even if I do say so myself."

The timer dinged in the kitchen and Mary Pat excused herself to get the lasagna out of the oven. While it rested for fifteen minutes or so, she would set the dining room table, pour glasses of ice water and heat up the garlic bread. She also thought about slashing her wrists but didn't want to ruin perfectly good lasagna or the new polo shirt that she was wearing. She had cut several rose buds from the bushes in her garden and arranged them in a low centerpiece on the table. She was using their finest silverware and linens. She could still hear Allen babbling away in the living room as she went about her preparations.

"Dinner is served," she called. "Bring your drinks with you, or I have some red wine if you're interested." They were interested, so she uncorked and poured the wine.

"Everything looks lovely, dear," spoke Cruella…oops, Nancy 1, as she seated herself and carefully placed a napkin on her lap. "I hope you haven't gone to too much trouble with meals this weekend. Whenever we have weekend guests, I always have them catered."

Mary Pat pictured herself, at this exact moment, shoving a fork into Nancy's left eye.

"Delicious, Mary Pat, delicious," blurted Allen. "Oh, this reminds me. Let me tell you about the last time I was in Rome. You've been to Rome, haven't you? You'll get a kick out of this."

Allen talked, between bites, for the next thirty minutes. But all Mary Pat heard was "Me…blah, blah, me…blah…me…blah, blah, blah…oh, and me!" She could have sworn she saw Derrick's eyes beginning to droop so, to play safe, she kicked him under the table. He gave her *that* look again.

Trying to bring Nancy into the conversation, Mary Pat asked: "So you'll be going on another cruise next week, I hear. You must like them." Mary Pat just noticed something. Nancy's nose had been in the air since she arrived. Mary Pat thought, at first, that perhaps it was a bit of a physical thing with her neck. Nope. It was that Nancy 1 was a first-class snob and she was a walking, talking cliché.

"Oh, yes," answered Nancy, "we simply adore them. Most of the captains on several ships know us by now, as does most of the crew. We're big tippers. We seem to get special treatment wherever we go, don't we, dear?" turning to still babbling Allen.

"Yes, dear, whatever you say," and he continued talking to Derrick.

"We get bumped up to the absolute best suites more often than not and don't get me started about the casinos. All the croupiers just *love* Allen!"

Why did Mary Pat just hear nothing but "blah, blah, blah, blah, Allen"?

Mary Anne had volunteered to feed Mary Pat's horse this evening and in the morning, so there was no need to rush out to CedarView today. In other words, there was no escape.

Things became a blur, from that point on, with story after story. By noontime the next day, Mary Pat and Derrick had heard inane details about a dozen different cruises, trips to thirty countries, lectures given and applauded, books written and awards won. Mary Pat was sure she heard, somewhere in the jumble, tumble of words, about a death-defying escape from a tribe of cannibalistic pygmies in Java and Allen's discovery of the lost Ark of the Covenant…but it could have been just her imagination.

Early Saturday morning, after feeding the two horses, Mary Pat's and her own, Mary Anne headed for the gym and her beloved Zumba class. Before starting her car, she texted her friend: Horses fed and happy. How R U doing?

Mary Pat shot back a two-word reply: DON'T ASK

Later Saturday afternoon, Mary Pat and Derrick said they were all going over to CedarView. It would be a nice chance to get out and see a small part of the countryside on the way. Nancy pointed toward the guest room and said to her husband "Please get my sweater for me, dear."

"It's 92 degrees out there," said Derrick, "I don't think you need a sweater."

"I get chilled easily," was the succinct reply.

You could get killed easily if I had my way, thought Mary Pat. Instead, she uttered, "Bless your heart."

On the drive over, Nancy began extolling the virtues of their daughter, Bitsy…the gifted child. Here she was, at 15, being approached by one of Allen's publishers to produce a series of little books for young readers based upon the journals she had written while overseas.

Mary Pat didn't want to tell Nancy about *their* sons' abilities to produce a series of dirty sports uniforms and smelly jock straps. And they could, at times, speak in somewhat coherent, oft-times complete sentences. It just didn't seem right to brag.

She also thought to herself that she'd been confusing education with intelligence. You could have a degree…or three…and *still* be an idiot.

They came to the top of the driveway leading down to the stable. Mary Pat waved to Mrs. Critchley, the widow who lived across the street. She was almost always working out in her yard, maintaining her property to the envy of all the neighbors. After they had parked and the car doors opened, Nancy immediately gasped.

"God! How can you tolerate the smell?" she asked.

"Smell? What smell?" Mary Pat asked in return, wondering what the concern was.

"Well…I *assume* it's manure," said Nancy, holding her nose.

What, you can't tolerate horseshit, thought Mary Pat, *but you can tolerate your husband's bullshit? What the hell?*

As soon as she stepped from the car, Nancy spotted the deck built into the end of the riding ring and headed for the steps.

"Wait," called Derrick. "Don't you want to come see the horses?"

"That's fine, dear, I can see them from here." She plopped herself down on a seat and pulled the sweater snuggly around herself.

Marty and Jessica Howce were trotting their two horses, Dan and Gemmy, slowly around the ring and both Mary Pat and Derrick waved to them.

The Phillips trio started walking from the parking area to the stable, leaving Nancy alone on the deck.

"I've been told that Marty is writing a book," Derrick said as he pointed toward his friend. "I think he's going to self-publish."

"Oh," said Allen, looking as though he had just discovered dog shit on his shoe. "I didn't have to resort to that. Several publishers sought *me* out."

Derrick was sorry that he had mentioned it.

Halfway through, Mary Pat thought…*another halfway to go.*

Meanwhile, it had turned into another pleasant evening. The temperature had already plummeted to a chilly (for July in the south) 82 degrees. Sitting side by side in a large chaise lounge, Mary Anne and her beau, Don, were enjoying margaritas on their back deck and listening to the loud chattering of birds as they were beginning to bed down for the night. Soon the chirping of the nighttime insects would replace that chattering. Cue the soundtrack. Something by Jimmy Buffett. *Anything* by Jimmy Buffett.

"Heard from Mary Pat yet?" asked Don.

"Only a short little text this morning. She was dreading the weekend, but I'm sure it's turning out *far* better that she thought. She was probably worrying for no reason…" she trailed off as she sipped her margarita, reaching for a potato chip "…and she'll be laughing about it for days."

She leaned into Don's chest and looked up at the beautiful waning moon just beginning to peek up over the treetops.

"I'm sure she'll be regaling me with humorous story after story following this weekend. She was probably worried for no reason and will feel guilty for doing so."

Don had already fallen asleep.

Sunday morning crept by; with Mary Pat's delicious French Toast Casserole reminding Allen of an "amusing experience" he and Nancy had had in Provence years before. You've been to Provence, right? Just when you think it's over, it's not.

Sunday afternoon crept along slowly, with Allen excusing himself to take a short nap. For some reason, he was feeling exhausted and had a bit of a sore throat. *Imagine that,* thought Mary Pat!

Sunday evening came along following a quick trip to CedarView to feed a horse. Mary Pat had gone by herself and was *so* relieved by the quiet. She thought, perhaps, that she had suddenly gone deaf, it was so quiet. Despite Allen's afternoon nap, the visiting Phillipses were going to retire early in the evening. They wanted to get an early start Monday morning... earlier than originally planned but welcomed by both Derrick and Mary Pat. They were eager to see MeeMee (that's what Nancy called her mother) and prepare for their *"fabulous"* cruise later in the week. They were certain that Captain Carlos would be *so* eager to see them as well.

Monday morning dawned and, after a sumptuous breakfast of scrambled eggs, bacon and toasted English muffins, Allen retrieved all five pieces of luggage from the guest room. They had needed only one piece for the weekend, but hadn't wanted to leave the other pieces in the car... not knowing, really, what kind of neighborhood it might be. The four of them paraded out to the Cadillac and said their goodbyes. The two guys shaking hands and the two ladies politely hugging each other.

"Thanks for a terrific weekend, you two," Allen grinned. "You're great hosts. We'll have to come back again sometime. Hopefully sooner than twelve years!"

Derrick felt his sphincter clamp shut.

"Loved that lasagna, dear," Nancy purred to Mary Pat. "Please, please, please remember to email that recipe to me. I'm so eager to see what my cook can do with it."

Mary Pat envisioned Nancy, up to her eyeballs, in a vat of steaming ricotta cheese.

Kisses, hugs and waves goodbye and then the verbose raconteur Allen and the chilled Nancy 1 headed off to MeeMee-Land!

It would be later that summer that Nancy 1 would be informed by Nancy 2 (aged 18) that she, too, was gifted...with child. A handsome young Swede named Arvid she met while in Paris had taught her a *lot* of things...except how to be careful.

AUGUST

Another Op'nin', Another Shoe

"Never underestimate the power you have to take your life in a new direction."

Germany Kent

Mary had stopped off at Panera Bread Company to pick up lunch for herself and Stet. She was now driving toward his house in Between with the anticipation of going over final arrangements for the big gallery opening. Her cellphone buzzed, she answered, hands free.

"Where are you?" asked Stet.

"Probably less than two minutes away, just turned down the road heading to your place," she answered.

"Great!" he quickly responded, then clicked off. *What the hell was that about* she thought?

She turned into his long, shaded driveway and came to a sudden stop. She gulped and nearly choked laughing.

Stet was standing in his open doorway, leaning up against the doorjamb with his arms folded across his chest, one ankle crossed in front of the other.

He was stark naked.

"What in the hell are you doing?" she gasped, as she got out of the car bringing the large bag of sandwiches with her. "Weren't you afraid that I could have been the UPS guy?"

"Nah," he answered matter-of-factly. "He's already come and gone. We had *such* a good time," he snickered.

Mary swatted him on the shoulder as she tried to squeeze by him to get into the house. "Smartass!"

"You really didn't need to bring lunch, Mary. You're my BLT."

"BLT? What?" she asked quizzically.

"Yeah. Bites. Licks. Tastes."

"Fresh!" she said as she reached out and tweaked his enlarged, supersensitive right nipple.

"Hey, watch it, lady! You just pushed the magic button!"

Ten minutes later, lying on the living room floor, they each let out a sigh. A few lingering drops of semen oozed from the tip of Stet's still-hard penis.

"Whew," Mary uttered softly. "That was a hell of a greeting. What was the occasion?"

"Do you realize," answered Stet, "that is was just about one year ago that you first accosted me at the Tack Shack?"

"Wait! What do you mean I accosted you? I did no such thing!"

Still lying on the floor, Stet turned his head and looked at her.

"Okay, so maybe I flirted just a little bit. But it was totally innocent," she said.

"Yeah, right. There I was, a sweet, naïve innocent young man and you tried to seduce me. Didn't you, Mrs. Robinson?"

"Roll over. I want to spank you!"

"Mmmmm, where's your riding crop?"

The preceding several weeks had been frantic. The renovation of Stet's gallery took up all of his thoughts, from dawn until dusk. Greg and Ash had supervised the build-out like champs, pleasing Stet and making Mary extremely proud. Sure, there were just a few disagreements about one small thing or another, but they were quickly resolved and eased over. The transformation of the old, empty warehouse space into a contemporary showplace was amazing. Greg had been staying at Mary's place for a few weeks, while Ash stayed at Stet's house. The two young men then drove together into Atlanta almost every day to oversee the work and make any adjustments, if needed, along the way.

Stet had thought, at first, that he would showcase his own work for the grand opening of the still unnamed gallery, but after speaking to Meagan at CedarView one afternoon, he decided to look at the paintings done by one of her friends and neighbors. A few photos taken on her smartphone had intrigued him. She had raved so much about the beautiful work that her friend had done, so he paid a visit to the home of JaNelle White.

After pulling into her driveway and exiting his car, he momentarily stopped as he heard the soft bleating of goats. Looking at him through a wire fence, three curious faces stared at him. He swore they were smiling. He smiled as one of them stood up on its hind legs to peer further over the fence. He couldn't resist. He went over and petted its head. And then the two others wanted their turn as well. By this time, JaNelle was standing on her front porch laughing.

"Better watch out," she called, "They'll rope you in and hogtie you if you're not careful. They love attention."

Although they had spoken on the phone, Stet formally introduced himself, and she ushered him into the house.

"Sweet tea?" she asked.

"But of course," he responded, "is there any other kind?"

He followed her into the kitchen where she filled two glasses with ice and poured the true nectar of the south to the brim of each. They chatted for a few minutes, getting to know one another a bit before Stet mentioned the reason for his visit.

"Please come this way, then," she said in her soft, melodious voice, as she turned and walked back into the main part of the house. She led him down a hallway and opened the door to what would, under normal circumstances, be a bedroom.

There was not a stitch of furniture in the room. Instead, leaning against each wall were paintings stacked back-to-back resting on the floor. She had them arranged by size, small in front, getting larger as the stack progressed back toward the wall. They were also arranged by subject matter. There was barely enough room to walk through the center of the room. The sizes varied from tiny 6" X 6" to quite large canvases of 45" X 60". He was blown away by the magnitude of her work and was shocked to learn that a gallery didn't already represent her. JaNelle was prolific, to say the least, but sold mainly to friends or showed her work at little local craft shows. He was impressed by the fact that she painted for a month or more zeroing in on one theme or subject matter: goats or other animals one month, landscapes another, and so forth. He was flipping through the canvases as he and JaNelle chatted about…

BREAKING NEWS: THE POLICE HAVE JUST ANNOUNCED THE ARREST OF A SUSPECT IN THE ALLEDGED MURDER OF LOCAL SCHOOLTEACHER JOSEPHINE THALES. ARRESTED WAS AARON HARDIN, 18, A RECENT HIGH SCHOOL GRADUATE AND FORMER STUDENT OF MISS THALES. HE HAD FLED THE COUNTRY AND WAS EXTRADITED FROM FRANCE EARLIER TODAY. STAY TUNED FOR FURTHER DETAILS AS THEY BECOME AVAILABLE.

…her work. He stopped flipping when he realized something intriguing.

He pulled out one painting. Then another. And then, yet another.

"JaNelle!" he exclaimed. "I love these. You have a very unique color palette. The juxtaposition of some of the colors are bizarre but, dammit, they work."

The works consisted of paintings with bold strokes…not wussy dab, dab, dab…but large swashes, laid on so thick in places that each painting had a rich texture. There were paintings of goats: blues, magentas, yellows, for example. And there were landscapes with bold, almost brash color schemes…sometimes there would be green skies. There were paintings of horses, with brilliant flourishes of purples, reds and greens. There were portraits with shadows of blues and greens falling across interesting faces.

"Honestly, JaNelle," said an almost breathless Stet, "You certainly see things in totally different ways."

JaNelle smiled. "Indeed I do, son. Indeed I do. I'm color blind."

"Get out! No way," Stet stammered. "You aren't."

"'Tis true, 'tis true," she repeated. "They call it Tritanopia. I have problems with blues and yellows. It's very rare, for sure."

"But…" Stet started, as he pointed to a few of the paintings around the room. "I see blues and yellows in these."

JaNelle laughed. "I didn't say I couldn't read. I pick out the color tubes of oils in the store. I use as many colors as I can. I'll squeeze blobs of paint out on my palette. They get mixed up when I move the palette around so then I have at it with abandon! What *you* see here isn't always what *I* see."

"Amazing," uttered Stet. "I am ever more impressed now. Okay, let's get serious and do some talking."

And they did.

Extraordinary advancements in DNA analysis have recently become an extremely effective investigative tool. But just suppose there isn't an existing DNA profile of an alleged perpetrator? He or she might not have a criminal record or be in any such database. But, then again, just suppose that your DNA evidence might be able to show you what your suspect looked like? Well, sit back folks and be enlightened. There is a new service called Snapshot DNA Phenotyping System. This system can predict the genetic ancestry, eye color, hair color, skin color, freckling and face shape of the "donor" of any particular DNA specimen. Seriously? Yes. And these epigenetic markers can be used to predict the donor's age within a three to four year range. Hence, one red pubic hair (that, and some very damaging evidence found on the victim's cellphone and laptop), led to a horny teenager named Aaron Hardin.

Although she ended up dead, which, of course, was a genuine tragedy, the victim was not without fault. She was not a sweet, innocent thing. She was a predator. She stalked and preyed upon virile young men. Aaron Hardin was not the first of her students to find his way into her bed. If only the other young men had bragged enough to each other, this story could have ended in a completely different way. She started with simple flirting in the classroom. If her prey was horny enough…unsuspicious enough… stupid enough to let his male ego be massaged enough to flirt back, things escalated from there. Flirtatious emails become steamy emails, which then led to meeting privately. Josephine (Josie) Thales craved young men. Young men craved her. Once she had spotted a guy who lit her fire, she planned and plotted their ultimate seduction. The one thing she had *not* planned, however, was an unwanted pregnancy. *How the hell did* that *happen*, she thought to herself? Condoms had never been used. She loved the sensation of semen oozing from her body. She was on the pill. Something went amiss but too late for questioning how. She knew it was Aaron's. She managed to space her conquests several months apart.

Aaron was panicky when she told him. His mother would have a heart attack. His girlfriend would leave him. His scholarship to Duke would probably be in jeopardy. Oh, and his father, the Reverend Philip Hardin of the First Methodist Church would explode.

She threatened to expose him. Accuse him of seduction and sexual harassment. It had just been a very cruel tease because, in actuality, she had already planned on getting an abortion. It was her own fault, after all, and she really wouldn't want to take this poor young guy down. Of course, Aaron didn't know that or he would have acted, or reacted, in a totally different manner. He had concealed a small pistol, a Colt Mustang, in his jeans on his last, fateful visit with the temptress. They had had sex and, while she was seated at her vanity freshening up following the romp, he pleaded with her, gun in hand, to recant her story. To do something, *anything*, to get rid of his baby. She had laughed and raised her hand quickly to fix her ponytail. Too quickly. Her hand hit Aaron's hand by accident, causing him to squeeze the trigger as he tried to not drop the gun. One problem solved but another *major* problem had just occurred. He stood there in total panic mode for 30 seconds before he raced to find a garbage bag and grab up what he thought was all the evidence that would connect him to the scene. Missing, of course, one tiny, messy piece of evidence. Obviously he had never watched "CSI". He walked a few houses away, through the woods behind the houses, until he spotted some trashcans along the curb. Nobody was around except some excited kids bouncing around an old ice cream truck. He then went home as quickly as he could. To be perfectly honest, he had not "fled the country" as the media reported. A month-long trip throughout Europe was a graduation present from his parents, planned months in advance. It just proved to be at a very opportune time. Sort of.

Fact: 20% of women who die during pregnancy are victims of murder. 67% of those die from firearms.

All of this came out in the trial, including the testimonies of four other virile, testosterone-empowered, yet embarrassed, classmates of Aaron who had also been bedmates of "Josie". The jury members were less than entertained by the photos that Josie kept on her smartphone and laptop: close-up shots of five teenaged penises in various states of erection, one of which had a flaming red bush at the base of the shaft. Josephine's past was vilified in the press. Aaron's future was now, as the expression goes, in the shitter.

Stet and JaNelle were still in the room of paintings when Bernie, her husband, came home from the office. He introduced himself, chatted with Stet for a while before he excused himself to get an evening drink, asking if either Stet or JaNelle would join him.

"Not yet, handsome," answered JaNelle. "In a bit. I think we're just getting started in here." And she would be right.

"So, okay," Stet began. "You've been selling to just friends and putting your stuff in dinky little local shows?"

"True," JaNelle responded with a sigh. "Look, I know my paintings are a bit weird, but they're my passion. I paint daily...well, not so much when Bernie is home but I paint a lot. Sometimes I can breeze through a couple paintings a day. Keeps my mind occupied, I guess. Our daughter, Esmé, is away at school and I miss her and worry about her constantly. Painting distracts me."

"When you *do* sell them, how do you price them?"

"Well, it all depends. If one of my friends likes something, I might charge them just a couple hundred dollars, basically for my time. If someone is a bit arrogant at one show or the other and wants to haggle unmercifully, then I might charge more just to be nasty." And she giggled.

"Ah, ha!" Stat blared. "So you charge via emotion, not logic. Perhaps I can set you straight with that one. I, too, just used to sell to friends or in dinky little shows. Folks who attend the Yellow Daisy Festival don't expect to pay for a Picasso. But I learned about a formula for pricing our artwork fairly and appropriately."

"Seriously?"

"Seriously," answered Stet. "Look. Figure out the total square inches in each painting. Then multiply that number by a set dollar value that you think is appropriate. Right now, looking at these paintings, I'd say, offhand, that you should use $7.00 per square inch. Then calculate your cost for the canvas and framing and double that number. I can get your framing materials wholesale. You certainly want to charge a paying customer for that; otherwise you're giving him a frame for free, in essence. Add all those numbers together. It might come out to a number that surprises you, but don't forget if you are going to be showing in a big gallery...ahem, mine for example...the commission will be 50%. That's pretty much the going rate."

"Whew!" whistled JaNelle, "you have my head swimming. Maybe I *do* need that drink!" They both laughed.

"Let's be logical, JaNelle, you and I both have been piddling around in small dinky shows. Sort of like we've been playing in off, off, off- Broadway houses. You and I are about to be stepping out on to the big Broadway stages now. And we need to be stepping out with gusto!"

"I'm not so terribly sure I have the gumption to be charging outrageous prices for my work."

"If you elect to come with my gallery-to-be, JaNelle, we can discuss the prices together and work out some deals. Sometimes it might be better to sell *everything* at reasonable prices than to sell little or nothing at outrageous prices. But. And that's a big '*but*'. Consider where this gallery is going to be. In Buckhead. Folks with big bucks will be coming in to these shows. Sometime these folks think that the more you pay for something, the better it is. I've seen it time and time again."

JaNelle laughed loudly. "You don't have to tell me that, son! I just about croak when I hear how much some of my friends pay for crap."

"Well, there you go," Stet stated. "And then you turn around and sell these same friends a painting of yours almost at give-away prices, right?"

JaNelle nodded.

"Okay, then. Look, I see a series here that I would *love* to use for my opening show. Actually I see a dozen shows here with your work. But this one in particular," and he started flipping through them again, front to back, "it's frivolous, outrageous, innovative, *so* far out there, totally fun and almost satirical. I think a couple of these are even making a social commentary."

"A what?" exclaimed JaNelle, "A social commentary? Ha! In that case I think *you* might be seeing something that *I* don't see. But, what the hell. Let's go for it."

"Great, JaNelle, I'm ecstatic. I have a standard contract form. I'll courier it to you tomorrow. I know your husband is a lawyer. Have him pass his wand over it and let's make magic together." They shook hands and then hugged.

"Let's go get that drink now," smiled JaNelle. "Look out, Bernie, here we come!"

The weeks had flown by since that first initial meeting between Stet and JaNelle. Several meeting had followed and then the transportation of thirty paintings to Stet's house in Between. He built his own simple frames and did the same for JaNelle, working the costs into the pricing for each painting. There had also been several meetings between him, Marty and Max…some of them a bit heated. The name for the gallery. Damn, why was this so difficult? Marty had shot down all of Stet's names weeks ago. Max had laughed at them as well.

"Look, guys," Marty finally said. "You're trying to make this far more difficult than it needs to be. You, Stet, are trying to make this a southern-sounding thing. I'm not so sure that's even relevant any more. Why not just cut to the chase and use your name?"

"What, 'Stet's Place'?" shrugged a tired and frustrated Stet.

"No. That's stupid. Besides, it sounds like a bar. Plain and simple. Keep it plain and simple. Your name is unique enough, take advantage of it: 'Brandson Gallery'. Plain and simple.

"Max and Camellia are major backers here," mulled Stet. "How about 'The Brandson-Holliday Gallery'? Plain and simple, right?"

They sat there staring at each other for a minute.

"Ha! Why the hell didn't we think of that five weeks ago?" blurted Max.

"Now I've got a shitload of work to do," Marty said as he got up to leave. "There's stationery to develop, press releases to prepare, posters to design. Name to register. Plus my entire regular shit…you know, like my freelance accounts? Get me a few photos of this JaNelle White's work and I can build my collateral material around it. Needless to say, we have to work fast. Pronto, pronto! Do you have a title for this show…for your grand opening?"

"Yes," said Stet, leaning back in his chair and clasping his hands behind his head. "Yes, I do. It's called 'Stepping Out'."

Invitations had been mailed, phone calls had been made, texts had been sent, and the media had been alerted. Months of hard work were about to pay off. Stet and Max took a final walk-through with Greg and Ash. The gallery was going to be a showstopper. Floor to ceiling windows fronted the space, letting in wonderful natural light during the daytime. Upon entering through a shiny black lacquered door, the visitor would see a long expanse of crisp white walls leading to a tall white reception desk halfway toward the back wall on the left. Flanking the door, on either side, were two big black lacquered pots containing very large split-leaf philodendrons. Industrial-looking floodlights were suspended from steel girders hanging from the raised ceiling with exposed beams overhead that were painted a matte black. The LED floodlights, for true color enhancement, could be individually controlled via a remote to direct their light on any hanging piece of art on the facing wall.

There was a small room off to the right, close to the entry, to be used for smaller showcases of artwork. Individual movable pedestals of varying sizes for sculptured pieces were placed around the room. Two black leather Barcelona Chairs for relaxing were set, back-to-back, dead center, on a large circle of white carpeting. Further back in the gallery, again off to the right, was a much larger space. The back wall of this space was a broad, sweeping curve. The flooring through the entire space was of the highest quality dark charcoal gray industrial carpeting with a crisp border of black extending two feet out from the walls. In the center of the carpet in the room with the curved wall was a big circle of black to match the border around the entire gallery, with two white leather Barcelona Chairs in the center. Suspended high overhead from the rafters, sleek, slim ceiling fans slowly, silently turned. They were the ultramodern MinkaAire Ninety-Nine models in brushed nickel. Each fan had nine slender blades and integrated LED lights. These, too, were controlled via a remote. Three fans spun in the main, entryway gallery; one spun in the smaller side gallery; and five spun overhead in the larger gallery area to the right.

A doorway on the back wall of the left-hand side of the gallery, opened to a long corridor flanked by bins where additional pieces could be displayed…additional pieces by the artist currently showing, pieces by other artists being represented by the gallery…and pieces by Stet. Further back were the restrooms, a small business office, a kitchen area and a storage room for cleaning supplies. Even these rooms, which would be rarely seen by the general public, were works of architectural art and design, with gently curving back walls. Greg and Ash were truly avant-garde in their designs and constructions. Stet had hung a few of his smaller paintings in each of the two restrooms. But he wasn't gauche enough to include price tags.

JaNelle's artwork had been delivered and carefully unpacked. She and Stet worked together for the installation, moving pieces from here to there to get the mood just right. They had worked on Stet's formula for the pricing of each piece ahead of time and JaNelle was still taken aback by what they have come up with.

"Frankly," she said, shaking her head, "I think some of these prices just might be totally out of line."

"I could agree with you," Stet answered, "but then we'd *both* be wrong."

As they decided the location for each piece and hung it, Stet placed a little card beneath it with title and price. The artwork ranged in prices from a low of $300 to the maximum of $18,000.

"Oh, Lordy," JaNelle shuddered when she saw that price card go up. "I'm sure that piece will still be hanging here after the show closes."

Stet laughed and continued placing the little cards.

Mary, who Stet had hired to be his manager, accompanied them. She, also, was just a bit concerned about the prices. But, what did *she* know, right?

STEPPING OUT: Opening Night! Mary Anne had been hired to cater the affair. No Cater-Tots kid stuff on *this* occasion. No balloons. No pony rides. Trays after tray of interesting-looking and great-tasting finger foods were created. Crystal champagne flutes were rented and cases of Moet & Chandon Imperial Champagne were ordered and chilled. A huge celebratory bouquet of exotic flowers, sent by Ash's parents, sat atop the reception desk.

Stet had a secret surprise. One that he had cleared with the Hollidays beforehand. He had reserved a two-bedroom suite at the Ritz-Carlton and told Mary to pack a small overnight bag. He knew that they'd be too tired and buzzed after the show to attempt to drive back out to Between. It was nearing show time!

Stet's clever title for the show actually had a double meaning. The subject matter for the entire series being shown at the opening, and throughout the following six-week run of the show, was...drumroll, please... *shoes!* Yes, shoes. JaNelle's paintings were all shoe-oriented. All shapes, styles, colors (oh, those incredible, fantastic color combinations!), close-ups, extreme close-ups, inside, outside, soles tattered, sneakers with holes worn through, juxtapositions of styles that were laughable. A huge canvass that looked like an abstract collage from a distance was actually a bird's eye view of a pile of dozens of shoes thrown together at random. It created a bizarre composition that was breathtaking in scope and imagination. The "social commentary" that Stet had seen was a gorgeous painting of a pair of dirty, dusty, beaten up work boots sitting in a puddle of mud next to a pair of high heels by Jimmy Choo, one of which had toppled over. The colors blared from the crisp white walls...magentas, turquoises, fire engine reds and stark blacks and blues.

Stet, in a tuxedo, and Mary, in a full-length, form fitting black dress with turquoise jewelry, stood side by side as they looked at the exhibit for the umpteenth time. JaNelle, in a sleek silk sleeveless floor length emerald green dress with matching emerald jewelry, stood hand in hand with tuxedo-clad Bernie. Max and Camellia, wearing the largest hat ever, perused the gallery, stopping from time to time to comment on one piece or another. Greg and Ash, both wearing classy business casual attire, stood at the back of the gallery, feeling very proud of their endeavor as they took in the whole colorful, eye-popping scene. Mary Anne, wearing a full-length sequined top cobalt blue dress, was standing, along with the two tuxedo-clad servers she had hired, waiting to play hostess with the hors d'oeuvres and champagne. Max had hired a trio for the event: a classical guitarist and two violins. They began to play in the small room to the right of the entry. Cue the soundtrack: "Samba De Orfeu" by Luiz Bonfá. Mary Anne struck a pose and the photographer who had been hired for the event started snapping several photos. The photos, along with a short story, would appear in the *Atlanta-Journal Constitution* and later would be picked up by the *Chicago Tribune*, Chicago being the home base for the two young architects.

8:00 P.M.: "Showtime, folks," announced Stet as he unlocked the doors. A few people had been waiting outside on this balmy summer evening, waiting for the refreshing air-conditioned air inside. Upon entering the gallery, patrons (well, perspective patrons) were met with an explosion of colors set against the brilliant white walls.

An hour later, the place was packed. And noisy. Conversations overlapped with laughter, which then overlapped with words of congratulations for Stet, Max, Camellia and the two architects. Champagne flowed like water. Stet was near the rear of the gallery when he saw him enter. He wasn't difficult to miss…he stood above most of the other people in the gallery. Mary noticed that Stet got a huge grin on his face and followed his gaze. A very handsome gentleman, probably in his early sixties, a full head of salt and pepper hair, wearing a beautifully tailored dark gray suit, with an open-neck pale blue oxford shirt, had caught Stet's eye. Stet slowly worked his way through the crowd, nodding to one patron or another, with a word or two to each. The two men stood facing each other for a brief second, and then they shook hands. The handshake turned into a warm embrace that was held for at least a minute. Stet said something to the man, he nodded, and then they both turned and headed in Mary's direction.

"Mary," Stet said, with tears in his eyes, "I'd like you to meet Ben. Ben Brandson. He's my Dad."

"You're right," Ben said, as he shook Mary's hand, "She's gorgeous, Stet. Simply gorgeous."

Mary dropped Ben's hand and gave him such a tight embrace that it nearly knocked him off his feet. She pulled back and stared into his face.

"Didn't think it was possible but, Mister Brandson, you're even better-looking than your son!"

"Hey, watch it!" joked Stet, wagging his finger at her.

They chatted and laughed for a few more minutes, with Ben complimenting the facility and the apparent success of the evening. He glanced around the room and spotted a large hat bouncing and turning to and fro as its owner was in active conversation.

"That can be only one person I know. Excuse me, kids, see you later," Ben said as he moved toward that bouncing hat.

Camellia saw him heading her way and nudged Max. "Here he comes," she whispered. "Didn't take him long."

Ben eased his way through the crowd and smiled broadly as he approached Camellia and Max. He leaned in and gave her a gentle peck on the cheek.

"Lovely, as ever," and he smiled.

"Well," answered Camellia, looking down at herself, "I've put on several years and a few pounds since you saw me last."

"I repeat," said Ben, "Lovely as ever."

He extended his hand to Max and the two men exchanged pleasantries.

"Stet sure has come a long way, hasn't he?" asked Ben.

"Indeed," answered Camellia, looking Ben up and down. "And so have you, I know."

Ben Brandson had raised Stet from the very beginning. He taught him everything he possibly could about life, about horses and how to become an expert farrier. They went on backpack hiking expeditions and horse treks all across the United States and parts of Europe. The strong father-son bond was enviable. They had remained inseparable until Stet grew up and moved out on his own. They communicated often, not as much as either had liked, but more so recently. Because of their respective schedules, they hadn't seen each other in close to five years.

Ben had been the permanent, and favored, farrier at SouthWind Farms, a premier horse-breeding facility in California. Camellia's father, Barratt

Starr, owned the very prosperous place up until his death. Ben Brandson, throughout the years, had become the son that Barratt, a widower, never had. Camellia had played an important role in the entertaining of prospective buyers of prized horses and their respective children but only up to a point. She had no interest in horses or the snobby horse people with whom her father dealt. Ben, with his good looks, suave charm (yes, even farriers can be suave!) and easy-going manner slowly filled Camellia's role. He travelled overseas to assure the horses purchased were well taken care of upon arrival, no matter what country, no matter what continent. Upon Barratt's death, Camellia received a substantial monetary inheritance and Ben had inherited SouthWind Farms. Only Stet knew that Ben was also the silent partner backing the gallery.

Mary and Stet were kept busy either chatting with patrons discussing this painting or that one, or writing up receipts. Credit cards flashed as quickly as teenagers' fake IDs at a bar. By the end of the evening there would be little red-dot stickers (signifying a sale) under half of the paintings in the gallery and three more paintings with the red-dots cut in half (signifying a 24-hour hold). Stet knew that those little red dots, once upon a time in galleries everywhere, were now considered gauche or tacky, but he was one to eschew current convention.

A well-dressed woman pulled JaNelle aside and asked question after question, almost giddy with enthusiasm. After a few minutes, JaNelle nodded and motioned for the woman to follow her. They went through that back door that led to the bins with other pieces of her artwork stacked back to back. They stood there flipping through the pieces. Five minutes later they came back out and JaNelle walked her to Mary at the reception desk and spoke to her. She turned to the woman, thanked her profusely and went to find Bernie. She leaned up along side of him, shoulder-to-shoulder, and whispered into his ear.

"I just sold a goddam purple goat for $4,000 to that woman over there," she said, matter-of-factly.

Bernie chuckled. "How'd you know it was purple?" he joked, looking at her, arching one eyebrow.

"Because she said 'Oh, I just *loooove* this purple goat', that's how!" And she swatted him playfully on the shoulder. "Smartass!"

Several of the CedarView "gang" showed up. Mary Pat, for once losing her faux southern accent, was beside herself as she walked around from piece to piece, with her husband, Derrick, by her side. Mary came up to her and the two linked arms as they continued to peruse the artwork.

"That cheapskate of a husband won't agree to buy my favorite piece here," as she pointed to a large canvas. It depicted long English riding boots leaning up against a pair of western boots. The riding boots were in shades of magentas and reds; the western boots were in shades of teal and black.

"It would be just perfect over our fireplace but he says he doesn't like it. Maybe I'll be able to convince him later. When we get home. You know what I mean?" she asked as she winked at Mary. Mary shook her head, rolled her eyes and laughed.

Megan Fairley grabbed Stet by the elbow. "I am so glad you took my advice and looked at her work. Isn't she fabulous?" she squealed.

Sometime during the middle of the evening, the White's daughter, Esmé, entered the gallery and searched for her parents. She wore a floor-length white dress that clung to her slim, toned body offsetting her smooth, tan skin. Her earrings and bracelet matched her deep ruby red stone necklace. Her long dark hair was pulled back and held in place by a black clip at the base of her neck. In essence, she was simply stunning. Greg saw her and was mesmerized immediately.

"Whoa," he whispered to Ash, "who is *that* goddess?"

"Calm down, lover boy, aren't you still on again, off again with Aideen," Ash smirked.

"Oh, come on, who the hell are you kidding? I know you and she are getting it on."

"Wait. What? How do you know that?" Ash responded with a mock shocked expression.

"Yes, Aideen and I broke up, but we're still friends. We still communicate. You tried to keep things quiet because you didn't want to hurt my feelings or jeopardize our friendship and working relationship. Come on, buddy, give me some credit. But she still doesn't want to move to Chicago, does she?"

Ash slowly shook his head. "No. But we're trying to work it out anyway."

"Yeah, well, good luck with that!" Greg said as he headed off to introduce himself to Esmé White.

Slowly, as the hours progressed, the gallery began to empty out. The finger food was gone, the champagne flutes had been washed, dried and repacked for return to the party rental facility and the musicians had packed up and headed for home.

Ben approached Stet and Mary. "The Hollidays are going to drive me up to the hotel. We're going to have a nightcap or two in the bar there. We have a lot of catching up to do. I'll meet you back there. I'll wait up for you two kids." And he disappeared out the front door.

"He seems like such a great guy, Stet. No wonder you turned out the way you did," Mary cooed into Stet's ear.

"I love that man so much, Mary. You have no idea what a spectacular time we had as I was growing up. I hope I can be half as good a father when *my* time comes."

JaNelle and Bernie came up beside them. Stet looked around. There was no one else in the gallery.

"Where are Greg and Ash?" Stet asked.

Bernie snickered. "Looks like our daughter hijacked them. She's going to show them a few nightspots around town. You know kids. They can keep right on ticking."

"They damn well better end up in Between sometime tonight, or at least by early tomorrow morning. Luger needs to get out for his nightly run and they promised to feed my horse breakfast," said Stet, shaking his head. "Ah, youth!"

Stet and JaNelle stood side by side in the middle of the now almost empty gallery. "Look at all those little red dots, JaNelle. Aren't they beautiful?"

Yes, she thought they *were* beautiful and surprising. There was even a red dot sticker under the largest painting in the exhibit...the one with an $18,000 price tag attached.

"Looks like we stepped out onstage at just the right time, my friend," Stet said to the bemused artist. "And we found just the right audience. Congratulations. You're a hit."

"And a great big congratulations to you, too, Stet. And an enormous thank you for believing in me and my work...no matter how weird the color palette might be." They hugged and he kissed her gently on both cheeks.

Bernie and JaNelle headed home. Stet and Mary finished with some paperwork, then turned out the lights, set the alarm and headed toward the Ritz-Carlton. Mary hadn't been aware that Stet had reserved a two-bedroom suite. She probably would have been suspicious if she had. They checked in and rode the elevator to the top floor. Entering the suite, Ben rose from the comfortable sofa in the sumptuous living room area and greeted them.

"You throw a hell of a party, son," Ben exclaimed. "Congratulations. You have done yourself proud. Very proud, indeed. You want to join me in a nightcap? The Hollidays just dumped me at the curb, practically, and drove off in their old Cadillac. Camellia had fallen asleep halfway between your gallery and here," and he laughed. "We'll play catch-up some other time."

"Thanks, Dad, but I think we'll pass. It's been a very long day."

"I completely understand. I'll see you both for breakfast in the morning. Pleasant dreams, kids," Ben said, winking at Stet, as he turned to go into his spacious bedroom. The door closed and locked.

Mary and Stet looked around their enormous bedroom, with a breathtaking view of sparkling downtown Atlanta from the floor-to-ceiling windows. Mary picked up her overnight case and headed for the bathroom.

A few minutes later, she emerged and saw Stet's tuxedo tossed into a heap on the far side of the room. He was standing at the end of the bed. Aside from a black bowtie around his neck, looking like a Chippendales dancer, he was totally naked. He was holding a very small pale blue box.

Stet, Mary and Ben had agreed to meet in the dining room for breakfast at 9:30. Ben would be flying from Atlanta to France later in the day. And from there, he would be flying off to Dubai later in the week. Although *he* looked perfectly rested, Stet and Mary looked a bit bedraggled when they found his table fifteen minutes late. He rose to greet them and assisted Mary with her chair. He gave Stet a particular look that silently asked "Well?" Stet got a big Cheshire cat grin on his face.

"She said 'yes', Dad." Stet glowed.

SEPTEMBER

Do Moles Look in Windows?

"If you're going to do something tonight that you'll be sorry for in the morning, sleep late."

Henny Youngman

Scenario 1: Part 1 - Mary Pat Phillips was in a pissy mood anyway, so when Derrick got off the phone with his brother she didn't feel very much like being sympathetic to anybody, for any reason. She hadn't had a good day at the stable. Mary Anne had criticized her for her awkward, careless riding and while she was grooming her horse, the beast had the audacity to step on her foot. Her riding boots had protected her only so much and now a big ugly bruise was forming on the top of her left foot. She had said a few very colorful words and swatted the poor horse with her crop. That had resulted in a simple but loud "Tsk, tsk" from Mary Anne and a wagging finger. Mary Pat rewarded Mary Anne with a finger as well, the middle one, followed by a resounding "Fuck off!" She put her horse back out into the pasture, put her grooming items away and got back into her car, slamming the door, without a goodbye or see ya later to Mary Anne.

"So what did your asshole of a brother want?" asked Mary Pat. "Did he suddenly remember a story he forgot to tell us while they were here?"

"No," answered Derrick, realizing that his wife was just a tad edgy tonight so he'd better tread slowly. "Actually he called about Nancy. His wife, not their daughter. You know, we both noticed and commented upon the fact that Nancy needed a sweater even though it was stifling outside. Well, come to find out that was a symptom of something called Hemolytic Anemia."

"Really?" asked Mary Pat. "Perhaps Allen and Bitsy, their gifted child, can collaborate and write a book about it." She regretted that the second it left her mouth. "I'm sorry. That was just plain mean. Just because I'm feeling bitchy tonight doesn't mean I have to take it out on your family. What is that? That thing that she has?"

"In a nutshell, it means her red blood cells are being destroyed faster than they can be made and replaced. She's on medication now, but she might need blood transfusions or bone marrow transplants. It's a wait and see situation right now. There are clinical trials being done in England on a drug that assists the marrow to produce healthy red blood cells. Not sure if they can get in on those trials or not. Allen might try. He's distraught, to say the least."

Of course he is, thought Mary Pat, *they'll probably have to cancel six cruises and disappoint Captain Carlos and his crew.*

"I'm sure he is," responded Mary Pat, "It can be devastating. How are their kids handling it?"

"Funny you should ask. When I mentioned the girls, he evaded the question entirely. He's usually so braggadocious regarding his little angels. I found that odd, considering they both must have had a marvelous time in Europe and experienced a ton of stuff."

Scenario 2: Part 1A - Graham Fairley came in from working in his yard. He started muttering under his breath. He was in a pissy mood. Megan came into the kitchen as he was finishing up washing his hands.

"What has *you* in such a tizzy, tonight, Graham?" she asked. "I thought you were in a good mood when you went out."

"I don't know why I even bother trying to keep the place looking great. If the drought doesn't fuck things up, then too much rain does it. And if that doesn't get you, then the hornworms will get your damn tomatoes. Or the deer will devour all your beautiful hostas. Now we have moles burrowing through the lawn. It's beginning to look like shit out there."

"Moles? Really?"

"Yeah, really." Graham sulked.

He had a flashback, albeit a funny one, regarding these creatures. He was probably no more than five years old, a bit older than his twin boys were now. He and his parents had gone early one evening to visit his paternal grandparents. He loved to read, so his Grandma had bought a special little picture book for him and he sat in a great big chair, next to a great big picture window slowly thumbing through the pages. He would pick up bits and pieces of conversation from time to time. His ears pricked up when he heard his Grandpa say "wicked little creatures. Ugly as sin and do a hell of a lot of damage." What was he talking about?

"They're out there in the yard right now, I have no doubt. Can't seem to get rid of those damn moles." Moles? What are moles? Are they big monsters? What do they do?

Graham, at that age, was afraid of the dark and always slept with a light on in his room. Basically, he was afraid of his own shadow. The conversation about moles continued for a few more minutes. He slowly turned his head toward that great big picture window he was sitting next to. It was pitch black outside now. Was he imagining something horrible looking in at him? What was out there? He slowly slid out of his chair, keeping one eye on that great big picture window with blackness and who knows what else outside. He cautiously sidled up next to his beloved Grandma.

"Do moles look in windows?" he asked nervously.

The adults burst into gales of laughter. He was assured that they didn't after being hugged by his grandmother. But that story and his question became a tale that was told, year after year, at family gatherings long after he had reached adulthood.

Scenario 2: Part 1B – Graham Fairley's pissy mood got even pissier when a short news segment aired on the 11 o'clock news. He had been involved in a local labor arbitration case that was supposed to be top secret until the issue was resolved. A key point that had been the pivotal argument issue was now announced, loud and clear, by an anchorman who had the airbrushed good looks of Barbie's Ken. *What the fuck?* thought Graham. *The shit's gonna hit the fan.* He realized that all the progress that had possibly been made up to this point was for naught. He was furious. He was beyond pissed off. Obviously they don't look in windows, but apparently moles *do* sit in on arbitration meetings.

Scenario 3: Part 1 - Jessica Howce was in a pissy mood. Her two sons and their constant bickering got on her nerves. It was almost a daily occurrence, starting with mild insults thrown at one another, and then poking that turned into pushing which, in turn, became punching each other. Jessie could hear the battles up in their respective rooms. They each claimed their own "turf", restricting his brother from entering his room. They each claimed to be the smarter one and they each boasted that he was "Mom's favorite". Marty found it somewhat amusing, although he remembered the situation, years ago, between him and *his* brother. He tried to reassure Jessie that the boys would eventually outgrow this sibling rivalry. Jessie wasn't totally convinced and mentioned something to the effect of "time will tell."

Scenario 4: Part 1 - Chips Tallman was in a pissy mood. He had just been called into Human Resources and was questioned about something he had said to a few of his co-workers. They were all having lunch together, a few days prior, and were complaining about one of the supervisors and being very critical about her. Chips made the offhand comment that he thought she was a strict, way *too* strict, micro-manager who didn't seem to respect or appreciate the talents and abilities of her own staff. He also joked about her inability to sit down considering the broom handle that

was so far up her ass. And then he had hummed the theme music of the Wicked Witch of the West. After being summoned to the HR Director's office, Chips wondered what was up. As he walked into that office, he knew *exactly* what was up: there sat the supervisor he had criticized, with her arms folded across her chest, staring at him with a glare that would have frightened Hitler. He had to do some fancy dancing to get around his comments and left the office, fifteen minutes later, with a dressing down, a mild wrist-slap and a stern look from that micro-manager. *Anyway,* he thought, *there's a mole amongst my co-workers and this taught me to keep my big mouth shut!*

Scenario 5: Part 1 - Stet Brandson was in a fantastic mood. By the end of Stepping Out's run, there were red dot stickers on every one of JaNelle White's paintings except one, with patrons clamoring for more of her work. Ironically, the lone remaining painting was the least expensive one, depicting a tattered and worn sneaker with what appeared to me a mouse (or could it be a mole?) peeking through a hole from inside the shoe. It would be kept hanging for the next show that Stet was now installing, but moved to a different location. The new show, entitled "Brandson and Then Some", comprised of works that were half of his own paintings and the other half being those of local young painters he had met throughout the years. The first painting that had a red sticker under it after the show opened was one of his paintings. Simply titled "George", it was a gorgeous painting of his beloved old horse that he had had to put down last year. The horse was walking away from the viewer through some tall grass blowing in the wind, but had stopped and turned his head looking back, ears erect, as though his name had just been called.

The art critic for the *Atlanta Journal/Constitution* had written a very positive review for the new gallery and its crisp, Spartan Minimalism design (whatever the hell *that* meant!). While she *basically* liked the show, "Stepping Out", and singled out several paintings for their "extremely brave use of color and inventive juxtapositions", a few she found pretentious. Ending her review on an upbeat note, she was "looking forward to seeing more of Ms. White's works and where this delightful talent may lead."

Stet penciled in on his calendar a show for sometime in January: "Getting Your Goat".

<u>Scenario 1: Part 2</u> – Mary Pat called Mary Anne to apologize and dredged up every excuse she could find, from the moon's phase to Starbucks messing up her latte that morning; after repeated reproachments still finding skid marks in her sons' underwear; and the cat had coughed up a huge fur ball into one of her favorite shoes.

"Don't be silly, Mary Pat," assured Mary Anne. "No need to apologize. Look, we all have those kinds of days. Even me! Although rarely. I love you too much to be offended by silly stuff. Don't worry about it. But…since when did you get a cat?"

Regarding her brother-in-law and Cruella, Mary Pat would take a wait and see stance. Her empathy was running on empty.

<u>Scenario 2: Part 2A</u> – Doing a search on the all-knowing, ever-amazing Google for getting rid of moles in your yard, Graham was faced with a conundrum. Moles could be bad…*or* good. Yes, they could damage lawns by destroying the roots. By the same token, they eat insect larvae and grubs, which could cause significant damage to plants. Moles also aerate the soil as they burrow. What to do? What to do? Spray the yard with castor oil? Moles hate the smell. Buy Whack-A-Mole (or something that sounded like that, anyway) at Home Depot for a gazillion bucks? Set traps and move them elsewhere (like your neighbor's yard, for example)? Fuck it! Considering the number of decimated chipmunks he had seen around his yard recently, he figured perhaps some neighborhood cat could take care of the situation. Case closed.

<u>Scenario 2: Part 2B</u> - In a strange twist of fate, the breach of confidentiality paid off. The mole in Graham Fairley's arbitration meeting never saw this one coming. The announcement that never should have been made public, actually forced the hand of the recalcitrant (and embarrassed) holdout in the negotiations. The issue was resolved early in the very next session. Case closed. *The mole,* thought Graham, *was probably a low-performing person who lacked the knowledge (or social skills) to realize how stupid he (or she) really was.*

Scenario 3: Part 2 - Jessica Howce was resigned to the fact that she'd have to listen to her sons' bickering and bantering for years to come. This sibling rivalry stuff was just plain silly. She raised her voice and shook a finger at them when she told them that she most definitely did *not* have a favorite – she disliked them both equally. This added a new dimension to their bickering, with each boy razzing the other, at times, "Mom dislikes *you* more!"

Scenario 4: Part 2 – Two days following his wrist slapping, Chips Tallman went out to his car to head for home after a long day at the office. The air had been let out of all four of his tires. He put his hands on his hips in exasperation. *Anyway,* he thought to himself, *good thing I have roadside assistance.* At that exact moment, the Wicked Witch of the West was summoned to HR. Surveillance cameras had caught her doing something mean in the parking lot. Evidently the baseball cap, oversized sunglasses and large jacket with the logo of her son's Lacrosse team on the back weren't enough of a disguise.

Scenario 5: Part 2 – The Brandson-Holliday Gallery was christened with champagne on opening night. The night the *AJC* review appeared, Stet and Mary christened the gallery again. After hours. Hot and steamy. In the back room. As a blue and green goat watched.

OCTOBER

Paradise or Pair O' Dice?

"We begin to learn wisely when we're willing to see the world from other people's perspective."

Toba Beta, Master of Stupidity

It was one of those beautiful autumn days, crisp mornings that turned into warm, if not hot, afternoons. Stet and his good friend Doc Morrison were discussing the plans for expanding his small stable and paddock area. Doc, also Stet's veterinarian, had been one of his friends who had helped build his fabulous, ultra-contemporary house a few years prior. He had taken a few days off to help his friend once again. It was obvious that Mary would soon be moving her huge horse, Thunder, from CedarView and would need much more space. Greg had flown in from Chicago the night before and was sleeping in. He seemed to be making trips to Atlanta every couple of weeks. Mary and Stet both knew why…and it wasn't to help with the construction of a new barn.

The two men were seated at the breakfast table, scribbling their thoughts on a note pad, enjoying their second cup of coffee when Greg stumbled, barefoot and sleepy-eyed, into the kitchen. The sound of Luger's toenails click-click-clicking on the hardwood floor followed close behind. The dog had taken to Greg right from the beginning and always slept up on his bed with him whenever he visited.

Greg stood there for a moment, in his boxers and a T-shirt, sniffing the air.

"I need some of that magic bean juice," he said, as he reached for a coffee mug from a shelf. "What time is it, anyway? I'm still on Chicago time, but maybe I overslept."

"It's seven," answered Doc, glancing at his watch.

"Seven!" Greg laughed, "Hell, that's too damn early. Why are you up and at 'em at the fucking ass-crack of dawn?"

"I guess we're just too eager to accomplish things today, young man," Stet laughed right back at him.

"Ha! There you go with that 'young man' stuff again, you old timer," Greg said, shaking his head. The two guys bantered like brothers when they were together, their bond growing stronger. Luger ambled into the room behind Greg and sniffed at his backside.

"Hey, cut that out," Greg said to the dog. "Haven't you got used to my scent yet? Jeesh! I'll fart in your face and *that'll* give ya something to sniff."

Greg filled his mug, then sauntered over to the table, pulled out a chair and sat down, glancing at the scribbled plans. He cocked his head to one side.

"Hmm," he said after a minute, picking up a pencil, "how about moving this around here and adding this?"

"Son of a gun, that's a great suggestion," replied Stet, "I hadn't thought of that but it's a terrific idea. Agreed, Doc?"

"Absolutely," he answered, after scrutinizing the rough sketch. "Why didn't *we* think of that?" And they all laughed.

The table became a hotbed of activity, with the plans being refined and a long list of the required material being drawn up. Crumpled pieces of notepaper littered the floor as they tossed one idea after the other aside as they refined and refined even further. By the time they were ready to set out, they had gone through two pots of coffee and a lot of laughter.

Marty had stable duty this morning and had gotten there early. His day was going to be a busy one, with two client meetings before noon and three projects that were due sometime tomorrow. Oedipus Pex, the old rooster, was pecking around on the ground and seemed to be getting closer to Marty's backside. Marty sensed it, jumped around quickly flapping his arms and shouting at the bird. The rooster squawked, jumped a foot into the air and ran off in the other direction, clucking loudly...probably something profane in chicken talk. *Damn bird,* Marty thought to himself. The commotion had startled the two barn cats, Shadow and Spook, and they ran in the opposite direction from the fluttering rooster. Design concepts were swirling through Marty's mind when he heard another car come down the driveway. It was a little black Miata, top down, but no music blaring. Sandi Prescott got out of her car and walked, not her usual bounce, toward the tack room.

Marty had just about finished grooming Gemmy by the time Sandi had gotten Fireball from the pasture and led him to his stall. "Good morning, out there," he called to her as she walked into the adjoining stall with her horse.

"Yeah, good morning to you, too, Marty. What's up?"

"The sun," he joked.

"What?"

"The sun. You asked 'what's up?' and I told you."

Silence.

"Are you okay?" asked Marty. He sensed that Sandi was not her usual beyond-perky self.

"Yeah, I guess so," she responded with a sigh.

"Are you sure? You're not yourself this morning, I can tell."

"Oh, yeah, I'm okay. I'm just a little upset. I'm not sick or anything. It's not me. But Dottie's husband was shot last night."

"What?" was Marty's sudden response.

"Dottie Washington. You know, your leading lady? Her husband was shot last night."

"Ah, ha! I knew it!" he almost shouted, jumping up and down. "I just *knew* it! I had him pegged the minute I first met him. It was mob-related, wasn't it? Is he the Godfather? He is, isn't he? Turf warfare? Was it drug-related?"

"What? No! Are you *crazy*?" She was incredulous. "Nate's the sweetest guy going, once you get to know him. Yeah, as a matter of fact it *was* drug-related, though. Nate is in the DEA. He was leading a major drug bust. Evidently it had been in the works for months."

The DEA...Drug Enforcement Administration. Marty's mouth dropped to the floor. First impressions can be *so* wrong.

"Are you serious?" Marty asked, mouth still agape. "Was he killed?"

"No. He'll be okay. I think he'll be getting out of the hospital in a couple days. He was wearing one of those Kevlar bulletproof vest things but somehow or other he got shot in the ass."

Mid afternoon, Mary came driving down Stet's street and turned into his long tree-lined driveway. They had hired a second manager for the gallery and today was, basically, Mary's day off. The new manager was doing a great job and Stet was impressed with her knowledge of the art world. Mary saw the three men hammering away on the roof of the newly enlarged barn. She also noticed that there was a strange car parked next to the house. The temperature had risen throughout the day and had gotten on the hot side. Stet, Greg and Doc Morrison were all shirtless as they worked; sweat glistening on their shoulders. She got out of the car and walked over to the barn, Luger running up beside her and giving her hand a sniff.

"I'm not sure I can handle all this testosterone," she called up to them, shielding her eyes from the sun. "Greg, you've changed a bit. I'm not sure your poor old mother is able to take this mature look. I can still picture you in diapers," and she laughed.

"Aw, hell, Mom, that embarrasses me, dammit!" he responded as the two other men snickered.

Mary was suddenly aware of someone coming up behind her. She turned to see Esmé White and she smiled.

"I think all that testosterone is just fine," the beautiful young woman purred. "Especially regarding that young one," pointing toward Greg.

Mary hugged her. "I *knew* someone else was up here," she said, "I just didn't recognize your car. And I knew damn well that Greg's frequent visits to Atlanta weren't to see his poor old Mom…or to help those two studs fix a barn." Pointing up to Greg again she said "He got that sexy hairy chest from his dad."

"Mom! Stop!" called Greg, with a chagrined look on his face. The two other men couldn't stop laughing.

"This sure isn't the same barn that I last saw here, guys. You work fast. I'm impressed. By the way, where was Gracie while you were doing all of this? She certainly couldn't have stayed in her stall or out here in the paddock."

"She's tethered out back. Way back there, where there's still a lot of tall grass," answered Stet. "She's a happy little mare, at the moment, I can tell you that! Just wait until she sees who her new stable mate is going to be. She sure won't be able to intimidate Thunder the way she did to poor George. Come on in; take a look at Thunder's stall. I think you'll like it."

"I'll change and be right back out," replied Mary. "Can I bring you guys anything to drink when I come back out?"

"Nah, thanks. We're good for now," called Stet. "We've been through gallons of water throughout the day. I'll be up peeing all night. We're gonna work until it gets too dark to see. The way we've been going today, I think we might be able to finish up tomorrow if the weather holds out. Next day, for sure. These guys," indicating Greg and Doc, "are the absolute best. Mary, you should be *so* proud of your son. Not only can he build out a drop-dead gorgeous gallery, but also his skills out here today blew me away. This kid knows what he's doing."

"There you go with 'kid' again, 'old man'," shouted Greg from the far end of the roof. "Doc and I will stay out here and finish up in a bit. Isn't it past your bedtime, you old goat?"

Mary just shook her head. It was so much fun having these guys around. She would surely miss Greg when he went back to Chicago.

"Come on back inside, Esmé, we'll fix these guys something to eat while they finish up here."

They turned and walked back toward the house, with Luger running ahead of them.

"You can call me Essie, Ms. Gordon. I hardly ever go by my formal name."

"And, please, call me Mary."

It was getting dark when three tired, shirtless, sweaty guys came into the kitchen.

"If I were Mary Pat," said Mary, grinning, "I'd be fluttering my hands in front of my face and saying 'Mah lawd o'mercy. Ah just might swoon from all this heah masculinity'!"

"Oh, stop!" said all three men, almost in unison.

"I assume, Doc," asked Mary, "that you'll be staying for supper tonight?"

"Nope. Thanks, though. That's awfully nice of you to ask. But I just called my wife and told her I was about to head for home. We promised the kids pizza and a movie tonight, so my long day is about to get longer. However, you *might* be able to twist my arm just a tad for tomorrow night. If I might be so presumptuous," and he smiled his great big handsome smile.

"We'll put in another long day tomorrow," said Stet, while washing his hands at the kitchen sink, "and you damn well better stay for supper then! Just sayin'!" He pulled his T-shirt over his head to put it back on, sweaty body or not.

"See you at seven," said Doc as he headed for the door.

"Seven? Shit," said Greg.

Earlier that afternoon, Marty had glanced at Caller ID on his cell phone and saw that it was Gary Smart, his former coworker at Compton Paperboard Packaging Company.

"Hey, Smart-ass," Marty said with a laugh, "you moved to Chicago yet, or what?" Gary, a top salesman at Compton, had been offered a decent promotion along with a transfer to Chicago. But that had been months ago and Marty hadn't heard from Gary since July.

"Nah," Gary sighed, "we turned it down. By 'we' I mean Linda and me. We did a lot of investigating and decided it really wasn't going to be such a great situation in the long run. The money was good…just not quite good enough. We looked at it from all angles, cost-wise, weather-wise… all that shit. I got something in the works though, that's why I called. Wanna grab a couple beers tonight? We can talk then. It's Trivia Night at the Vortex. The one in Little Five Points. Wanna go with me? Linda can't make it tonight; she has something with a bunch of her friends. We're a great team and we usually win. I know *you* know a lot of trivia shit. You used to razzle-dazzle us at our sales meetings with your silly pieces of nonsense just to lighten things up. Whaddya say?"

Marty chuckled to himself. Yes, he remembered how he loved to throw out little pieces of nonsensical trivia peppered throughout his presentations. "Did you know that the tongue of a Blue Whale weighs as much as an elephant?" "In 1905 there were only two cars in the entire state of Ohio. They collided." "Did you know that the wingspan of a Boeing 747 is longer than the first flight of the Wright brothers?" "Did you know that it's illegal in Arizona to have more than two dildos in your house? Any more, and it's considered a brothel." (Seriously? Do they have a Dildo Inspector going from house to house taking count, or what?) "What was Mickey Mouse's original name?" Gary Smart liked that one. He collected watches and his favorite was an original Mickey Mouse watch in pristine condition.

"I love that place and haven't been there in ages. Let me check with Jessie. I'm sure it'll be fine. I'll get right back to you. What time?"

"Trivia starts at 9 o'clock. I get there around 8:30 or so. I like to get a slight buzz on first."

Marty texted Jessie, who texted him right back, saying "Have fun!"

"C U there, Gary," Marty texted Gary.

Marty was lucky enough to find a newly vacant space in the parking lot right next door to the restaurant. He enjoyed this part of town, one of Atlanta's hippest neighborhoods. A wild conglomeration of shops, restaurants and bars, there was always activity (legal or otherwise) to be found here. Locking his car, he made sure there was nothing worth breaking in for left visible. He smiled as he walked through the famous laughing skull's mouth/doorway. The place was packed, as always, and noisy, as always. Nothing had changed: there was a mishmash of strange artifacts hanging everywhere and especially a lot of skulls. He saw Gary sitting at the far end of the short bar and tried to make his way through the mixture of races, colors, accents, clothing styles and aromas. He was grateful that the place had initiated a "No Smoking" policy within the past year or so and was also glad it strictly enforced its "Nobody Under 21 Allowed" policy as well. Gary looked up over the surrounding heads and spotted Marty, motioning for him to come on. He didn't want to lose his spot at the bar, obviously. The two men vigorously shook hands and tried to summon the bartender. Marty preferred gin and tonics, but made the wise decision that this place was better suited for beers.

"Hey, man," Gary practically had to shout over the cacophony around them. "I'm sorry. I fucked up. Trivia Night was *last* night. I'm so screwed up with my days that I lost track. If you want to go someplace else, that's okay."

"Hell, no. Are you kidding me? This place is great and I've been looking forward all afternoon to one of their fabulous burgers. It won't be a total loss. I brought a couple of new trivia questions for you anyway." And they both laughed.

"Great," shouted Gary. "You never let us down, do you, sport?"

Three beers later, Gary was still sitting, and Marty was still standing. Eventually, the man sitting next to Gary turned to look at Marty. "Okay, junior," he said with a booming voice and a friendly smile. "I'm about to head out into the *real* world. Wanna sit down before you fall down?"

Marty couldn't really tell what ethnicity this guy was, but it was obvious that he was a mixed breed. Although he was somewhat neat, with no noticeable aroma aside from alcohol, he clearly hadn't shaved since the last royal wedding. There were strange little do-dads tied to the end of his beard. If he were walking through Buckhead, he'd be avoided. Here in Little Five Points…? Well, he'd be considered the norm.

"Thanks, my friend!" Marty said, extending his hand for a shake. The man stood up, towering over Marty and bowed graciously.

"Je t'en prie, monsieur," he said, shocking Marty. "Bon nuit." And with that, he departed, leaving Gary and Marty agape.

"You just never know down here, do ya?" muttered Gary, studying the bottle, and then lifting his beer to his lips. "Ya just never know."

"Hey, guys, we're going too," said one of the two young men who were sitting at a small table for two next to the bar. "You can have our table if you want it."

"Great, thanks. We'll do just that," responded Marty, as he got ready to switch places.

As the two young guys stood up, one turned to smile at Marty and winked at him. *You're barking up the wrong eggroll, Mr. Goldstone,* thought Marty with a broad smile. Gary saw the wink.

"If you play your cards right, stud, I'll bet you could get lucky tonight," he smirked.

"Shut up!" Marty shot back, shaking his head.

Gary and Marty each ordered one of the burgers for which this place is famous…with fries for Gary, tater tots for Marty.

"Okay, so what's going on with you, Gary? Something interesting?"

Before Gary could answer, Marty felt a tap on his shoulder. He turned around to see a smiling, familiar face.

"Remember me?" laughed Peter Scott, the young designer that Marty had hired at Compton.

"Well, I'll be damned! Peter Scott, the kid with two first names." The two men embraced, then shook hands.

"How the hell have you been, my young friend? You've changed a bit. You look…"

"Like Chris Evans, right? Yeah, I get that a lot." And Peter laughed.

"No, actually I wasn't going to say that," answered Marty, "although I guess, if I stretch my imagination, I could *possibly* see that. I meant that you look different, sort of. You've changed your hairstyle and it looks like you've been working out."

"I have," answered Peter, bending to look around Marty. "Hey, Gary, how's the Smart-ass?"

"I was wondering when you were going to acknowledge me, you little twerp." Gary reached across the table and shook Peter's hand.

"I've been meaning to call you, Marty, and thank you profusely for helping me to get that job at *Atlanta Today Magazine*. Everything you taught me helped *tremendously*! You have no idea how much. I mean it. I started there at just the right time. I was there for, what, six months and their art director left for a job in New York. And today *I* got promoted to art director! Can you fucking believe that? I'm sort of celebrating. Scott's over there," he said, pointing to a table full of young men at the far side of the room. Peter's partner, Scott, waved at Marty and Marty waved back. Marty snickered at the combination: Peter Scott's partner was Scott Peters. One could get tongue-tied, or confused, after a few drinks.

"Holy shit, that's awesome, Peter!" Marty exclaimed. I am so freakin' proud of you. I am impressed as hell. Good luck…now I *will* have to buy that damn magazine."

"Want to join us?" asked Peter.

"No, thanks anyway," responded Marty. "Gary and I need to discuss some business and crap. Go back to your friends and have a great time. It was awesome running into you like this, Chris…oops, I mean Peter!" And they all laughed.

Peter worked his way back to his table through the jumbled crowd. Their burgers were set down before them and both Marty and Gary dove right in, each letting out a loud "Mmmmmm!" after their first bites.

"And, now, Gary, what's up?"

"Well, it's about damn time you got around to me. It's always about you, isn't it?" Gary laughed. "You, you, you."

Marty put down his burger, rested his elbow on the table and cupped his chin with his hand. "Speak, oh great one, I am *all* ears."

"Hey, guys! What the hell are *you* doing here?" came a familiar voice from behind Marty.

"Oh, for shit's sake," Marty muttered as he turned to see Sandi Prescott bouncing toward their table.

"I came into town to visit Dottie's husband at Grady Hospital. Anybody who gets shot in Atlanta ends up at Grady, you know. And this is one of my favorite watering holes. Aren't you guys a little overdressed for this place? Jeeze," she said, as she eyed them up and down. "Don't you know they sodomize preppies like you down here all the time just for fun?" and she giggled loudly.

"See? I told you that you could get lucky tonight, Marty," sneered Gary.

"Shut the fuck up, dammit!" Marty sneered right back. "Okay, so how *is* Dottie's husband?"

"Nate's going to be fine. Sore ass for a while, I guess, but he'll be getting out tomorrow. Hey, can I have one of your fries?" as she reached for Gary's plate. He playfully slapped her hand. "I see a table opening up over there," she said as she pointed across the room. "Your friend Jeff Pringle is with me too, Marty. We both went to see Nate. He's trying to find a parking place right now. See ya!"

Oh, great, thought Marty, *someone else after my "eggroll" tonight!* He turned to look at Gary and gave him the look that said: "Well?"

Gary shook his head. "Nope. Not saying a fucking word until this fucking parade of your fucking followers stops marching up to this fucking table."

"Hey, watch your fucking language," laughed a woman at the next table. "There are two fucking genteel ladies sitting right here within hearing range, you know, and you're driving us bat-shit crazy!" as they both laughed like hyenas. The two women looked to be somewhere in their 40s, wearing jeans and tank tops, with colorful tattoos up and down both arms and multiple piercings. One of them had spiked blonde hair; the other had hair the color of raspberry Jell-O.

"While you're trying to calm down, Gary, and being that you screwed up on Trivia Night, I'll give you a trivia question. Breathe deeply, just relax. Okay? Here it is. There is only one state in this country that borders just one other state. What is it?"

Gary sat back, closed his eyes, trying to picture the United States in his mind. One of the "fucking ladies" from the adjacent table leaned her chair back on its two rear legs and turned to Marty.

"Maine," she said. "I'd *better* know that one. I'm from Boston where I pahk the cah and go into the bah. And here's one other little piece of trivia to add to your question, cutie-pie. Maine is the *only* state in the union with a one-syllable name. Ta, dah! What do I win?"

"My undying affection and admiration for life. I just fell in love again," Marty said sarcastically, clutching his hands to his heart.

"Yeah, well, don't get too carried away, big guy" winked the Bostonian. "You're just not our type, if you catch my drift."

"Well, just shit!" announced Gary loudly. "I forgot why the hell I even came here tonight. Fuck it! I'm going home!" and he slammed down a wad of cash on the table to cover the tab and stormed out of the door.

Both Greg and Stet had retreated to their respective rooms to shower and change before dinner. Mary and Esmé prepared a large salad with a conglomeration of fresh vegetable that Mary had picked up from a local farmer's market on the way home. She grilled a couple of large boneless, skinless chicken breasts and thinly sliced them, spreading them across the salad. Esmé created fresh raspberry vinaigrette and uncorked a chilled bottle of Chardonnay. Cool jazz was playing in the background. Ellis Marsalis on piano. Stet padded, barefoot, into the kitchen. He was wearing tan shorts and a navy blue T-shirt.

"Something smells good in here," he said, sniffing the air. "Looks like you two lovely ladies have conjured up some magic out here." He came up behind Mary and nuzzled her on the neck.

"Stop harassing the chef, mister, or I'll have to report you to management!" Mary laughed.

"Go ahead, report me," answered Stet. "I can hardly wait to see what my punishment might be." And he winked at Esmé.

A few moments later, Greg padded, also barefoot, into the kitchen. He was wearing tan shorts and a navy blue T-shirt.

"Well, well, well, don't you look like the Bobbsey Twins?" laughed Mary.

"Who?" replied Stet, Greg and Esmé, almost in unison.

"Never mind," said Mary, shaking her head. "They were before my time, too."

Marty caught up to Gary in the parking lot next to the Vortex.

"Gary, wait. Slow down. Hey, I'm sorry for all that nonsense in there. Who knew that we'd run into that situation? It's quiet out here, now tell me what's up."

Gary was leaning against his car, arms folded and legs crossed at his ankles.

"I'll give it another minute or so out here, Marty," he said, as he made a big production of looking up and down Moreland Avenue. "I'm sure you must know half the denizens of Little Five Points and the parade should start any second now."

"Oh, stop. You're acting like a petulant little girl. Look, it's late. Tell me or *I* will go home."

"Okay," answered Gary, with a resigned look on his face. "It's actually a two-part thing. Sort of. A couple of friends of mine started a large-format printing company up in Cumming a couple of years ago. They do great stuff. Wall graphics for restaurants, businesses…even at the airport, too. They were doing it all. The selling and the production. Well, their little business isn't so little any more and it's running them ragged. They want me to join them, as a partner, and be responsible for all their selling. They intend to go nationwide. The business is expanding and they have to get huge, new equipment. And they're looking for new, larger office space It's exciting as hell."

"That sounds fantastic," exclaimed Marty with enthusiasm. "Cumming isn't that far away…not like Chicago…and a lot warmer during the winter, for sure. So, are you doing it? And what's part two?"

"Yeah, I'm having a lawyer friend look at all the legal angles, you know, with the partner aspect. Linda and I are really excited about it. We won't have to move and little Alex will still be able to root for the Braves. Oh, and about part two. This is where *you* come in."

"Me? What?"

"Their young, little designer has been overwhelmed with the growing business and she gave her notice. She'll work until the end of the month and then it's adios, amigos. They actually need a couple of designers, frankly, and someone to oversee that aspect of the business. Someone who can accompany me, the sales person, out on calls to present our credentials to new prospects. There are all kinds of collateral material that needs to be designed and produced. A shitload of stuff. I told them all about you and what you've been doing for the past several years. I extolled the virtues of your presentation skills and I showed them printed samples of your work. They were impressed as hell. Look, at this point, you don't even have to be interviewed, believe it or not. The guys wanted me to approach you first. They're going to offer you a fulltime position. Okay, look, I know you have a lot going on with your freelance shit, but this means something permanent. And with benefits. If you're interested, we can all have a nice big pow-wow to discuss details. You know, like money. A little detail like that. There, I said it. And not one freak has come by to greet you with love and affection."

Marty laughed and shook his head as if to loosen the cobwebs.

"Wow. I mean *wow*! This lightning bolt came outta the clear blue sky. I'm going to have to give this a *lot* of thought, my friend. A lot. My freelance stuff is keeping me pretty busy for the moment, but that may or may not last. And Jessie and I will do a lot of talking about this. She does *not* do well with change at all. She's still rattled about me getting cut from Compton last December. My severance package ran out in August and she's still nervous about it. Before I make any decision, obviously, I want to visit that place up in Cumming. I want to see what those guys actually do. *Then* we can talk."

"I understand, I understand completely. No problemo, amigo," replied Gary. 'I know you and Jessie will be thinking long and hard about this, but the opportunity is…or can be…amazing."

Thirty seconds later, Jeff Pringle came stumbling out the door of the Vortex and spotted Marty.

"Hey, Marty!" he called out loudly, waving his hand.

"Oh, for shit's sake!" exclaimed Marty, closing his eyes.

Sandi and Jeff had, indeed, visited with Nate Washington in the hospital, but Sandi was excited about a text she had received that afternoon and then a meeting later in the day. She wanted to share this bit of information with Jeff…with Dottie…with whoever…but she forgot to tell Marty before he left the restaurant. By sheer chance, an Atlanta talent agent had seen the production of "Gypsy" a few months before. He was visiting with his sister who lived in Snellville and she had a couple extra tickets. He was impressed by the vivaciousness and uncanny stage presence of this young woman called Sandi Prescott. He returned a few more times over the ensuing months when he knew she would be, again, onstage. Somehow he was able to get her phone number and texted her about a meeting. They met at a Starbucks, one of her favorite spots, and he laid it out for her. He wanted to know more, résumé, headshots, etc., but was sincerely interested in representing her as her agent. He also mentioned that she should think about furthering her abilities via some acting classes. He mentioned the Alliance Theatre in Atlanta and she squealed. She attends almost all of their shows and has often fantasized about appearing on their stage.

"What a bunch of pigeon poop!" Sandi said out loud to herself as she slid into her car in the Starbucks parking lot. *It's gotta be a con job,* she thought. *That guy must think I was born yesterday or something. Well, I'm not going to be suckered in, for damn sure! Things like this don't happen in real life. The movies, maybe.*

As soon as she got back home she booted up her computer and headed straight for Google to do some research on "that guy". She pulled up page after page of information. Website after website of information. Her eyes popped and her mouth dropped open.

This wasn't a con-job. He had gotten Sandi's phone number from Gus Mansard, the director, who was a good friend. It was the real deal. This man was serious.

"I can't believe what you guys accomplished in one day already," exclaimed Mary. "I said it before and I'll say it again, I am impressed.'

"Thanks," beamed Stet, "it was fun today. Really. And your son is simply amazing, Mary. First of all, you obviously did a great job in raising him, but also his talents are impressive as hell."

"You *do* know that I'm right here in the room, don't you," snickered Greg. "That kind of shit embarrasses me."

"I think his talents are impressive as well," interjected Esmé, with a broad smile.

"Wait, wait, wait. We *are* talking about his architectural talents, right?" asked Mary, raising an eyebrow.

"Oh, Mom, please," sighed Greg. "None of us are kids in this room now, are we?"

"Honestly," said Stet, "Greg's suggestions about some of the changes and alterations actually streamlined the procedure. I know that you didn't come back out this evening to see what we had done, but look at it first thing in the morning. You won't believe how great it all looks. Doc was impressed, too. We really and truly had a blast out there today. And now, before I fall asleep in mid-sentence, I'm going to bed."

With that, he stood up, stretched and yawned. "Oh, and don't forget, kiddo," he said, directing his comment to Greg. "We start at seven. Not *thinking* about getting up at seven. Not getting up at seven. Not kissing someone goodbye at seven. But dressed, caffeinated, and out there, hammer in hand, at seven."

"I don't love you anymore," Greg said, folding his arms across his chest.

Sandi Prescott felt overwhelmed. She also felt elated and renewed. She had never considered acting lessons before. Everything she did, onstage or in front of her Zumba classes, came naturally to her. But she had signed up and just completed her first full week. There were eleven others in the class with her, ranging in ages from 18 through 76. Yes, 76! Men and women, multiple ethnicities and sexual persuasions. The drama coach, Jonathan Pope, introduced himself and asked everyone in the class to do the same. He was a large man but carried himself with grace. He asked them to introduce themselves twice, telling a little about themselves each time. One time being themselves and the other time trying to be someone else. But not to let on to the group which was which.

"Oscar Wilde once said 'Give a man a mask, and he will tell you the truth'," announced Jonathan Pope in a voice that made windows rattle.

Sandi was the last one and she introduced herself first as if Dainty June from "Gypsy" were talking, and then as herself as a Zumba instructor. She was extremely animated each time. The class laughed along with the instructor.

"Try that last one again, dear," said Jonathan, "but don't use your hands. Sometimes being still is just as effective."

Sandi froze.

Jonathan laughed again. "Don't worry. We'll learn movement here as well as diction, by that I mean articulation, and, of course, projection. We shall also learn to trust our instincts. Now that we all know a little bit about each other, let's *really* get the ball rolling. We're going to play a little warm-up game…well, more of an exercise really. It's called Zip, Zap, Zop. It's all about focus and energy. This will get us to relate to each other and get more relaxed with each other as well. Speed counts here and, Sandi, you'll get to use every part of your body...especially those hands."

The class was instructed to form a circle, facing each other, and repeat the words "Zip, Zap, Zop" together as a group three times.

"Alright, then," said Jonathan after they had done so, "Imagine that you are holding a bolt of energy in your hands. You are going to throw it to someone else in the circle. As you do so, with force, yell 'Zip' using your voice, arms, body, eye contact...whatever. That person, who you toss it to, should quickly send it right off to someone else yelling 'Zap' and *that* receiving person should yell 'Zop'. The tossing should continue as fast as possible...no pausing, no hesitation. Like an invisible dodge ball, if you will. 'Zip'. 'Zap'. And 'Zop'...remember. The challenge is to go very quickly and stay consistent with the rhythm. This will give you the opportunity to explore pace and specificity of choice. If you use the wrong word, you're out, so pay close attention! Let's see how long we can go without anyone getting called out. Ready? Three...two...one...go!"

It was slow going at first, until they really got into the swing of things and then it continually picked up speed. It was five minutes before anyone got tagged as "out" but they were all dripping with sweat by that time and the laughter was infectious. And it was the 18-year-old who messed up. He zipped when he should have zapped. Sandi's adrenaline was pumping and she just couldn't stand still. She was loving this!

Later in the week, the coach introduced the class to The "Machine" of Emotions. To start with, they had to write down a list of things that made them angry. They would have to use images connected to this list to call upon their acting skills at the appropriate moment in whatever scene they were playing. Hmmmm...Sandi was actually stumped. She tried to think of things that made her angry and came up blank. *I'm too happy-go-lucky for my own good,* she thought. Then she remembered something that Mary Anne had talked about several months ago: the two old annoying men in her Zumba class. Barry and Walter made Mary Anne angry...or, well, annoyed, to say the least. So Sandi put herself in Mary Anne's shoes. Within five minutes she was seething inside. She wanted to punch their lights out...both of those guys! *Wait,* she thought, *was Mary Anne out of line for getting angry over nothing...for kicking at raindrops...or was I foolish for not getting angry with those guys?* This exercise was working. It was very effective. Then the class was given several other emotions to work on. By the end of the day, Sandi was so emotionally drained she could hardly think straight.

By the end of the day, Stet, Greg and Doc were so physically drained that they could hardly walk straight. A few more finishing touches were needed, but they were minor and could wait. The enlarged stable and paddock area were almost ready and waiting for Welcome Thunder to come to his new home. Stet felt a slight tinge of emotion as he thought how much his beloved old horse, George, would have loved this new area. Doc drained what little water was left in his thermos, gathered all of his tools together and headed back toward his truck. Luger followed him as he went and sat watching him as he loaded up his tools in the back. Doc leaned over and scratched the awaiting dog behind his ears and under his chin, leaning over to give him a soft kiss on his snout.

"Come on back into the house, Doc," Stet said, as he also gathered up some tools. "I'll get a pot of coffee going. Or we can have something stronger if you'd prefer. I think we all certainly deserve it, don't you? And dinner? Didn't you say last night that with a twist of the wrist you'd stay tonight?"

"Nah, but thanks, anyway. Coffee or whatever sounds great but, at the moment, a nice hot shower and soft bed sound even better. Rain check?"

The three men stood back and surveyed their handiwork for a moment. They were extremely pleased with what they had accomplished.

"You know," Greg said, "We may have pushed it just a bit to get it finished so quickly but, damn, that looks great, right?"

Doc and Stet could do nothing but agree completely. They shook hands, patted each other on the backs and Doc headed to his truck, waving over his shoulder as he went. Greg and Stet headed into the house, with Luger running on ahead of them, as Doc slowly drove away.

"I don't know about you, Greg, but coffee sounds like a winner right now," Stet remarked as he headed for the kitchen. He glanced at his watch. "Mary won't be back from the gallery for at least another couple of hours. Is Esmé coming out here tonight?"

"Nope. Not tonight. She has a couple of late classes and then a very early class in the morning. I'll be sleeping solo tonight, sorry to say. I'll hit the shower then come join you for that coffee," he said, over his shoulder, as he headed for his room. Luger, and the click-click-click of his toenails on the hardwood floor, pranced after him.

Stet got the coffee brewing then he, too, headed to his room and a long, hot shower. Stet had planned his house well, with guests in mind. Each bedroom had its own private bath.

Greg stood under the shower, letting the hot water flow over all his sore muscles. Dirt and sweat swirled around his feet as it went down the drain. He closed his eyes and faced the showerhead and he nearly fell asleep standing up. He quickly lathered up, and then just as quickly rinsed off, leaning against the glass-encased shower stall. Shutting off the water, he opened the door, reaching for a soft, fluffy towel. He dried off, dropped the towel on the floor, and then padded, naked, back into his bedroom and fell face first onto his bed. Within ten seconds he was fast asleep with Luger curled up beside him.

Stet padded, naked, from *his* shower and looked at his bed. He inhaled and smelled the coffee that was brewing down the hall in the kitchen. He thought about it for about ten seconds and then fell, face first, onto his bed. And that's exactly where Mary found him, snoring softly, when she arrived two hours later.

"Well, now *that's* a sight," she chuckled to herself as she quietly closed the bedroom door and headed back to the kitchen for a cup of coffee.

Sandi had just finished conducting her second Zumba class of the day and felt like heading for a long hot shower. But, instead, it was time to head for the stable and feed Fireball. By the time she arrived at CedarView it was almost dark, but there were lights on and several cars still parked in the lot. She saw Mary Anne's car and was eager to share with her all that had been going on this past week. She hopped out of her little Miata and practically jogged to the tack room. Mary Anne and Mary Pat were chatting as they put away all their grooming equipment and covered their saddles.

"Well, here she is, world!" shouted Mary Anne when she saw Sandi enter the tack room, "the next toast of Broadway!" Sandi laughed so hard she snorted.

"Yeah, right!" she answered, still laughing. "Hey, let me tell you something…this acting stuff is a hell of a lot more than just memorizing lines. Jeesh!" She stood there, shaking her head. "I had *no* idea. Evidently I don't talk right…I don't move right. Well, maybe I move too much. Anyway, it's a blast, these lessons. And I'm learning things like crazy. *Crazy*, I tell you!"

"What do y'all mean, dawlin'," drawled southern belle Mary Pat, "that y'all don't tawk raht? Y'all sound fine to mah po' li'l eahs."

Sandi laughed again. "None of us talk right. Well, I mean for the theater or whatever. We run words and sounds together when we talk. It's natural. We don't realize that we're doing it, of course, simply because that's our normal speech patterns. All of us. My drama coach stopped me countless times the other day while I was doing a scene with another actor. Actually, the other guy was stopped several times as well. We were reading from scripts and I was talking the way I always do…"

"You mean, fast as hell?" interrupted Mary Anne.

"Ha! Yeah, well, that too," chuckled Sandi. Not only do I have to slow down but I have to learn not to run words together."

"Example, please?" asked Mary Pat with nary a hint of a drawl.

"Hmmm, well," started Sandi, "for example I said 'don't you know' but it sounded like 'don't chew know'. I ran those words together. Oh, and another one. I said 'yes, I am' but it sounded like 'yeh, siam'. See? We all do it. I am so aware of it now that it's not funny. Notice how I enunciated that last sentence? Normally it would have sounded like I said 'it snot funny'. Mary Anne, I know you're always correcting peoples' grammar in your head, so you must have been going bonkers all these years."

"That snot funny," giggled Mary Anne. "I'm gonna getcha for that, just you wait!" And they all laughed.

"Oh, and another thing," continued Sandi. "Line readings, for example. How to get several different meanings out of the same word or phrase just through inflections. Think about it for a second. How many meanings can you get out of a simple word like 'hello'? You can say that one stupid little word a dozen different ways and get a dozen different meaning or intentions. It can be inquisitive, seductive, sarcastic, frightened…whatever. These classes are amazing, dontcha know!"

"What's going on at the gym, by the way?" asked Mary Anne. "I've had a lot of my kids parties lately, so I haven't been able to stick around after Zumba to chat with you. Didn't I see you and Trevor talking the other day? What's up with that?"

"Oh, it's a casual thing, really. We go out maybe every few weeks or so. No big deal. Just movies or a burger. I didn't want to tell you, but he asked me to Dragon Con last month."

"Seriously?" asked Mary Pat and Mary Anne, almost in unison.

"Would this face lie to you? I kid you not. I went as Harley Quinn, can you believe it? I looked great, even if I do say so myself. It was fun, really. Trevor, as you know, is a Georgia Tech grad and very clever, actually, went as a Lego version of himself. His costume was awesome. I have some pictures here," and she whipped out her smartphone. "Girls were drooling all over him."

The three women ogled the photos for a few minutes as Sandi explained what was going on. The two Marys laughed but had to admit that Trevor *did* look pretty hot, if in a sort of clunky, Lego sort of way,

"Well, don't get too worked up, girls," Sandi said. "It's not…see, I pronounced that correctly, not sounding like 'it snot'…it's not going to turn into a long term relationship. He's a nice guy. We like to hang out. But that's as far it's going. Just friends. End of story."

The three of them chatted for a few moments more before both Marys had to head for home and dinner. They had been riding in the ring for at least an hour prior to Sandi's arrival and they were tired. They said their goodbyes and drove away. As Sandi headed toward the gate to get Fireball from the pasture, Oedipus Pex, the old rooster silently strutted his way toward Sandi's backside. He was just about to peck her leg when she spun around quickly and blared, "Dontcha even think about it, you big dumb cluck, or I'll fry you up faster than Colonel Sanders!" A loud squawk and a flutter of wings and the bird was gone, running for cover.

After taking care of Fireball, Sandi and her Miata headed for her apartment. Ten minutes after arriving back home, she hit the shower. Standing there, letting the hot water flow over her sore muscles, she let out a long sigh. It had been a long day. Oh, that water felt *so* good. She dried off, dropped the towel on the floor and padded, naked, into her bedroom. She fell, face first, onto her bed. Within ten seconds she was sound asleep and didn't wake up until the sun was peeking through her window several hours later.

The bright morning sun was poring through the large skylight in Stet's kitchen making the whiteness of the room even brighter. He and Mary were standing side by side already into their second cup of coffee. He was dressed up and ready to head into Atlanta. He was going to be managing the gallery singlehandedly today and Mary was "just going to goof off", as she said earlier. Suddenly, Greg came running down the hallway from the bedrooms, bare-chested and just in his boxers, cellphone in hand and Luger in hot pursuit.

"What the hell…" started Stet.

"I'm waiting for Ash to pick up," he announced, holding the phone aloft, "I'm on hold."

Ash had just sent a text: *CALL ME ASAP…NOW!* Greg put the phone on speaker mode as he laid it on the counter and he reached for the coffee and poured it into a mug.

"What's up?" asked Stet, and Greg just shrugged as he gulped down a big swig of coffee.

"Greg?" came Ash's voice.

"Hey!" responded Greg, almost choking on his coffee, "I'm here, man. What's up?"

"You finished playing cowboys and carpenters out there yet?" asked Ash. "How quickly can you get your ass back here? And I mean *today!*"

"Yeah, basically. We finished for the most part last night. I repeat, what's up? By the way, you're on speakerphone here. Stet and my Mom are right here, so keep it clean," and he laughed.

"Good morning, Mary and hey to you, too, Stet," Ash called out.

"And good morning right back at you," answered Stet. "It's a tad early where you are, something big happening, or what?"

"Good morning," Mary interjected before Ash could answer.

"Could be. Well, yes…emphatically, yes," Ash responded to Stet's question. "Greg, remember that huge office complex deal we bid on several months ago? I thought it had died, didn't you? We never heard a word."

"Agreed," nodded Greg. "So?"

"So, I recently heard the scuttlebutt that they had narrowed it down and we were in the running with only one other small firm. Then they saw the photos from the opening night at Stet's gallery in the *Tribune*."

Stet and Mary exchanged glances. Stet arched his eyebrows. Greg straightened up.

"I guess that cinched it. It's been narrowed down again, my friend. It's just us. We got it. We fucking got it! They called fifteen minutes ago and they want to meet with us tomorrow, in their offices, at noon. They're having lunch brought in. I repeat, *to-mor-row*."

"Whoa," Greg said. "Seriously? This is *some* shit."

"*Some* shit," Ash repeated.

"Hot holy damn, this is so fucking fantastic! Okay, I'll get to the airport as quickly as I can," Greg said, his heart racing. "I'll catch whatever flight I can and text you."

They all shouted their goodbyes and Greg clicked off.

Stet looked at his watch. "Sorry, but now I've *really* gotta get outta here. Morning traffic into town is going to be a bitch. Wow, sounds like something big is happening for you, young man. I'm proud of you."

Greg let out a big sigh, "Damn, that 'young man' tag will drive me bats, you old goat! But you're right. This could be *some* shit!"

"I take it," chuckled Mary, "that '*some* shit' means a gigantic opportunity, right? That term confuses me."

"I guess that's a sort of private joke Ash and I made up when we were in college," Greg sort of giggled. "I don't know if you've ever been constipated for a couple of days. Then, all of a sudden, you're *not* constipated and that great, wonderful, relieved feeling you have? And you just say to yourself 'whoa, that was *some* shit'."

Mary just stared at him. "That's the weirdest thing I've ever heard," she said, shaking her heard.

"Oh, hell, yes, Mom. This is certainly gigantic. We're figuring on a two to three year build-out. This complex will be on a grand scale. And we're talking many millions here. *Multiple* millions! Ash and I have done some large projects before, but never done anything of *this* size before. I'm trembling right now. I'm excited as hell and scared shitless at the same time. Whoa, this is *some* shit!"

Stet shook his head and laughed. "Now I *really, really* have to get out of here!"

The two men shook hands and Stet headed out the door, calling back, "Thanks a million for all that work out there at the stable. Keep us posted as soon as you know what's what. I mean it. As soon!" And he was gone.

"Mom, can you get me to the airport or should I Uber it?"

"No, no…I'll get you there. But let me suggest something a bit more than your boxers for your flight back home?"

Greg looked down at himself.

"Consider yourself lucky that I pulled *these* on before I dashed in here a few minutes ago!"

Mary Anne was already in the Group Fitness room at the gym, waiting for Sandi to come bouncing in and get the Zumba class underway. She was going to try a completely different attitude and tactic, from a totally different perspective, hoping that it wouldn't backfire. Everyone was chatting like magpies, as always, before the class began. The room buzzed with conversations ranging from the weather to one's health issues, of which there were several, evidently. Mary Anne greeted everyone with a smile and then winked at Barry (the harmless, innocuous non-lecherous flirt). His eyes popped open wide and he turned around to see if that wink might have been intended for someone behind him. He nodded to her and offered a weak little wave of his hand. He looked confused.

Sandi came rushing into the room, apologizing as she headed to the raised stage for the instructors.

"So, so sorry I'm a wee bit late, folks," she said. "It's not like me to oversleep…but, oh, well. Guess I did."

She hooked up her smartphone to the speaker system and with the playlist for today's class. The music started. By the time they had reached the third song, a frantic merengue, sweat was pouring and the entire room was bouncing. Mary Anne was waiting…hoping…that "Gangnam Style" was on today's playlist. It was.

Three-quarters of the way through that song, Sandi glanced at Mary Anne. She smiled, but knew that Walter would blare his usual announcement and Mary Anne would cringe. The moment came closer… then closer. Mary Anne was watching Walter. Just as the song hit that particular spot and he was about to call out, Mary Anne yelled at the top of her voice: "One! More! Time!" Sandi's jaw dropped. Walter looked shocked. The rest of the class hooted and hollered and applauded.

"Another country heard from!" called a voice from the back of the class. "Finally!" called another. Walter looked deflated. Mary Anne actually felt sorry for him, but she loved the looks that she got from everyone else. Sandi just stood in the center of the little stage, hands on hips, shaking her head and laughing like a hyena.

It might be for only this one day. Probably Mary Anne wouldn't do it again. But it had felt great to do so. Maybe that's why Walter blares out like that. It just simply feels good to yell at the top of your lungs "One! More! Time!"

"If you say 'some shit' one more time," laughed Mary, "I'll swat you, Greg!"

"Sorry, Mom, I'm just excited, I guess. I can't help it. Ash and I worked so hard for this. Looks like things are beginning to fall into place. Yeah, this is huge…truly, it's some…aahh…big, big deal!"

They were zipping down the highway, heading for the airport. Greg had been working his smartphone continuously trying to book a flight out of Atlanta and into O'Hare. He had an open-ended ticket and was hoping that there would be no restrictions to prevent him heading out today. Soon. If not sooner.

"Ah, ha!" he shouted. "There it is. That's the one flight I need…oh, shit, only one seat available. I'm booking it."

"Wait!" blurted Mary. "When's the flight? Remember this is rush hour and we're heading towards the Perimeter which is almost always a parking lot by now."

Atlanta's Perimeter, I-285, encircles the city, joining two separate north-south interstate highways, I-85 and I-75, with I-20, an east-west highway crossing through the middle. It is often called the most heavily traveled highway in the United States. It has also earned the dubious distinction, in some surveys, of being the deadliest interstate in the union. At rush hour? It's a nightmare.

"Where are we now, Mom? I mean, how far from the airport?"

"Probably about twenty, maybe twenty-five miles. Time-wise for Atlanta at this hour? Two hours. Maybe more."

"I hope you're kidding. I just booked the flight. Had to. Departure is just a little over two hours."

"Well, shit…yep, Greg, that's *some* shit, but not in a good way!"

All of a sudden, all they saw in front of them was a sea of red brake lights.

Zumba class ended, and the members were slowly heading out of the room. Mary Anne, usually one to hurry out and go home, held back for a few minutes. She ambled over to Walter who was mopping his brow and swigging water from his Yeti. Sandi was chatting with a group of members about some personal training sessions.

"Walter," said Mary Anne a bit weakly. "I'm sorry I stole your thunder. I know you seem to enjoy that song…especially the ending. And I know that you must like the attention. I was actually surprised by the reaction from the rest of the group. Frankly, I was surprised in myself for doing it. Please accept my apology."

"Don't be silly, Mary Anne. Please. No need for an apology. If anyone should apologize it's me. I know that I irritate some of the others in the class. I see their expressions, trust me. It's kind of ridiculous, really, why I do it all the time. Yes, you mentioned 'attention'. Right. I like the attention. I'm just a silly old guy looking for a little bit of attention. Yes, I was stunned when you did that. But, guess what? It felt good, didn't it? Didn't you feel a jolt of excitement when you did it?"

"You know what, Walter?" Mary asked, "Next time Sandi has that routine and that song, let's yell that together, shall we? I won't be stealing your thunder, we'll be making a bit of thunder and lightning together, shall we?"

As it so happened, the very next time Sandi programmed "Gangnam Style" into her routine, when that particular part of the song arrived, the entire class called out, in unison, as loudly as they could: "One! More! Time!"

Two miles in front of them, a car had either stalled out or run out of gas right in the center lane. Fortunately there had not been any collisions… not yet, anyway…so traffic simply had to slow down to pull around the stationary vehicle. It made for very slow, cautious going. Mary was getting a bit edgy, glancing at the clock on her dashboard as the time moved closer and closer to Greg's departure time. Greg had texted Esmé to apologize for the rapid departure. Then he had texted Ash to alert him to the anticipated arrival time. He pulled out his laptop and opened up the documents for the office complex proposal. He wanted to refresh his memory and see if he could suggest any revisions to Ash prior to tomorrow's meeting.

Finally they passed the vehicle in distress and the traffic began to pick up speed again. Mary breathed a momentary sigh of relief and Greg lost himself in the proposal. She stepped on the gas, trying to make up the lost time, passing several cars in doing so.

"Shit!" exclaimed Mary loudly ten minutes later, applying the brakes and making Greg's head jerk upright suddenly, looking straight ahead, bracing his hand on the dashboard, expecting to see an accident or to be in one.

"What the fuck, Mom?"

"We're finally moving at a good clip and now there are flashing blue lights coming up behind me. A few cars behind us, but I *was* going a bit fast. Shit!"

She eased her foot off the gas just a little.

The flashing blue lights sped right past their car and disappeared off the next exit ramp.

"Damn it, Mom, don't do that! I would have felt safer in a self-driving Uber!"

"Ingrate," Mary smirked, and they both laughed. "Look. *There's* a good sign. We're getting close now." And she pointed up into the sky, over the highway.

A large airplane was coming in for a landing, flying low over the highway as it made its approach to the runway. Greg could see several planes behind it in the same landing pattern in the sky, slowly descending and approaching the airport.

"Ten minutes, max, Greg. Are we good?" asked Mary.

"Yeah, so far. Flight departs, supposedly, in forty-five minutes. If I can get through security pronto, I can squeak in. Won't feel comfortable until I can fasten that damn seatbelt and put my tray table in its full upright position."

Traffic leading up to the departure drop-off zone was jammed. Slowly moving vehicles crept up the ramp.

"Shit, shit, shit!" exclaimed Greg, getting just a slight bit nervous. He kept glancing at his watch. "Move it, goddamn it!" he yelled inside the car and to no one in particular.

Mary maneuvered her car around a large group of people standing in the road, blocking other cars as they unloaded luggage from their minivan. "Fucking tourists!" she muttered and Greg laughed. She found a place to squeeze her car into the curb to let Greg out.

"Don't get out, Mom…gotta dash. You're the best Mom *ever*! I mean it. I love you to pieces. Oh, and tell that old goat you're living with that I love him, too. Forgot to tell him this morning."

He leaned across to the driver's seat; grabbing his backpack as he did so, and gave Mary the biggest hug he could give her while she was still wearing her seat belt. She kissed him on both cheeks and said, "Run, dammit! Don't miss that flight." And he disappeared into the throng.

Thirty minutes later, as she was stuck in non-moving traffic on I-285, Mary received a text from Greg: WHEELS UP!

Thirty hours later, two handsome young men, one black, one white, former college roommates, business partners, best friends, walked up Michigan Avenue, passing the Art Institute of Chicago and turned eastward onto East Monroe Street. They entered Grant Park and found an empty bench. Dressed in their absolute best suits and ties, they sat in silence for five minutes, not believing what had just happened in the preceding hour. Trying to process the situation, they both inhaled deeply, feeling the moisture and breeze from the lake. It was a beautiful, crisp day. A pair of seagulls swooped down and were squabbling and squawking over a half-eaten discarded sandwich on the ground a few feet away. The men chuckled and shook their heads.

"Want to head over to Kasey's Tavern?" asked Greg, with a big, happy grin on his face.

"Damn right, I do," answered Ash. "Damn right."

"This is *some* shit, isn't it?" asked Greg.

"*Some* shit!" answered Ash.

NOVEMBER

The Sound and The Furry

"I should get a dog. I would get a rescue dog. I like mutts; I don't care. I would probably get a three-legged dog no one else would want."

Simon Cowell

Although none of her stable friends even knew this about Mary Pat, she was a sentimental sap when it came to dogs. They weren't even aware that she and Derrick even *had* a dog. Well, that wasn't totally true. Mary Anne knew that her friend had, and lost, her beloved furry friend after nearly fifteen beautiful, love-filled years. That was three years ago. Mary Pat had grieved for weeks. It had been Zara, Remy Major's late wife, who had told Mary Pat about a terrific rescue facility about an hour's drive north of Atlanta. Only natural: Zara rescued horse after horse while she was alive. Why not help rescue dogs as well? Derrick was hesitant at first. He, too, was grieving over Dexter, their black Lab. It was sheer coincidence that they loved the TV show by that name as well.

Zara had texted a photo to Mary Pat of a five-month-old pup from the shelter that was still available for adoption. Of course, Zara had been up there to check out a horse. Tears started flowing and the photo was shown to Derrick. And then shown to their four sons. The vote was unanimous. Following a few phone calls and emails to and from the shelter to check out this sweet little thing, the Phillips family piled into their SUV and headed straight for TLC Farms & Rescue in Cedartown.

Fast forward to the present: Jasmine (aka Jazzy) was now three years old. And shy. *Terribly* shy. The attractive young woman who owned the shelter had told them that she thought the poor pup must have had a very traumatic start to life. Jasmine and her littermates were, basically, feral dogs when they were first found. Her backstory, as much as was known, was told to the Phillips family. All of her littermates had been adopted but no one seemed to want this puppy for some reason. Perhaps it was because she was so apprehensive of people. To this day, she was frightened of just about everything and everybody (except the Phillips family, of course) and strange sounds would send the dog running for cover. The 4th of July holiday always proved to be one minor step behind thunderstorms as far as the fear factor was concerned. Jasmine would not come running to greet them when they returned home. She would run and hide if anyone came to the front door. The UPS truck threw her into a quivering mess. When Derrick's brother and sister-in-law visited, they never would have known a dog was even in the house, except when Jazzy had to be taken out. For the entire weekend, aside from her "duty-walks", she hid in one corner or another, away from the strange visitors. This was *not* the dog that Mary Pat and Derrick had hoped for, but they loved her, if only in a sort of standoffish way. The boys, especially Jake, their youngest, treated her with loads of love and affection to compensate. They tried their best to play with her but she wasn't very responsive to most of their attempts.

Mary Pat had done a load of laundry and was taking a stack of fresh underwear and T-shirts to the boys' rooms. When she entered Jake's room, she saw an empty Coke can sitting on the desk next to his computer. She shook her head. The boys had been admonished about bringing food, especially cans of soda (so easily spilled…from past experience) up to their rooms. She put the clean clothes into their proper drawers and then stepped to the desk to retrieve the empty can. As she leaned over, she caught sight of a couple of papers that had been printed out from Jake's ink jet and then stapled together. *What had he been working on,* she thought? She wasn't aware of any recent school assignments that required printouts. She slid the papers out from under the small book that it had poked out from. She started to read. Then she sat down on the edge of the bed to read some more. By the time she had reached the fifth sentence, she covered her mouth with her hand and her eyes filled with tears.

"Who Rescued Who?"
by Jacob Phillips

Right from the very beginning, they started calling me Jasmine. I guess that's my name. Sometimes it's Jazzy. I'm happy now, in my own funny way. But I wasn't always happy. Or lucky. I was mostly frightened.

I don't know what happened to my Mom. One day she was with me and my four brothers and sisters and then she was gone. We were scared. We didn't know what to do. We were hungry. There were some humans around but we didn't like them. We had seen them hit my Mom with sticks sometimes and she would cry. So we decided that we would all run away. Finding something to eat wasn't always easy. There were dead, smelly things that we found along some houses and sometimes there were big round things that had some kind of old food falling out of the openings in the top. My brother knocked one over once and it made a loud noise. It scared me and I hid behind one of my sisters. We drank from water that moved through the woods on the ground and we got our paws wet. We chased small furry things with bushy tails that looked like they might be good to eat, but they were fast and climbed up trees before we could catch them. There were great big things that stayed together in a group. They ate grass and leaves and were very, very fast when we chased them. They were able to jump over fences and get away from us. We heard a loud noise one day and one of those animals dropped to the ground and didn't move any more. My brothers and sisters sniffed at it. I did too. We started to eat a little bit of it but somebody started coming and we backed away. The person had a big stick with him and he pointed it up at the sky. It made a horrible noise and scared me so much I cried. We all ran away again and hid in the woods. Sometimes water would fall on us from the sky and we would huddle together to stay warm. I didn't like what was happening to us. I cried a lot.

One day several humans in big trucks started chasing us. They were trying to catch us. I didn't know what to do. I was so scared. They had to use something they called traps to get us. They put each one of us into cages on their trucks. One of my brothers was trying to be brave and he barked and snarled at these men. They hit him with straps. I closed my eyes. I didn't want to watch. I wanted to run away again and hide in the woods. The trucks came to a big building and were all put into a large cage. We huddled together again but I could tell my brothers and sisters were scared too. It wasn't a very nice place. One of the humans said something to us. It sounded like he said, "Welcome to the kill shelter, mutts." But I didn't really know what he meant. I didn't like him. We got some food and water but it wasn't very good. We had to eat it because we were so hungry. There were other dogs in other cages and they were barking and crying too. I guess they were scared too.

A couple days later, a very pretty lady came into our area. She was very angry with the men. She came into our cage and started petting us and talking with a soft, nice voice. One by one, she put something around our necks and attached a long rope thing to it. She led us out to her truck. I didn't like that thing around my neck. It scared me but my brothers and sisters went along so I did too. I didn't know what was going to happen to us so I cried as we bounced over bumps in the road. When we got out of the truck again, all I could see was beautiful countryside and woods. I saw some big animals with a man sitting on the back of one of them. He waved to the lady who had been driving the truck. She had some other people help get us into a big pen. Then we all got wet with sweet smelly stuff making bubbles on us. They dried us off with fluffy cloths and machines that made a noise and blew hot air. And we got food. It was yummy. And fresh water.

This was a nice place and we were happy. But all of a sudden one day I began feeling sick. So did my brothers and sisters. We didn't want to eat. We just wanted to sleep. The pretty lady came to us with another man. He did things to us. The lady looked sad. The man said a word that sounded like "parvo" and the lady shook her head. We were all separated and put in cages far away from the other animals. Things were stabbed into us and we were forced to swallow things. This went on for weeks. Finally, I started feeling better. I was getting hungry again and I felt like running. One day I saw my brothers and sisters again and we were able to play together. But I looked around and couldn't find one of my brothers. Where was he? I never saw him again.

We were all feeling so much better and we got to romp and play together again. A couple weeks went by and I was taken to another place. A man in a white coat examined me and talked to that pretty lady who had saved us. They both used a word that I didn't know, but it sounded like "spay". Or "let's play"…I didn't know. The next thing I knew, I woke up and I was in a small cage. My belly felt funny and I was a little dizzy. So many things had happened to me over the last several weeks. I felt better but too many things still made me afraid. I didn't want to be scared but I couldn't help it.

I was feeling better and better by the day. I noticed that, one by one, my brothers and sisters would disappear. People came to see us and then drove away again in their cars. I never got to say goodbye to any of them. But the pretty lady and a few other people who must work here at this place treated me with love. I got petted often. And got treats, too. One day a big car drove up the long driveway to the barn. I had a funny feeling about this, for some reason. I hid behind a tree and watched as the people got out and looked around. The pretty lady came to greet them. I think they called her something that sounded like "Jeanne". She saw me hiding and came to get me. I ran away a little bit and she must have thought I was being playful. She laughed.

Hardly before I knew what was happening, I was being hugged and kissed. They hooked up that rope thing to that thing that was around my neck and led me to their car. I didn't want to get in but they helped me. Where was I going now? Would it be a place that scared me even more? I just plopped down and tried to sleep. It felt like I was crying on the inside. When I woke up the car was stopped and I was being led out and into a house. It wasn't a big barn. There were other houses around. I didn't see or hear any other animals, like the ones that Jeanne and that man rode. What was next for me? When we got inside, they unhooked that rope thing from my neck. This was scary. I looked for someplace to hide and found a great big chair and went behind it. The people just laughed and tried to calm my nerves with gentle talk. They seemed nice enough and it didn't look as though they were going to hit me with sticks or anything. The two big people smiled and left the room. The four smaller people stayed with me for a while, trying to pet me and coax me to come out. I didn't budge. I just stared at them for a while. The house smelled nice. It wasn't an outdoors smell, though.

A few days later, I was beginning to feel a little bit more at ease. I was taken out for walks, still hooked up to that rope thing. I guess they were afraid

I'd run away. I would, too. The food was good but the water didn't taste like the same stuff I drank out in the woods. I still hid behind that chair but, from time to time, I would come out and explore the rest of the house. That's when nobody else was around. I found a small basket thing in one of the rooms that had some strange stuff in it. There was something that looked like a bone and it had chew marks on it. It smelled like another dog. There were other things in it too, things that looked like balls or rubbery-feeling things with different shapes. I had no idea what this was all about.

The weeks went by and, although loud noises still scared me, I was feeling more comfortable. They would take me for long walks in something they called a "park". That scared me. There were strange people there, lots of strange sounds and things that people were riding that had two big wheels on them. Those things scared me the most. Every time we got into the car to go to the park, I got the awful feeling that they might not be bringing me back home. I don't know why I felt that way. I had the feeling that the two big people I was living with were disappointed when we came back from our walks. I guess they noticed that I really didn't enjoy the "park" as much as they had hoped. The four smaller people of the house wanted to play with me. They would throw a ball and want me to go get it. I had never learned how to play. I didn't know what I was supposed to do. I just wanted to sleep. I missed my brothers and sisters but I soon realized that I was never going to see them again. I felt safe here with these people, but I just hadn't felt truly happy. Yet.

A couple years have gone by and I am really feeling at home by now. The smaller people are getting bigger and they still love on me every day. That's when I feel the happiest. I heard the lady of the house say she was glad they rescued me but she still missed Dexter, whoever that was. She also said I wasn't the dog that she had hoped for. Whatever that meant. The smallest person in the house seems to love me the most. He lets me sleep up on his bed with him and he is always hugging me and kissing me on the nose. He gives me belly rubs almost every day, too. Oh, I really like those belly rubs. He always talks to me. He told me that he had been so sad when Dexter went away and he had cried for a long time. He told me that I have rescued him from his sadness. He tells me several times a day that he loves me. He also tells me that I'm a good girl, so I guess I'm a good girl.

I know silly stuff still frightens me. Strange sounds make me want to hide. I can't help it, but I'm trying to get better. I'm really trying. It will take time.

I have grown to love this family. And maybe one day I <u>will</u> be the dog they hoped I would be.

Mary Pat sat there with tears streaming down her face. When she turned around, Jake was standing in the doorway. She stretched out her arms and he came to fill them. They sat there, embraced and rocked back and forth for several minutes.

"You sweet, sweet boy," Mary Pat said to her youngest son. "You sweet, sweet boy."

She couldn't wait for Derrick to get home from work. She was so eager to show him Jake's short story and to let him know that they, too, had a gifted child.

DECEMBER

Major Changes – And New Endings

"If you want a happy ending, that depends, of course, on where you stop your story."

Orson Welles

The phrase "We need to talk" is one that sends the shock of trepidation through the recipient. Amber recognized the fact that Raymond had been somewhat distant the past couple of weeks. Well, actually, the past couple of months. She also realized that she had kept herself extremely busy, with not much time for being truly social. Her classes at school had kept her hopping, with long hours of studying and homework. And her job at the restaurant had been taking up what little time she had left in the week. She was working double shifts, on occasion, to earn some extra cash. She barely had time for poor Flapjack. Raymond had not actually uttered that fateful phrase when he called, but Amber could sense that something was afoot. But, was she being too negative? Could he really want to take the next step in their relationship, such as it was? She was doing the closing shift at the restaurant tonight and then they were going to meet at the local Waffle House. From the sublime to the ridiculous. Was she going to be scattered and smothered or over easy? She loved the Waffle House, but was this the right venue for a serious discussion?

Raymond was already seated at a corner booth by the window. Amber saw him as she pulled up front and parked. She entered and as she approached the table, a waitress with a hairstyle that went out the year John Lennon was shot delivered a Coke and set it down in front of Raymond. "What kin I getcha, sweetie?" she asked Amber.

"Sweet tea, please," answered Amber. "The largest ya got."

She sat down but couldn't read Raymond. Was he up? Down? Somewhere in between?

"How ya been?" was his opening question. "I know we haven't seen too much of each other lately, have we?" Second question.

"What's up, Raymond?" was *her* first question. "And, no, we haven't really been all that sociable lately, have we?" An answer *and* a question, all in one.

The waitress reappeared to take their orders. Raymond ordered three eggs, over hard, bacon, and a double order of hash browns, scattered and smothered. Was this an omen? Amber said she was fine with just the sweet tea. After smelling and delivering food all evening, she wasn't really hungry. Obviously, no matter what Raymond had on his mind, his appetite wasn't affected. Raymond turned to look out the window into the darkness beyond. He shrugged his shoulders and sighed. Might as well jump, feet first.

"Amber," he began haltingly, "I am very, very fond of you. We've had a lot of fun and you've helped me in more ways than you can imagine."

Amber frowned. Yep, there's a *"but"* in there somewhere and it's about to hit.

"I'm moving back to St. Simons." Period. Crash.

"What? When? Why?" came out of Amber almost all at once. "What the hell?"

"Look, Amber, I'm not breaking up with you. That's not what I'm saying, really...but..." and he stammered for a minute. "I realize long distance relationships take a bit more work but we'll only be five hours apart. I mean, if you still want to and everything. But I really don't like it up here. Too many people, too many cars…too much freakin' noise, if you know what I mean. You have your schooling to finish. And, if we're still friends after that, you know there *are* vets on the island. You might be able to find a job there. Perhaps. If you're interested, that is."

"Well, what are *you* going to do?" asked Amber, still reeling from his announcement and shaking her head.

"I've been offered a job at one of the marinas. My Grandpa has a fishing boat and I've worked with him since I was a kid. I know a lot about boats and this is a good opportunity. And…well…please don't laugh…but I'm going to take flying lessons and get my commercial pilot's license and maybe then get a job at the airport there. One of my buddies is doing just that right now."

"Are you moving back in with your parents?"

"Oh, heck, no! I love 'em and all that, but, nope, not moving back in. That buddy at the airport said I can bunk in with him. He has a nice little house on the northern part of the island. His girlfriend dumped him recently for some jerk from New York City, so he has plenty of room. Might even take Rocky with me."

"Do your parents know about this yet?"

"Yeah," he sighed, "my Mom is really disappointed. She really, really likes you and was hoping…well, she was hoping. She's hooked on all those sappy Hallmark Channel movies and she told me this is *not* how our story is supposed to end." He laughed. Sort of. "It doesn't really have to end, Amber. Just postponed. Maybe."

Amber sat there stunned by this revelation. This sudden, almost *too* sudden, change of events rattled her brain. She felt adrift. Raymond's food had been delivered as he was talking but he hadn't touched it. She leaned back in her seat and turned toward the large window, now *her* turn to stare out into the darkness beyond.

The waitress came back to the table. "Sure I can't getcha anything, sweetie?" she asked Amber. "More sweet tea?"

Amber slowly shook her head. "No, thanks. I'm fine."

She wasn't fine. She was crestfallen but not totally surprised. Raymond hadn't been the same vibrant self he was when they visited the island months before. But she had never suspected that he would pick up and head south for good. They both sat in silence, staring out the window.

"I really wasn't expecting a goodbye tonight, Raymond. But I don't know what else to say."

"Amber, it's not a goodbye…more of a see ya later type of thing, right? We don't have to stop being friends. I don't want that. But, seriously, haven't you noticed that in all the months we've been together, neither one of us has used that 'L' word?" He looked at her and cocked his head.

"You're right, Ray-Ray," she joked, with a tear in the corner of her eye. "You are so right. We like each other, but…" she let that drift off into a long sigh. He had told her, not long after they first met, that his friends called him Ray-Ray. She hated it but now, somehow, she found it endearing.

"Okay, so when are you leaving?" she asked. He glanced at his watch.

"At sunup," was his terse reply. "I didn't want to drag this thing out until it hurt any more than it does already."

"Well, just shit!" blurted Amber. "You didn't wait until the patient died, you just went ahead and pulled the damn plug anyway!"

She got up and was ready to storm out but stopped and turned.

"Tell your folks 'hi' for me and give Rocky a big hug as well. Maybe I'll come down for a visit some time. Then again, maybe I won't. For the record, this was a pretty shitty way to say 'see ya later'." She bent over and gave Raymond a soft kiss on the cheek and headed out.

"Ya want a to-go cup for your tea, sweetie?" called the waitress. But Amber didn't hear her as she went out the door, into the darkness beyond.

"What were you doing out there in the dark?" Mary Pat asked her youngest son, Jake, as he walked through the back door into the kitchen. "You should have been in bed hours ago."

"I heard a cat."

"Excuse me? What? A cat? There are no cats around here. None of our neighbors have cats. Were you dreaming, or what?"

"Mom, I swear I heard a cat. It was almost under my window. And, no, I wasn't dreaming."

"Did any of your brothers happen to hear this mysterious cat as well?"

"How should I know? They're all asleep."

Mary Pat shook her head. All of a sudden, Jasmine appeared, coming from Jake's room. She started whimpering…the happy, excited kind of whimpering that the Phillips family had come to recognize. It was not the nervous kind of whimpering that this dog exhibited when she heard strange sounds or saw strange people. And her tail was wagging.

"Well, what's up with *you*, young lady?" Mary Pat asked Jazzy. "You're looking awfully perky right now."

Then she heard it.

"I'll be damned," Mary Pat exclaimed. "That sounded like a…"

"A cat!" shouted Jake. "I told you!"

Mary Pat opened the back door, and both Jake and Jazzy ran out. As she was reaching for the back porch lights to turn them on, she heard a commotion…a lot of scuffling, a yowl of a cat, a low bark of a dog and her son uttering a very foul word.

A few moments later, Jake appeared, arms fully extended out in front of him, holding a small, squirming kitten. His arms had scratches on them and one cheek seemed to have been visited by a cat's claw as well. Jasmine was wagging her tail faster and actually appeared to be smiling up at the kitten. Dogs *do* smile, you know.

"What in the hell…" was Mary Pat's first comment, "Surely you're not bringing that thing in here, young man."

"Aw, Mom, Please? I think he…or she…might be hurt. When I tried to catch it, he limped away. Maybe a dog got it or something. One of its legs is hurt, I think. We can't let it stay out there, can we?"

"We can. And we will. First of all, we don't have any cat food. Second, we don't have any cat litter. I certainly don't want any cat peeing in my house. Cat pee stinks like cat pee."

Within a matter of minutes, alerted by all the commotion, Derrick appeared from the living room. His hair was disheveled and he was scratching himself. He had fallen asleep in front of the television during the 11 o'clock news. Not thirty seconds later their three other sons appeared in the kitchen. They all stared at the kitten, a small ball of orange and white fluff. The orange was as bright as a shiny new penny.

"Did we just get a cat?" asked Derrick Jr., the eldest, as he yawned.

"We did not," answered Mary Pat abruptly.

Jake was still holding the now squirming kitten at arm's length.

"I can't hold this thing forever, you know, Mom. Why can't we keep it just until morning and see if it belongs around here?"

"I already gave you two reasons, young man. That's that."

"Sure is a cute little thing," said Derrick Sr., with a big goofy grin. "Wal-Mart is open 24 hours. I can run down and get a small bag of feed and some litter. What would it hurt?"

Mary Pat gave him the stink-eye. "Are you serious? Don't you know what happens when you feed a stray cat? The damn thing will stick around for the next…oh, thirty years or so, that's what!"

"Okay, good. I'll be right back," said Derrick as he reached for his car keys.

The kitten that was as shiny orange as a new penny was named Copper before they all went back to bed. No one in the neighborhood had lost a kitten so, apparently, the Phillips family had gained a feline resident. It took a lot of hissing and arching of one's back, but the kitten, within a few days, had become best buddies with Jazzy. Jasmine loved this little thing, her very own furry companion. Within a week, they curled up, side-by-side, and napped together and, at times, romped and played like little kids. How it got to the window under Jake's bedroom that night was anybody's guess. So he took credit for rescuing it from untold dangers in the darkness beyond.

It was still dark when Bryan and Brandy Dennison were awakened by the telephone.

"What the hell? Who's calling us at this hour?" Bryan stammered as he fumbled for his glasses. Brandy saw the Caller ID and her heart stopped. It was her father calling. At 4:37 A.M.

"Dad, what's wrong?" she blurted into the phone. There was silence. Then she thought she might have heard a soft sob.

"She's gone, Brandy," her father answered, almost in a whisper. At first, Brandy thought that perhaps her mother had wandered away from the house during the night. She had done that a couple months prior and was found, in her nightgown, sitting on a neighbor's front porch swing.

Then it hit her. Her father wouldn't be calling at this hour to tell Brandy about her mother's wanderings.

"Dad," she gulped, "where are you?"

"I'm at the hospital. Things started happening fast. Too fast. Your mother woke up around one and started acting erratic. Well, more erratic than usual. I couldn't coax her to get back into bed. And then she collapsed and I couldn't lift her. She was like a limp rag doll. I called 911 and in a flash we were headed to the hospital. I was going to call you, but things were happening so damn fast. Her blood pressure was through the roof and her eyes were…well, they looked so strange. They had all kinds of tubes pumping into her. I don't know what all that shit was. It seemed to calm her down and she was lying as still as can be in her bed. All of a sudden her eyes popped wide open and she sat straight up. It looked to me like she saw something…or somebody…but she was looking toward the door to her room. Nobody was there. She reached out her arms and got the biggest, happiest smile on her face. 'Bud', she said. 'Oh, Bud, you've come for me' and she plopped back against her pillow and simply died right then and there. And you know what, Brandy? For no more that a fraction of a second, I swear, I actually thought I saw him.'"

At this point, Brandy was sobbing and Bryan had his arms around her shoulders trying to comfort her as best he could. They knew it was inevitable. We are all aware that none of us gets out of here alive. The comedian Woody Allen once said that he wasn't afraid of death. He just didn't want to be around when it happened.

Memories flashed through Brandy's mind. It all goes too fast. The roller coaster had come to a stop. Arrangements needed to be made. Another chapter comes to a close and a new one begins. Life goes on. Tears will dry, only to resurface again sometime in the future. Brandy closed her eyes and saw her mother, youthful and happy, years before, many years ago…many tears ago. Her mother, who had been the light of Brandy's life, had now entered the darkness beyond.

The sun had long gone down and it was dark outside but the lights and camaraderie shone brightly at Stet's house. There was the rumble of distant thunder as a storm had just passed. On his return from his business trip to Germany, Ben Brandson was staying at his son's place for a few days to get reacquainted. They had a lot of catching up to do. Stet had also invited Max and Camellia who also had a lot of catching up to do with Ben.

Mary had prepared a huge dish of moussaka for dinner and then presented everyone with the enticing dessert of homemade baklava.

"I don't get the chance very often to make either of these," she said as everyone oohed and aahed when she set down the tray. "These are best for a large crowd and it would be too much for just Stet and me."

"Gracious, Mary," Camellia stated as she stared at the dessert, "Maybe I should hire you to do my annual New Year's bash. This is just fabulous. There you go…you for dinner and dessert and then Marty to do the singing!" They all laughed, except Ben who looked confused. Stet had to explain about Marty Howce's surprise hidden talent.

A couple of bottles of Mavrodaphne were polished off along with the dessert and everyone sat back in their respective seats to take a deep breath.

"So, Mary," Ben began with a huge smile, "obviously you know Stet's backstory by now, but I don't know *yours*. Aside from being a fabulous cook, an expert equestrian and the love of my son's life, who, exactly, is Mary Gordon? I can definitely tell that you're not from the south. Am I picking up a hint of New England?"

Stet had heard this story several times during the past year, at the stable and at the gallery because of inquisitive patrons and boarders, so he started clearing away the dirty dishes and then cleaning up the kitchen.

"I'll help, too," said Greg, starting to stack dishes on top of one another to take to the dishwasher. "I've heard this story practically from the beginning. Well, sort of. Should make a zinger of a movie some day, don't you agree?" Stet laughed and just shook his head.

"Good ear, sir," Mary said, responding to Ben's query about New England. "I'm impressed. Well, let's see…where to begin? First of all, my actual name is Myrina. My mother, who was Greek, just *loved* Greek mythology. Do you happen to know who Myrina was by any chance?"

Everyone shook their heads.

"Myrina was a queen of the Amazons. I thought that was pretty cool until kids in school thought it was funny and razzed me for being a *marina*, you know, where boats are moored. So, from that point on, I decided I was going to be Mary…just plain Mary. I was born and raised, for a while, anyway, in a tiny town in Vermont. Pittsford. Not too far from Rutland. Hence that bit of New England, I guess. Didn't realize that it was still noticeable. My maiden name was Minor, which led to another funny situation that I'll get to in a second. Actually, I thought Mary Minor sounded like a nursery rhyme character. When I was about five or six, my Dad joined the military. The Air Force…that's how I eventually met Frank Gordon, my husband, by the way. The military has always been a part of my life. And that's why I have lived in various parts of the globe over the years. My beloved late father rose to the rank of major so, until his dying day, he was addressed as Major Minor. Doesn't that sound like something straight out of Gilbert and Sullivan?"

And everybody chuckled at the thought.

"So, both parents are deceased; Dad from cancer and Mom from a broken heart, I'm certain. She died less than two months after my dad. And, as you probably know, my husband was killed in the Middle East. My handsome son, Greg, looks so much like Frank it's uncanny. And then, Ben, your great big brute of a son sexually harassed me at the Tack Shack and just look where *that* has led!"

"Hey, hey, hey," called Stet starting back in from the kitchen. "I heard that and just *who* did the seducing, you vixen, you?" He came back into the dining room, dish towel in hand, and stood in the doorway with his arms folded across his chest…and with a big, broad smile. "I didn't stand a chance, Dad. She would have had me right then and there…right on the floor…if Brenda, the manager, hadn't stepped in to save me."

Max shook his head. "Why do I think that the wine has gone to everyone's heads and this story has gotten *way* out of the realm of plausibility?"

Everyone laughed and Ben applauded.

"Mary, Myrina, whoever…great story. Well, a story indicates fiction. I don't mean to say that your backstory is such, but it's great knowing a bit more, now, about the person who made a lovesick fool of my son. I am so glad that you'll be a part of our lives from now on…no matter who seduced whom."

"Dad," whimpered Stet, "I was a helpless, innocent, sweet young thing when I was viciously attacked from behind by this Amazonian queen!"

"Bullshit!" laughed Ben. "You have *never* been helpless or innocent. Sweet? Hell, I wouldn't call you sweet, either, young man!"

"Ah, ha!" shrieked Greg all the way from the kitchen. "Look who's being called 'young man' now, you big old goofball!"

Max and Camellia just looked at one another and howled, shaking their heads. Mary turned to look at Stet with that "see there?" stare.

The aroma of coffee filled the air as they all convened in the living room for further conversation. Another hour went by, punctuated with raucous laughter and remembrances from years gone by.

"Okay, dear," said Max, putting down his empty coffee cup, and speaking to Camellia. "It's past our bedtime and it's a long drive back into town. We'd better get going."

"I have four bedrooms here, guys, if you'd like to spend the night you're more than welcome. Then we can stay up until dawn," said Stet.

"No, no, thanks for the offer, dear. But our poor old cat will worry if we're not home," answered Camellia. "This was great fun. Great fun. Max and I appreciate the invitation. It's so nice to be a part of your life again, Stet. I am so proud of the fine man you've become. Ben, you did a marvelous job with this guy. This poor, helpless, innocent, sweet, sweet young man," and she winked broadly.

Goodbyes, with hugs and kisses, were said at the front door and they all stepped out onto the broad front porch. A sudden gust of wind blew Camellia's hat off her head and it went tumbling across the driveway. Greg went running out to retrieve it. Brushing it off, he handed it back to her.

"Well I'll be damned!" Mary exclaimed. "You actually *do* have hair. All this time I thought you always wore hats because you were bald!" And they all laughed.

"Don't be sassy, Mary," Camellia said with fake haughtiness, and patting the back of her blonde head. "How do you know this isn't a wig?" With a big wink, she stepped off the porch.

Waving goodbye, Max and Camellia got into their old Cadillac, drove away from the house and into the darkness beyond.

It was almost dark by the time Bryan drove the final nail into his impressive new wooden archway of an entrance to the stables. Yes, Mrs. Critchley had issued a complaint but the permits had been granted and the plans approved by all the appropriate committees in town. It was a genuine work of art, and Bryan stood back and admired his handiwork. As he was building it, he had planned on having a sign, resembling a branding iron symbol, hanging from the center at the top that would read, in bold type, **CVS** (for CedarView Stables, of course)…but then, coming to the conclusion that it sounded like the pharmacies that are on practically every street corner, he decided against it. Mary's son, Greg, who visited the stable as Bryan was finalizing his plans about the archway, had given Bryan a couple of suggestions to make the archway even more beautiful and more stable. Bryan had mentioned about a sign to hang from above. As a nice gesture, Greg contacted a friend who made laser-cut metal signs, sketched out a rough design, and had it produced. It took Bryan's breath away when Greg, Mary and Stet presented it, as a farewell gift, a couple days ago.

Bryan pulled the ladder away from the archway and stood back, staring up at it and the classy, shiny new stainless steel sign, in a beautiful bold font, announcing the entry to CedarView Stables. He sighed. He was eager to see what that sign would look like with the daylight shining on it, and with the bright sunlight beyond.

Bright morning sunlight shone through all the windows and myriad skylights in Stet's house. It was going to be a beautiful winter day here in the south. Mild temperatures and sparkling clear blue skies. Stet had the coffee brewing already as Mary came out to the kitchen to get stacks and stacks of pancakes made. It wouldn't be too long before their guests wandered into the kitchen from their respective bedrooms. Probably the scent of coffee would do the trick.

Ben Brandson was the first one to appear, smiling as he greeted Mary and his son.

"No matter what time of day, Stet, your place is just dazzling. You and your friend Doc are so talented. Both of you, in so many ways. This place is an art gallery unto itself, much less a great place to live. Impressive... impressive."

"I agree, Ben," said Mary. "When I first drove down his driveway last year I simply could not believe it was real. Now that I'm finally living here too...well, I pinch myself occasionally to make sure I'm not dreaming." She turned to Stet and gave him a sweet kiss on the lips.

A couple minutes later Greg sauntered, barefoot, into the kitchen in his boxers and T-shirt.

"Nice to see that you dress for the occasion, Greg," laughed his mother. "You couldn't have pulled on some jeans first before coming out here?"

"What the hell?" grinned Greg. "We're all family now, aren't we? Damn, that coffee smells great. Is it ready yet?"

Before he had a chance to pour his coffee, Esmé padded, barefoot, into the kitchen. She, at least, was wearing jeans along with her T-shirt. She had had a late class last night and couldn't get out to the house before dinner was over and the Hollidays' departure. Greg had waited up for her after receiving her text with arrival time. She came up behind Greg, put her arms around him and gave him a kiss on the back of his neck.

"Hey, watch it!" he exclaimed. "I'm standing here in my underwear. I don't want to get too excited...in front of my Mom and the entire world here, ya know!" And they all laughed.

"Greg!" Mary said, shaking her head. "Behave. Don't embarrass yourself, especially in front of Stet's dad."

Greg and Ben exchanged glances, shrugged and rolled their eyes... then laughed.

Ten minutes later, there were stacks of fluffy, made-from-scratch pancakes on everyone's plate. A can of Vermont maple syrup was passed around, and the strips of crispy bacon in the middle of a large platter disappeared faster than drinks at an open bar wedding. Greg had managed to slip into a pair of jeans before he joined them all for breakfast.

"Stet, you lucked out, son," said Ben as he downed his third piece of bacon. "I know it's a cliché, but this one's a keeper." Stet agreed. "I know that you've already moved here, Mary, but I haven't heard any mention of a date, if you know what I mean."

"Yeah, I know," answered Mary, "but, frankly, there really isn't any need to rush, is there? This big lug," indicating Stet, "and I are here for the duration. I already know that he snores on occasion and farts, at times, so there aren't too many more secrets. When the time is right…when we feel that it's time…we'll make it official. We'll alert you before the media so, don't worry, you'll have plenty of notice."

"Okay," said Greg with a big grin, "I don't care when…or even *if* you two make it official. I just want to tell you right here and now…" and he pointed straight at Stet… "I will not *ever* call you 'Daddy'."

"Jeeze," sighed Stet, "I was *so* hoping you would, you little whippersnapper!"

"Hey, as long as I can come back here anytime, to your little mansion in the woods, I don't care one way or the other about a marriage."

Stet laughed. "Well, I wouldn't actually call this place a mansion, but thanks for the compliment and you know damn well that you're welcome here anytime, young man."

"Ahhhh…there you go with that 'young man' crap again!" Greg said, rolling his eyes and throwing up his hands.

Breakfast dishes were cleaned and put away. Ben and Greg retreated to their rooms for a morning shower and shave…and to pack for their respective flights home.

"Essie is driving us both back to the airport," Greg said, "Our flights are only about thirty minutes apart. We need to be leaving in about ten minutes or so. Man, this is going to be tough. I've had a blast with you guys the past few months but I'll try to be back whenever I can," as he turned to look at Esmé. "I shall call this my second home. However, that office complex deal will be extremely time consuming, I hope you all realize. Things are starting to gear up with that, and that's exciting as hell. It's going to be in full swing very soon, now. So, unfortunately, my visits may be pretty sporadic. And yes, Mom, Ash and I still refer to it as '*some* shit'."

Luger slowly came up beside Greg and sat, looking up at him.

"Aw, I'm gonna miss you, buddy, You're a good boy," Greg said as he leaned over and gave the dog a big, rough hug. Luger responded by licking Greg's face.

"Well, damn…you didn't think my face was clean enough, eh? Protect these two old folks while I'm gone, will ya? Good boy."

The car was loaded with Ben's luggage and Greg's backpack. Stet and Ben shook hands and that melted into a warm embrace. "I love you,

Dad," said Stet with tears in his eyes. "I'll miss you. Please come back often. Please."

"I will, son, I promise. And I love you, too. But why not plan a trip out to California some time? It's been ages since you were back and we've made several nice changes at SouthWind since you were there last."

"You know what? That sounds like a terrific idea," answered Stet. "I know the springtime is gorgeous out there. Mary and I will *definitely* schedule a trip out there then. Oh, man, I'd love to take her riding through those hills. All three of us for that matter, Dad, could go for some spectacular rides, right?"

"Absolutely," responded Ben, reaching out to embrace Mary. "I shall look forward to it. You'll be impressed...I can guarantee."

Ben and Mary held their embrace for at least a minute. When they broke apart, Ben saw the tears streaming down Mary's cheeks. He tried to hold back his own tears as he walked to the car and got into the back seat. Esmé had started the engine and was waiting for Greg. A few seconds later, Greg came running from his room with a large, thin package wrapped in what appeared to be wedding paper.

"I know there really isn't going to be a wedding, not yet anyway, but this is special for you guys. It's for you both, actually, but I'll hand it to you, Stet. Ash will just have to get used to the fact that he has been knocked down a peg. You're my new best friend."

Stet cocked his head to one side and exchanged glances with Mary. He slowly unwrapped the gift. Greg had had his friend create yet another elegantly designed laser-cut sign of brushed stainless steel. There was a subtle, soft-ground pattern sweeping across the sign that resembled tall grasses blowing in the wind. Stet stared at it for a moment, and then turned it, holding it aloft as Mary let the tears flow. The sign, that would soon be mounted on the fence post at the entry to Stet's and Mary's driveway read **The BRANDSON MANSION** in bold type and underneath that in an elegant script, **Love Lives Here**. Mary grabbed her son and held him tight for a long time. He, in turn, held her just as tightly. She kissed him on both cheeks and relinquished him to Stet. The two men embraced for a minute.

"Oh, jeeze, I gotta go before this gets any sappier," Greg said, shaking his head, as he turned to leave and go to the car. Stet took hold of Greg's shirtsleeve to stop him and looked into his eyes.

"Hey, thanks again for everything. You're the best. I mean it. The absolute best. I'm sure going to miss you, *young man*," Stet said, smiling.

"And I'm going to miss you, too, *young man*," responded Greg as he stepped off the low porch, giving Stet a fist bump.

Greg turned and jogged backwards toward the car as he called out.

"But you better treat my Mom right or I'll come back and beat the shit outta ya, you old goat!" and he spun around, laughing and hopped into the car, slamming the door.

Esmé put the pedal to the metal and the car zoomed up Stet's shaded driveway and out into the brilliant sunlight beyond.

The sunlight almost blinded Marty as he turned into the parking lot of 3H-Grafix in Cumming, Georgia. He had traveled on shaded, tree-lined streets up to this point and had removed his sunglasses. Evidently he had removed them too soon, as he turned directly into the blazing sun when his GPS directed him to turn right in ten feet. The three Hanson brothers (hence the name 3H-Grafix) were awaiting him and Gary Smart. Marty had visited their website and had even found some of their work in local establishments. He was impressed. Extremely impressed, for that matter. He had been in communication, via Facetime, with all three brothers on several occasions within the past couple of weeks. He and Gary had also been burning up the phone lines. Well, the cellphone lines. Marty knew that a deal would be presented to him today. And he would have to make a fateful decision. He and Jessica had discussed this over and over, hour after hour. Jessie, who did *not* do well with change of any kind, fretted over this for days. He would be facing different pressures from either decision: **Plan A**- Constantly looking for freelance work to keep himself busy, with fluctuating income or, **Plan B**- becoming fully employed again (with benefits, Gary reminded him over and over again), beating the bushes, so to speak, to generate new business for the Hanson brothers.

Gary's car pulled in alongside Marty's. They got out, shook hands, exchanged a few words and entered the building.

Several hours later, Marty emerged from the building and took a deep breath. He leaned up against his car and texted Jessie: I start Feb 3. Great $$$ CU Soon! LuvU.

He got into his car and drove off into the setting sun.

The sun was setting as Stet and Doc stood side-by-side admiring their handiwork. The stable, with the newly enlarged stall for Thunder, was impressive, to say the least. The paddock area had been extended and an entirely new riding ring had been built with white fencing surrounding it. Stet and Greg had built several jumps which had been placed strategically throughout the ring. It honestly looked as though they were going to host a hunter/jumper event there. Mary was so impressed she cried when she saw them. She knew that Thunder loved to jump and Stet was eager to see if Gracie would like to as well. *Ah, Gracie,* thought Stet, *just wait until she catches sight of Thunder.* What will be her reaction? She had been lonely since her longtime companion, George, had been put down the previous year. A new adventure lay ahead for her, no doubt.

"I'm gonna miss Greg," Doc said as they strolled back into the house for a beer. "He was a smartass but a lot of fun. It was great working along with him, side by side. Sure knows his stuff, that's for damn sure."

"Yeah," Stet sighed, "I'll miss that twit myself. Don't worry, though, he'll be back from time to time. Next time he's here we'll have you and your wife up here for that dinner that you never got."

"Deal!" smiled Doc. "He sure left his mark around here, didn't he?"

Greg had had his friend create laser-cut metal name signs for the stall doors. **Welcome Thunder** and **Gracie**, in brushed stainless steel, hung on each door. Evidently, Greg *really* liked those laser-cut signs! They appeared to sparkle in the late afternoon sun.

The late afternoon sun was quickly disappearing behind clouds as Mary slowly drove her truck and horse trailer down the gravel driveway to CedarView. Moving day! There were a couple other familiar cars parked there. The bright blue sky of earlier in the afternoon had melted into a milky white mass of clouds. Bryan had just finished repairing the railing around the deck at the end of the riding ring and was cleaning his tools. He waved to Mary and she waved back.

"We'll sure miss you around here, little lady," Bryan said as he gathered up some remnants of wood. "Come back and see us from time to time."

"I shall definitely do that, Bryan. And, please, you and Brandy come up to see us every once in a while, too. Perhaps sometime in the spring Stet and I will throw a big party up there for all the CedarView folks."

She went into the tack room to gather up all her gear.

Mary Anne and Mary Pat were in the tack room, waiting for her. They had known what time Mary was planning on moving Thunder. Group hug.

"This isn't goodbye," sniffed Mary Anne. "This is a 'see ya later' thing, right?"

"Well, of course," answered Mary. "Hell, I'm only going to be, what, ten, fifteen miles away? Come on up to Between and we can all go riding. Or I can come back sometime and trailer Thunder down here. I haven't gotten my fill of Yahoo Hill yet! And you damn well better not forget about us next May...you know...Derby time, just sayin'."

"Mah lawd," drawled Mary Pat, "Ah could stand one of them day-um juleps raht 'bout now, couldn't y'all?"

"Don't ever change, Mary Pat," laughed Mary. "Don't ever change. That's the fakest southern accent since Vivien Leigh and I love it."

"We'd better let you go before it starts raining," said Mary Anne. "And we've got to get our babies in from the pasture and fed."

Mary gathered her gear and made a few trips out to her trailer, loading it up in the truck.

The three Marys walked together to the metal gate leading from the pasture and retrieved their respective horses. Mary Anne stopped at her stall with her horse and Mary Pat stopped at hers.

"We're going to stay in here with our horses," said Mary Anne. "We don't want to be a sorry, sobbing mess as you drive up and away."

"I completely understand," said Mary. "I love you both. We've had a lot of fun here this past year, haven't we? Don't be strangers. Oh, that sounds so trite, doesn't it?" She hugged each lady one more time then led Thunder down past all the other stalls toward the awaiting trailer.

Thunder was loaded into his trailer with ease. He was a champ at this. He immediately started munching on the hay that hung in the bag in front of him. It would be a short ride but one that would lead to new sights, new horse scents, a new future with new adventures. Mary hopped up into the cab of her truck, taking one last look around CedarView. As she started to pull up into the driveway heading up to the street, another truck, pulling another horse trailer, started to come down the driveway. She stopped and waited. New boarders. As the truck approached the side of hers, she rolled down her window. There was a young family…a man and his wife and two young girls sitting in the back seat of the truck. The girls were bouncing up and down with excitement, eager to start *their* new adventures. A horse nickered from inside the trailer and loudly stomped a hoof. The man opened his door and hopped down, smiling at Mary.

"Welcome to CedarView," she said, smiling back at him. "If you guys have half as much fun here as I have had, then you're in for a treat. Good luck to you. Savor every moment."

"Thank you, ma'am," said the young father, tipping his Stetson. "We sure do appreciate those encouraging words. We're looking forward to it, for sure."

Mary noticed that Bryan was coming out of the tack room, heading to greet his new arrivals. He waved to her, once again, as she rolled up her window and pulled up and out of the driveway. Thunder let out a loud whinny, as if it was a "goodbye" to his friends in the pasture behind them. Cue the soundtrack: "Happy Trails To You"…Roy Rogers, of course. She drove slowly down the road, away from the stable. The CedarView archway reflected in her rearview mirror, and then slowly disappeared from view as she turned the curve in the road. But she didn't look back. She was only looking forward. She was eager for *her* new future to begin.

Sometimes there are happy endings. Sometimes there are not. And sometimes there are no endings at all. That's life.

It was late in the afternoon, and the horses were getting restless. The sky, which had been milky white earlier in the day, was turning a darker gray and becoming heavy with the threat of rain. The horses could sense that it was nearing feeding time. They jostled for position at the battered metal gate leading from the pasture to the stable area and their awaiting stalls. Their only instincts now were hunger and impatience, with neither a thought about yesterday nor a care about tomorrow.

EPILOGUE

It would be at least two years in the future, but Marty Howce eventually published his book. Six months later, while browsing through Barnes & Noble, Quentin Tarantino found the book on the "Reduced Price" table, bought it and loved it. He acquired the film rights, casting himself as a lead character. The resulting movie was universally panned, causing the studio to lose countless millions of dollars. Tarantino never made another film again.

It would be at least ten years in the future, but Greg Gordon, Ashton (Ash) DuRand and their respective wives, Esmé and Aideen, would attend an awards ceremony where the two men would receive the AIA Gold Medal…one of the most prestigious prizes in the world of architecture, bestowed by the American Institute of Architects.

The following year, they would win The Pritzker Prize, often referred to as the Nobel Prize of architecture.

It would be at least fifteen years in the future, but Sandi Prescott, who had moved to New York City and changed her name to Sondra Da Moire (Italian for "to die for"...or something like that), won the Tony Award for Best Lead Actress in a Musical in the fifteenth revival of "Gypsy" on Broadway. She played Momma Rose. It was noted by the host, Neil Patrick Harris, that she was the shortest actress ever to play that role...and the most energetic.

It would be at least twenty years in the future, but eventually things would come full circle. Upon Ben Brandson's death, his and Camellia Starr Holliday's son, Stet, inherited SouthWind Farms.

AUTHOR'S NOTES

I, personally, have been involved in the world of horses and graphic design for decades. The pleasures and rewards that I've derived from both are immeasurable. The people and horses I have met on my journey have left indelible marks on my heart, and I am forever grateful.

For the sake of "dramatic purposes", my departure from realistic time frames must be explained and then excused. I have severely compressed the amount of time required to select a site, secure all the required permits and legal folderol and then build-out a location for a magnificent art gallery. And the dealing with artists in arranging openings, showings, etc., can take months of painstaking preparation. To say nothing of the marketing/advertising/media excitement-building/ass-kissing that goes along with all of this! Oh, and to set the record straight, there are *no* 2-bedroom suites at the Ritz-Carlton in Atlanta, either location.

If I have been cavalier in my story involving a murder and subsequent DNA investigative procedures, I shall wait until I receive a formal complaint from Harlan Coben, Lee Child or James Patterson.

Again, as I previously stated, I've taken some liberties with reality and logic. Here's another such departure. Should a potential blockbuster movie (or TV mini-series) ever be made from this insightful book, following is my very large, fantasy all-star cast for all my characters:

Jeremy (Remy) Major – Tommy Lee Jones

Marty Howce – Armie Hammer

Jessica (Jessie) Howce – Evangeline Lilly

Sandi Prescott – Lady Gaga

Dottie Washington – Patti LuPone

Nathaniel Washington (practically a walk-on) – Joe Pesci

Amber Givings – Sandra Dee

Raymond Futtz – Andrew Rannells

Jeannie Futtz (Raymond's mother) – Blythe Danner

Tom Futtz (Raymond's father) – John Lithgow

Mary Anne Forde – Reese Witherspoon

Mary Pat Phillips – Jennifer Lawrence

Derrick Phillips – Chris Pine

Allen Phillips (Derrick's brother) – John Malkovich

Nancy Phillips (Derrick's sister-in-law) – Glenn Close

Mary Gordon – Gal Gadot

Greg Gordon (Mary's son) – Alden Ehrenreich

Stet Brandson – Henry Cavill

Ashton (Ash) DuRand – Alfred Enoch

Josephine (Josie) Thales – Mila Kunis

Aaron Hardin – Lucas Till

Megan Fairley – Saoirse Ronan

Graham Fairley – Hugh Dancy

JaNelle White – Lupita Nyong'o

Bernard (Bernie) White – Ewan McGregor

Esmé White (their daughter) – Jessica Jarrell

Inspector Harold Black – Joseph Gordon-Levitt

Don Edwards, an EMT – Philip Seymour Hoffman

Ingrid Schumacher – Nina Arianda

Charles (Chips) Tallman – Jake Gyllenhaal

Felicity Tallman – Michelle Williams

Doctor (Doc) Morrison, a veterinarian – Alexander Skarsgard

Julia Constance (Rance Hurakon's wife) – Bryce Dallas Howard

Bryan Dennison – Kenneth Branagh

Brandy Dennison – Emma Thompson

Cliff Ambridge (Brandy's father) – Hume Cronyn

Sara Ambridge (Brandy's mother) – Jessica Tandy
Peter Scott (Graphic Designer/Art Director) – Chris Evans
Gary Smart – Ryan Gosling
Linda Smart – Emma Stone
Gus Mansard (a director who over-acts) – J.K. Simmons
Jeff Pringle (an actor looking for "eggrolls") – Ricky Gervais
Jonathan Pope (Drama Coach) – Orson Welles
Max Holliday- Monty Woolley
Camellia Holliday – Shelley Winters

And **Liam Neeson** as Ben Brandson

ACKNOWLEDGEMENTS

"Tomorrow is the most important thing in life. It comes into us at midnight very clean. It's perfect when it arrives and it puts itself in our hands. It hopes we've learned something from yesterday."

John Wayne

This has been an extraordinary experience, and one that took me totally by surprise. I had assumed that my first book, *Horse Scents*, would be my *only* book. This sequel practically wrote itself. My characters took me by the hand and guided me. Without the wonderful tool called the Internet, a few of the actual, true facts mentioned in my book would never have played a role in my storytelling. Of course, maybe you didn't believe any of it anyway. Hey, would this face lie to you? But you can't put anything on the Internet that isn't true, right?

I must acknowledge a couple departed acquaintances from a few decades in my past. The late Jere Frutchey and the late Dean Gillette, superb artists and long-time partners, were co-owners of the long-shuttered and much-lamented popular art gallery, Image South, in Buckhead. My wife and I attended many openings there, and spent more than a few dollars there over the years. Their gallery was partly the inspiration for Stet's gallery. In fact, if it had not been for Jere, I might never have ended up in Atlanta.

My two sons, Gregory and Christopher, continue to make me proud with their respective talents and distinctive personalities. I always thought that kids outgrow their sibling rivalry. I was wrong. I continually shake my head, roll my eyes and laugh hysterically.

Saving the best for last, I have to thank and commend my loving wife, Gaylin, for putting up with my shenanigans for fifty-five years of marriage plus seven years of friendship prior to that. She will always be the absolute best friend (and critic) I have ever had. Her patience is amazing. Without her, Jessica Howce couldn't possibly exist. She's also quite an accomplished equestrian, by the way.

Printed in the United States
By Bookmasters